APOCALYPSE RISING

END TIMES CHRONICLES SEASON 2
EPISODE 1

J. A. BOUMA

EmmausWay
PRESS

CHAPTER 1

SOUTHERN ROMA. AD 2125.

WITH A SUDDEN, painful thud to his backside, Alexander Zarruq tumbled face-first into the hot, rocky sand along the Mediterranean. His mouth filled with the gritty beige soil of the sea and the taste of salted dead fish and rotting algae that had come to define his life the past year.

Bouts of laughter from vaguely familiar voices rose from behind as he struggled to upright himself in his half-sleepy, groggy state. He spit out the invasive sand from his mouth and blew it from his nostrils, but made little headway. Compounding the confusion was a wicked headache throbbing at his temples, his eyes aching from the light, and a chalky mouth from dehydration. Was he hung over?

For a second, he had forgotten where he was. But then it all came back. The lapping of wind-blown waves and the annoying cawing calls of those wretched seagulls overhead he had come to loathe suddenly snapped him back to reality.

He remembered stumbling back to his place of employ from a night on the town up the coast, a seaside town still stuck in the 21st century yet offering all of the pleasurable accommodations of the 22nd, particularly his pleasure of choice. The synthetic narcotics that went for a few Republic *merca* credits crudely nicknamed "hosts," after the thin unleavened wafers that served as the memory marker of Christ's Body, broken on the cross for the sins of the world. Narcowafers were what they were actually called on the street, going for less than the packet of gum they mimicked. Though illegal, Solterran streets were flooded with them, servicing a ready market for the relief they brought upon contact with saliva.

A market that included the former priest who had taken to them since his mother's death at university. Anxiety had had a strong grip on his family, taking his mother away from him, and the feelings of helplessness and insecurity had strengthened its resolve, sending him to secretly self-medicate when he started his seminary graduate work at Oxford. Not often, but enough that he knew where to find it on the street when he needed to. Whether back home across the Great Sea in North Alkebulana or in his new abode on the run.

A packet of narcowafers and a bottle of Roma's finest wine had been his companion the night before. Somehow he made it back to the wharf that had also become his home, where he must have passed out on the shore out front. Surprised he didn't end up in the Mediterranean, given where he had spent the night drunk and high and everything in between, numbing away the pain and confusion, the hopelessness and helplessness that had become his reality.

A strong hand dragged him to his feet, proof positive of that reality.

Mateo, his boss from the fishing yard he had joined up with months ago, a tall, stocky brute made of solid muscle with leathery bronze skin and a wide flat face, and dreadlocks spun up into a hive above his head that meant business.

"Thought I might findchya here, *Martin*," the man growled, spitting out Alexander's fake name he had been using while on the run, his father's, and spinning him around. The brute set him on unstable feet, then he got in his face: "Snoozing on the job—*yet again!*"

Alexander swallowed hard, then regretted it, that blasted sand clawing at his throat now. He spit to the side and wiped his mouth, then his face, Oscar and Elias and Kye, the brawny brutes he'd nicknamed the Three Amigos, throwing up another round of laughs. At his expense.

Running an embarrassed hand through his unwashed hair thickened by time, Alexander offered a weak, "Sorry, Mateo. Won't happen again."

"Sleeping off another late-night binge, were ya? A lass up the coast keepin' ya busy all night, givin' ya a workout that left ya plumb tuckered for another day of work, did she?"

Now he laughed. "Nothing like that. Just overtired is—"

One of Mateo's hands at the end of an arm bulging with cords of muscle grabbed the front of Alexander's dirty white shirt, twisting it into a knot and yanking him forward.

Alexander was met by the man's hardened face, a flat nose flaring with indignation and menacing eyes, one shot through with the haunting milky center of blindness. A mouth of chapped lips and several missing teeth, the others stained yellow from neglect and tobacco, offered up a growl that signaled trouble.

"I don't care what yer excuse is, *mystik*," Mateo spat at him with revulsion, "you *sanguinazi* piece of marine trash deserving of nothing more than a Republic reprogramming camp, as far as I'm concerned!"

Alexander's heart stopped at the twin words that had become curse words for followers of Jesus, for members of Ichthus, the remnant of the Church in the 22nd century.

Mateo leaned in, his breath hot and sour, whispering: "That's right. Heard ya mumblin' something about that dead god of yers in yer sleep. Jesus, this. Christ, that. Something about Father Jim and Thaddeus. But don't worry, your secret's safe with me, *canis*."

Panic began welling within Alexander, his head growing faint at the massive slip of the tongue in his hungover state. Could get him killed for it, or worse: sent off to some Solterra reprogramming camp, given that Ichthus had been deemed a threat to the Republic. Deemed Unfits, even. Men and women who Solterra Republic deemed a burden or menace on society.

But those words...*Mystik. Sanguinazi.* Neither meant anything good, the epithets of hate and intolerance in a world increasingly hostile toward Ichthus. Mocking, contemptuous slurs for those who claimed the name of Christ as *'blood-eaters'* who practiced superstitious ways and bigots who believed regressive ideologies harmful to the Republic.

It was more than that, though. Because the pair of words were connected to a distant memory from a season of his life he'd soon forget.

Last time he heard those words he had been heading off to meet Father James Ferraro in modern-day Nicaea after his cathedral had been blown to bits by a pseudo-spiritual organization called Nous, a resurgent archnemesis of the Church that resurfaced to wage war against the faith. And this was a week after he had received a cryptic message requiring his presence at a clandestine conclave of Ministerium officials answering the threats of a new pseudo-religious entity that threatened the Christian faith itself. Which then led him on a wild goose chase through time collecting the testimony and memory of the once-for-all faith entrusted to God's holy people with some contraption straight out of a bargain bin DiviNet sci-fi ebook. All of which eventually led him to being christened the Master of a lost religious order of the Church stretching back to one of Christ's apostles, Jude Thaddeus—right before it all went to Hades on a hot breath of bad luck and devilish designs.

That was over a year ago. Since then, he had nearly gotten killed by said pseudo-spiritual ecclesiastical archenemy, got stuck in the past, then nearly got locked away in the time-space continuum—or rather, the space-time continuum as his good buddy and brilliant physicist who had discovered time travel to begin with, Sasha Pavlovich, would correct him.

But that wasn't even touching on the worst of it, what had sent him spiraling back for those blasted synthetic narcotics: discovering his dead father, who he thought had committed suicide, was in fact in cahoots with the Republic to destroy Ichthus with the one world religious entity known as Panligo. It was no wonder he had been passed out on the beach in the middle of the day at the wharf where he had been hired to clean the undersides of the ultramodern hydrocraft fishing boats with all that had happened.

With all that he had been through and witnessed and endured.

A searing pain bloomed from inside his head from standing and the heat and light of the day, reminding him of an aftereffect of four rounds of time travel he worried meant more than he had cared to admit.

Suddenly, a headache was the least of his worries.

Mateo violently shoved Alexander in the chest. He stumbled backward and landed hard on his back in the wet sand, the Three Amigos striking up another round of laughs at his expense. He went to sit when the rush of an ebbing wave flowing back toward the shore overtook him.

Sea water flooded his eyes and mouth and nose, sending him into a choking fit that felt like he was going to drown.

Which instantly surfaced another memory from over a year now, far sweeter than sour—the time Rebekah had rescued him from the clutches of Poseidon after jumping phases from the early Church back to the future, landing them out along the shore of ultramodern Solterra and nearly sending him to Davy Jones's locker and an early reunion with Saint Peter himself.

Alexander struggled to sit and climb out from the shore on the southern tip of Roma, what had been the boot of Italy but had washed away in the climate and political changes of the 22nd century. It was no use. The undertow was stronger than his hungover self, sucking him back into the sea and sending another wave crashing over his entire body now.

He couldn't breathe. His mouth was filled with the twin tastes of salted dead fish and rotting algae again. His lungs burned with salt water, and he couldn't see anything but the high-noon sun and clear blue sky refracted through a prism of watery eyes—which soon began to dim from being dragged below the surface of the water and being starved of oxygen.

Then the moment hit, when he stopped struggling, stopped trying, stopped grasping for life. Because let's face it: there was nothing left of it. Why not just let the sea drag him down under? So he relaxed and set out his arms and stilled his legs, his body sinking even as it tumbled under the violence of Mother Nature.

Until another hand was yanking him back above the surface, and a string of Romish was being hurled at him, and another bout of laughter from the Three Amigos was pulling his consciousness back to the surface.

Alexander was thrown back to the hot sand, and a hand was slapping his back, then again. Soon, he was retching and coughing up that blasted sea water, its burn just as wicked coming up and out as when it went down and in.

He collapsed to the sand, heaving desperate breaths and wanting nothing more than to have left his godforsaken life that had turned sour.

Because surely God was nowhere in the hellhole that was known as Solterra Republic, including Alexander's corner of it.

Another pair of strong hands pulled him to his feet, one of them giving his face a good slap. Mateo, again.

"Now back to work, ya mangy mutt!" Then the man got in his ear, whispering on a hot breath of sour beer and boiled cabbage: "Before I turn yer sorry ass in to the Republic. Might fetch a pretty penny for yer head, the way things are going. And I might, too, if the big boss wouldn't have my hide." Then he yelled again: "Back to work!" He gave Alexander a shove toward the sodding warehouse, a metaphor really for his lot in life.

A cold, dark, dank prison that amounted to little more than indentured servitude for what little he had left to live.

The others went their way as Alexander stumbled inside the vast warehouse where three large hydrocrafts of gleaming titanium were moored, along with a few other smaller personal submergence vehicles that had come to define part of 22nd-century living, the world having settled that vast underwater world that had gone unexplored for millennia. It stunk to high heaven, too, the dead fish compounded by the suffocating heat, temperatures reaching into the mid 110s Fahrenheit, maybe into the 120s given the cloudless sky.

Alexander sauntered over to the larger vessel, its underside covered with barnacles from weeks of service on the open seas and waiting for him to do his job. A bucket sat next to it on the cracked concrete floor, filled with some concoction the owner of the fishing company had cooked up to clean away the pests that slowed down his operation. And it was his job to scrub them away.

He grabbed a steel brush and dipped it inside the bucket, then slapped it against the underside littered with the beige cone-like crustaceans—when something caught his eye at the mawing entrance.

A dark shadow, passing across the threshold, extending out across the sand and into the sea and dimming the light inside.

Figured it was a storm rolling in soon, the gathering clouds blotting out the sun that had been mercilessly beating down for weeks, bringing welcomed relief.

And me without my surfboard.

Alexander huffed in annoyance at not being able to jump on a new pastime, but relented and returned to the boat. A rusted tripod lamp with flaking yellow paint from last century was standing by. He flipped it on. He half expected it to lie dormant, given the shaky reliability of power in those parts. Solterra prided itself on '*peace, prosperity, progress...For Humanity!*' its triple promises that usually fell far short. But the LED bulb flickered to life with a bright orange glow that offered him a better viewing of the bloody sea vessel and its barnacle-covered underside.

The rest of the warehouse filled with faint light as well, a two-story space of corrugated metal. The stench of oil and gasoline and dead fish mixed in a putrid mess that threatened to turn his stomach inside out again. It was so thick, his mouth filled with the sour taste, brought on by the suffocating heat pressing in against him now. It was probably heightened by the sleek metal hydrocraft orbs that hoovered up the sea, spitting seawater out the back while retaining their catch inside, their metal skin holding and magnifying the heat.

Alexander wiped his forehead with the back of his hand, a line of sweat beading at his hairline and dirty white linen shirt beginning to stick to him now. Still wore the clothes on his back when he ran off those many months ago on that beach in Lebanon after receiving the shocking news about his father, leaving Father Jim and John Mark Ford and Rebekah and Sasha in his wake.

"Best get to it," he grumbled, stuffing the metal broom back into the bucket of cleaning agent and slapping it against the unsuspecting crustaceans. He pressed the brush back and forth, their poor little bodies throwing up a briny flair of protest as he scrubbed them away.

This is what his life had been reduced to, cleaning the underbelly of a fishing boat, on the run from the Republic and Ichthus. Running from life, really. *His* life, after discovering he'd been living a lie. One perpetuated by his father.

He kept at it, anger rising at what Martin Zarruq had put him through by faking his suicide on that bloomin' bridge back home in Tripolitania. Leaving him all alone to tend to his church and minister to his flock, all while Ichthus reeled from menacing threats inside and outside the Church. And then to find out his father was orchestrating it all—from the rising apostasy to the threat of persecuting violence. It was all too much.

Alexander supposed he should just be thankful he had a job. He had tracked down the son of a man he had known from childhood who had left Tripolitania a decade ago to start the fishing business he was now working. It was all he could think to do to survive. After all, he needed to eat, needed a place to sleep. Took some doing, stowing away on a freighter from the coast of Izmir in Arabia-Persia, the ancient town of Smyrna that had been a central city to early Christianity, and making his way to southern Roma, old-century Italy. But he'd managed. The son of Tareq had wondered why the son of his father's old priest had showed up at his doorstep, but he didn't ask questions, offering him the entry-level job and a bunk at the on-site migrant housing.

That was over a year ago now. Seemed like a lifetime ago. He'd paid neither attention nor mind to anything going on outside the area, having ditched his DiviNet device in the sea and vowing to keep out of the politics of it all, including whatever Ichthus had gotten itself into. No, it was now a matter of self-preservation, of living his life on his terms. Sure, it was self-ish. But what more could he do? If he couldn't trust the truth of his dead father, trust the integrity of the man who raised him and made him the man he was, what could he rely on but himself?

His throat suddenly grew tight with emotion and a wetness sprang to his eyes. He heaved a breath and a halting cry climbed out. He set the brush on the floor and leaned against the handle, glancing out into the dimming afternoon in embarrassment, hoping no one had heard his weakness.

No one there but him and the barnacles and his bloomin' brush. Pretty well summed up his lot in life.

Alexander wiped his eyes on his sleeve and thrust the brush back into the bucket of cleaner.

When a clang sounded from behind the sleek, hulking hydrocraft.

He jumped back with a start, his breath catching in his chest at the sudden sound. He glanced over his shoulder—when another thud snapped his head toward the rear.

Picking up the metal brush, he inched along the sleek titanium hull, gripping it like a weapon for any would-be thieves. Had been having some trouble of late with some vagabonds from the village up the coast rummaging around for spare parts to sell on the black market, even discarded fish.

Alexander neared the back, gripping the handle tighter and raising it like a sword.

When a seagull *caw-cawed* and bolted toward him from under the hull.

He swung at it, this way and that. The buzzard *caw-cawed* again, wildly flapping its wings at him and sending a plume of white feathers cascading down before rising high and circling.

"Come back here, you little—"

Another *caw-caw*, and another wild flapping before darting out of the entrance and into the dimmed afternoon.

He mumbled a string of curses under his breath, mostly grumbling about his lot in life, defined by sea buzzards and barnacles. "Sodding buzzard..." he mumbled from behind the hull.

Then he stopped, drenched with sweat now from the exchange and his conscience convicting him with one of several Psalms he had memorized, Psalm 9: *'I will give thanks to you, Lord, with all my heart; I will tell of all your wonderful deeds. I will be glad and rejoice in you; I will sing the praises of your name, O Most High.'*

He frowned. *Hear you loud and clear, Lord. I do thank you and praise you and rejoice in you and your deeds over my life. Buzzards, barnacles, and all...*

Alexander smiled to himself at the truth of those words, then sauntered back around toward the front of the—

"BOOO!" someone shrouded in the shadows yelled, hands out and arms wide and body looming over Alexander, who shrank back with arms over his face in fright.

The man laughed, stepping back with arms grasping his gut as if in pain, the tripod lamp catching his face and revealing all.

Kye, one of the Three Amigos and another immigrant who had arrived shortly before him. Tall and lanky and a decade younger than Alexander, the olive-skinned man with black hair and the immaturity of a teenager kept at it, stoking Alexander's embarrassment from the earlier ordeal and giving him an excuse to vent.

Alexander raised a fist and punched at the kid. Who raised a shoulder just in time to take the brunt of his anger.

"Ooh, tough guy now, ehh, brotha? Not so tough back at beach." He laughed again, then raised his hands in surrender when Alexander raised another threatening fist, his face twisted and reddening with anger. "Alright, alright. Chill, brotha. Just making sure you still had breath in your lungs after nearly drowning."

"I'm fine," Alexander said under his breath, shoving past the man and sauntering back to the boat covered with those blasted white lumps. Looked like the thing was covered in leprosy, it was so bad. And disgusting, hard work. Not to mention humiliating, the man who was Master of the Order of Thaddeus reduced to a pleb, the underclass of Solterra. Not that his former life of a priest was any better, but still. How the mighty had fallen.

He grabbed the metal brush handle and stuck it back in the bucket of solution meant to ease the cleaning.

Kye came up to his side, crossing his arms and leaning against the hydrocraft. "You know, Mateo ain't so bad, once you get to know him."

Sloshing the brush around, Alexander pulled it out and slapped it on the underside, ignoring Kye while working the brush against the polished underside, a patch beginning to gleam through the leprosy now.

"If you are wanting my advice, I'd stay away from the booze, and the women." Kye jabbed Alexander in the arm and smiled, before continuing: "And make sure you don't pass out on the beach. Because next time—"

A vibration suddenly seized the floor, interrupting the man as a tremor worked its way up through the craft and rattled the tripod lamp until the entire building was shuddering under the quake.

Kye bolted from the boat and threw out his arms for support. "Hot damn! What the devil is going on?"

Alexander glanced at him without answering. He knew the dangers such seismic activity in the earth's crust brought for those left inside buildings. A wicked quake had decimated a town near his own back home in Tripolitania, sending older buildings crumbling within seconds and doing a number on the newer ones of gleaming glass and titanium constructed to the Republic's specifications. Several members of his parish had helped with the recovery, and they had set up a temporary shelter at his parish for those in need of food and housing. The death count had been catastrophic, which meant they needed to get out into the open—pronto.

"Let's get out of here," he said, throwing the brush to the floor and turning toward the entrance.

When his breath seized in his chest and fear flooded his veins at what he saw unfolding outside.

"What the heck…"

CHAPTER 2

Alexander threw his hands on the top of his head, face twisted up in horror at the scene playing out in front of him.

The beshadowed entrance threshold was shrouded in darkness now. Except it was still early afternoon, when the sun was brightest, most merciless. And the darkness wasn't that of an incoming storm, but of the dead of night.

The tremor suddenly shifted into overdrive, the shudders turning violent now. Kye cried out in the tongue of his homeland and shoved past Alexander, who was planted to the floor with petrified immobility.

Something crashed at the back of the warehouse; same for the light stand that had been offering him light, the blasted thing slamming against the hull of the fishing boat before clattering to the floor. It shattered and flickered off, plunging the vast space further into darkness.

A cry rose from outside. Kye again, his arms waving frantically around and pointing at the sky, his panicked voice joined by others, a chorus of confused shouts and fearful screams coalescing into pandemonium.

Another crash jolted Alexander from his frozen stupor, a beam from on high smashing into the bridge of the hydrocraft he had been scrubbing and toppling it to one side, threatening to come unmoored altogether and trapping Alexander inside as the building continued convulsing.

He received it as his final warning from the good Lord above. He ran outside to join the protest.

Then stopped dead in his tracks at the fuller picture.

Men and women, his fellow fishermen and some others from the village just down the coast were standing at the edge of the Mediterranean awash in a faint crimson, the color of diluted blood. They were staring up into the sky; some were pointing and screaming and crying out on frightened breaths.

Trees snugging the warehouse property line were blocking his view, so he ran across the still-shaking ground to join his fellow crew members. Then sank to his shaking knees in the sand at what he witnessed.

The sun had indeed darkened. Not just from an invading storm cloud, but from a blackened sky, as if night had suddenly descended upon them. But that wasn't all of it. A full moon was shining back at him, bathed in the darkest of red. A blood-red moon, full and menacing and portending a wickedness no one had spoken of in decades, even inside Ichthus. And a sky that should have been blanketed by stars was giving way to a blank canvas—literally, as the tiny specks of ancient light began falling from their perches high above, some with blazing tails that reminded him of the comets from childhood he and his father had spent countless hours watching. Only this time falling to the earth.

A word started ricocheting across the beachhead that described the truth of it. From various tongues and in various languages, but all expressing the same exact sentiment.

Apocalypse.

Alexander sucked in a shaky breath as the ground continued its violent convulsing, the very center of the earth seeming to give way as the heavens themselves gave up any notion of what was sane and whole and real—the sun blinking out and moon shedding its blood and stars giving way. He threw his hands up on his head again and closed his eyes, his head filling with one resounding thought.

It has begun...

Immediately, a passage from the Holy Scriptures surfaced. Something John the Seer had witnessed, who Alexander had visited over a year ago now to retrieve the memory of the Church to bolster the faith and combat the rising apostasy plaguing Ichthus. From the Book of Revelation, chapter 6:

> *I watched as he opened the sixth seal. There was*
> *a great earthquake. The sun turned black*
> *like sackcloth made of goat hair, the whole*
> *moon turned blood red, and the stars in the*
> *sky fell to earth, as figs drop from a fig tree*
> *when shaken by a strong wind. The heavens*
> *receded like a scroll being rolled up, and*
> *every mountain and island was removed*
> *from its place.*
> *Then the kings of the earth, the princes, the*
> *generals, the rich, the mighty, and everyone*
> *else, both slave and free, hid in caves and*
> *among the rocks of the mountains. They*
> *called to the mountains and the rocks, "Fall*
> *on us and hide us from the face of him who*
> *sits on the throne and from the wrath of the*
> *Lamb! For the great day of their wrath has*
> *come, and who can withstand it?"*

The sixth seal. The final seal, unleashing a cosmic catastrophe to bring the world to the brink of the end times.

The beginning of the end...

The world continued rumbling around Alexander, even as the moon continued shining blood-red and the stars faded from view. Even as Alexander himself reeled inside, his brain going haywire at the turn and thirsting for narcotic relief, that wicked headache blooming into pain and sending his bowels into watery weakness.

A lesson from a class he had taken on the Book of Revelation under Father Jim's tutelage at Oxford sprang from memory. He taught that the seals surrounding the scroll were the normal forces operating through the course of history, signaling both the brokenness of the world and picturing the redemptive, judicial purposes of God. War, murder and radical conflict, economic depressions and recessions, famine and plagues, the persecution of Christian brothers and sisters—all of it was history's ongoing suffering.

Then there was the sixth seal. The one before the final one opening the scroll to unleash the Great Tribulation itself. Using language that was thought to be merely symbolic and apocalyptic to describe the end of the world. The language of cosmic catastrophe. Father Jim had insisted that John's use of such language was completely poetic and symbolic of spiritual realities—the blotting out of the sun, the blood-red moon, the falling away of the stars. So had most everyone else, brushing away such language as not at all describing the end of the world as we know it.

And yet there it was! All of it. The darkness of the night in the middle of the day. The bloomin' full moon bleeding crimson. The fiery contrails of stars as they fell from view, hundreds and thousands blinking off now for Pete's sake!

Father Jim was wrong; they were all so bloody wrong...

What was he going to do?

What was the world going to do?

An arm seized Alexander's own, a familiar vice grip that wrenched him from the fast-cooling sand under the shroud of darkness and dragged him to his feet.

It was Mateo, face beet red with that corkscrew vein popping out, swinging wild arms and pointing at the sky, shouting at the top of his frazzled lungs what everyone was wondering:

"What the bloody hell is going on, mystik!"

Alexander didn't answer, his wide, frightened eyes darting up above to take in the apocalyptic scene unfolding.

He was slapped in the face, pain and blood blooming from his nose. Then Mateo grabbed both shoulders, centering Alexander's gaze to his, the man yelling again: *"I'll ask you one more time, mystik, because surely you're the only one in these parts with sense enough to interpret this hell unleashed on our beach. Answer me this: What the bloody hell is going on!"*

A crowd had gathered, Kye at Mateo's side with the two other Amigos behind, the faces of each and every man, woman, and even child echoing Mateo's freaked-out plea for answers.

Alexander swallowed hard, a sudden courage and peace gripping him, and the force of the Holy Spirit himself leading him forward. As much as he might want to run from his calling as a priest and hide in anonymity, it dawned on him that he had trained for such moments.

Lord Jesus Christ, Son of God, don't fail me now...

He swallowed hard and began quoting the words of Jesus from memory: *"So when you see standing in the holy place 'the abomination that causes desolation,' spoken of through the prophet Daniel—let the reader understand—then let those who are in Judea flee to the mountains. Let no one on the housetop go down to take anything out of the house. Let no one in the field go back to get their cloak. How dreadful it will be in those days for pregnant women and nursing mothers! Pray that your flight will not take place in winter or on the Sabbath. For then there will be great distress, unequaled from the beginning of the world until now—and never to be equaled again."*

The crowd hushed even as the world continued to quake, not a word being spoken, not a breath being breathed as Alexander continued with the words of Matthew's Gospel: *"If those days had not been cut short, no one would survive, but for the sake of the elect those days will be shortened. At that time if anyone says to you, 'Look, here is the Messiah!' or, 'There he is!' do not believe it. For false messiahs and false prophets will appear and perform great signs and wonders to deceive, if possible, even the elect. See, I have told you ahead of time."*

Mateo twisted up his face and glanced at Kye. "What the bloody hell are ye jibber-jabbering on about, *mystik*?"

"I'm trying to tell you!" Alexander yelled. He took a breath and huffed it out, running a shaky hand through his hair. "The words of Jesus, the founder of Ichthus, as you would say—that's what these are. His word about the beginning of the end of the world."

That got his attention, and the others, their faces draining of color and mouths falling open with a mixture of intrigue and panic.

Mateo nodded for Alexander to continue. So he did, quoting: *"So if anyone tells you, 'There he is, out in the wilderness,' do not go out; or, 'Here he is, in the inner rooms,' do not believe it. For as lightning that comes from the east is visible even in the west, so will be the coming of the Son of Man. Wherever there is a carcass, there the vultures will gather."*

Alexander took a breath, then explained, "And here's where it gets interesting, especially for the crazy we're experiencing right now."

Cutting off his homily, the back half of the warehouse threw up a collapsing shudder, the roof caving in and one side collapsing in a palsy that threw an exclamation point at the end of what he'd said.

Mateo looked back to assess the damage, groaning and smacking a meaty palm against his flat forehead before turning back to face Alexander with pleading eyes. "Go on, then!"

He did, reaching back into the recesses of his brain for the Gospel of Matthew, chapter 24, that he had memorized years ago:

> *"Immediately after the distress of those days*
> *'the sun will be darkened,*
> *and the moon will not give its light;*
> *the stars will fall from the sky,*
> *and the heavenly bodies will be shaken.'"*
> *"Then will appear the sign of the Son of Man in*
> *heaven. And then all the peoples of the earth*
> *will mourn when they see the Son of Man*
> *coming on the clouds of heaven, with power*
> *and great glory. And he will send his angels*
> *with a loud trumpet call, and they will*
> *gather his elect from the four winds, from*
> *one end of the heavens to the oth—"*

Mateo grabbed Alexander by his shirt with both hands before he could finish, yanking him from within a few centimeters of his face, his breath still reeking of beer and boiled cabbage. The man looked like he was on the verge of a manic episode, his eyes wide and forehead wrinkled with panic, his mawing mouth quivering and his hands gripping Alexander weakly now in a way that reflected the same panic. Probably was one foot into a complete psychotic break, given what he was experiencing—what they all were experiencing.

The man whimpered, "What does it all mean, Martin?"

His eyes filled with tears, and his lower lip started quivering. He repeated with a whisper: "What does it all mean?"

Alexander went to offer a reply when he was cut off by another voice, high and shrilly and hysterical.

"Incoming!" someone shouted from view, near the beachhead.

Mateo turned toward the shout as a chorus of screams arose behind him. Alexander caught sight of the man pointing frantically at the sky.

He squinted, not understanding what it was. Then Alexander's eyes widened and another bout of cold panic drenched him from head to toe, his brain not being able to process the fiery object quickly descending from the heavens.

'the sun will be darkened,
and the moon will not give its light;
the stars will fall from the sky,
and the heavenly bodies will be shaken.'

The blazing ball of fire was fast approaching from above, aiming for the wharf or the warehouse.

Or them...

The inflamed orb was growing in size by the second. Had to be the size of a magnacar. Which sent the crowd surging toward the beachhead down below, the waters foaming now as the earth continued its own psychotic break with reality.

Alexander joined them, pressed from behind with the surge of bodies. He offered his own pressing insistence, shoving past a pair of women holding wailing babies, feeling slightly bad about his rude, almost inhumane gesture. But it was every man for himself.

'the sun will be darkened,
and the moon will not give its light;
the stars will fall from the sky,
and the heavenly bodies will be shaken.'

Twisting back for another look, those words of Jesus from Matthew's Gospel ringing in his ears, he hiked up his legs and pumped his arms and made for the water. It was automatic, primal, his body carried along by something buried deep in his lizard brain from an ancient, ancestral instinct to survive. He splashed into the water, the waves slamming into his torso as he waded farther out, mere seconds before—

It hit.

The force of impact by the alien rock, its phantasmic fire and fury was unbelievable. The pressure like one of those Queller disruptors that Solterra Enforcers dropped against threats to the Republic. But a thousand-fold worse, the moment being overcome by pressure and heat and light and sound and a radiating wave of all four that threatened to undo the beach.

The blast radiated out from the point of impact a beat later in a blinding, deafening explosion that sent everyone sailing from their feet and into the wicked water boiling from the seismic convulsion.

Alexander hit the surface hard, his chest stinging with a smack. Then he was grabbed down under by a mauling wave, the undertow fierce with continued seismic convulsions. He sank beneath the water but kicked and clawed with all his might for the surface. All the while the invisible claws of the water's depth clung to him like a magnetic attraction, beckoning his legs and torso with yanking invitation to succumb to the darkness down below.

For a second, he considered accepting the invitation, letting it all just fade away. The world was on fire anyway, literally. While he had no earthly clue what was transpiring above, whether it was the apocalypse as some were shouting or some natural phenomenon or something spawned from the loins of Satan himself—all he knew for certain was that his place of employment and housing had just been obliterated in an instant. His life was over, for a third time in quadruple as many months. What was the point in continuing on?

But then his suicidal ideation was chased by another thought, something Father Jim had said to him: *All things worth fighting for demand a leap of faith.*

Something seized in his chest. An ember of responsibility and purpose that had grown cold the past few months, dowsed by a cascading set of circumstances but that had been preserved with just enough energy to come back to life.

And it did, blown back into a force by the Holy Spirit himself—first blooming into a will to live, and then into a desire to find out what the heck was going on. Whether it was all connected to what Jesus and his beloved apostle John had foretold.

'the sun will be darkened,
and the moon will not give its light;
the stars will fall from the sky,
and the heavenly bodies will be shaken.'

Those words clanged inside his head like a clarion call to arms. So Alexander fought against the current dragging him down and out to sea, using every fiber of his being to kick and claw toward the surface—mostly for himself but also for the charge he had been given to preserve and guard the once-for-all faith entrusted to God's holy people by Jesus Christ himself.

Because if the space rock that slammed into his life was any indication, Solterra was in a world of hurt. Which only the gospel of Jesus Christ had any hint of ameliorating.

With a sudden burst from the water, his powerful legs propelling him quickly to the surface. He twisted back toward the wharf to glimpse the damage.

A hell ten times worse than Dante's vision was splayed before him.

Belching flames spewed from every direction, the heat of a

thousand furnaces scorching the air and everything around it. Bringing the warehouse to its knees and sending the surrounding buildings of ultramodern gleaming glass and titanium along with previous-century brick and wood into inflamed piles of heaping rubble. But that wasn't all of the destruction.

Those who hadn't made it to the water before the incoming explosion had been caught in the hellish maelstrom, their bodies burnt to a blackened crisp littering the shoreline now. Some large, some small—even infant-like.

Other chunks of space rock continued falling farther out toward the village, and others yet beyond on the hilly horizon. Flowers of fire bloomed and plumes of ash and soot rained down.

Emotion seized Alexander's throat and threatened his eyes, his mind reeling from the violent, vengeful display before him.

The world was on fire. And there was nothing he could do about it.

"*Alex!*" a voice rose with a shout above the din of chaos.

His heart leapt and sank in tandem; hope rising at the sound of his former life while sinking at being recognized.

What did it portend? And who on earth could recognize him all the way out in the middle—

"*Alexander Zarruq!*"

His breath seized in his chest, and throat constricted with a sudden rise in emotion.

He knew that voice! Seasoned, with a polished lilt from Britannia.

No, it couldn't be...

Alexander spun toward the sound, searching the blood-red waters with a splash for the voice connected to his former life.

When he caught sight of it.

A yellow submarine several meters out, bobbing up and

down like one of those rubber ducks he'd adored as a child. And perched on top was a tall, trim man with wide shoulders in a black cassock, sporting a mane of silver hair and a wide grin of invitation outmatched only by his wide, open arms.

Father James Ferraro.

At last. Help!

And hope...

CHAPTER 3

THE WORLD around Alexander continued to foam and slosh with vibrating indignation, the darkened world of the horrific blood-red moon and fading stars inflamed by a furnace of a hundred fires.

Until it wasn't.

The full moon that had '*turned blood red,*' returned to its whitened luminescent brilliance. The stars, many of them still dimmed and darkened, missing now from their former place of perch, they had ceased to '*fall to earth, as figs drop from a fig tree when shaken by a strong wind,*' the flaming balls of fiery rock no longer slamming to the earth now either. The sun itself, which had '*turned black like sackcloth made of goat's hair*' began to regain its shine as well, the world brightening as in the dawning light, the sun itself regaining its blinding brilliance. Even the earth no longer shook, although the waves still crashed, a delayed response from being stirred for what seemed like the better part of an hour, but no longer foaming and churning with menace.

The world seemed back to normal. Perhaps a new normal, given the apocalyptic happenings. For now.

Who knew how the Republic would function after what had just transpired. Whatever it was that had just transpired.

Alexander couldn't make sense of it. He spun back toward shore, the coastline still on fire with towering flames and acrid smoke filling the skyline from every direction. Continuing to tread water, he spotted the Three Amigos several meters out, then Mateo, the man screaming and carrying on in full manic mode. Sounded like he'd finally snapped.

"Homefry!" someone called out across the waving water, another familiar voice. Strong and commanding, lilting with the Southern twang of Noramericana from south of the former United States, before it was broken up during the Reckoning.

John Mark Ford.

Alexander spun back toward the yellow submarine he had spotted earlier with Father Jim perched on top. The cardinal was joined now by Ford, ex-Solterran soldier and former elite Purifier who had been deep with the Republic's paramilitary arm before becoming chief of operations for the Ministerium, the remnant of ministers and priests and pastors for the Church, for Ichthus. That is, if there was any Ministerium left after what had happened over a year ago, the Republic having destroyed it in the crucible fires of persecuting destruction.

The man had also saved Alexander's life and journeyed with him back in time to retrieve the memory of Jude Thaddeus. Yes, Ford plucked his nerves. And he could do without the Southern swagger and military bravado. But he was a man of integrity who handled himself well, putting it all on the line for the Church when it needed him most.

And there he was, motioning Alexander to swim toward the yellow personal submergence vehicle and calling out again for him to kick it into gear.

A smile flashed across his face, and tears edged to the corner of his eyes. He was being rescued. He glanced back to look for Mateo and Kye and the others, catching sight of them wading up the shoreline now. Satisfied they were as safe as could be under the circumstances, he swam for his friends, his family.

Reaching the underwater hydrocraft, strong arms pulled him up top the slippery submarine. He fell against the yellow surface trying to bring a leg up top, smacking his jaw with a clatter. It hurt something fierce, but he'd live. He *had* lived, several times over after enough brushes with death to last a lifetime.

Soon, he was being ushered through a narrow circular hatch and down a red ladder into the belly of the fish—a cramped, narrow space of dim LED lighting and steel girding that extended back to front before splitting into a T at the rear. Seats ran along the sides, with a functional tin-colored aesthetic punctuated by navy. The steady hum of engines and fans and Lord knew what else filled the aural void.

A noise caught his attention up top just as his boots hit the floor with a wet slap. Ford had sealed the hatch and was descending below.

A chorus of voices greeted him, snapping him back to his new reality.

"*Bratishka!* You are still being alive!" Sasha grabbed him from behind, wrapping his arms in a bear hug before Alexander could turn around.

"Move it, would ya?" Ford bellowed from above. "We've got two more incoming fellas." The pair shuffled out of the way as Ford and Father Jim descended.

Alexander turned around and returned the embrace. Before long, Ford was joining the reunion, as was Father Jim and Rebekah, the woman who had traveled with him last through time to the early Church, who had begun to steal his heart, who he had left at the beach along with the others. Jin

Sung and Luciana Jane were standing off to the side, smiling and waving their greeting as well.

It felt like ages since he had felt real joy and anything close to human connection. He wasn't embarrassed to admit it, at least to himself, that he had cried himself to sleep more times than he'd care to count the past few months in the darkened aloneness of hiding and running, wanting nothing more than to return to Father Jim and Rebekah and Sasha, even Ford, joining the cause and fulfilling his role as Master of the Order of Thaddeus.

But the news of his father being alive after believing him to be dead, of the man apostatizing from the faith and architecting Ichthus's destruction; the burden of bearing the mantle to reclaim and retrieve the Church's memory, to preserve and protect Ichthus and its faith; the fear over what traveling through time was doing to him physically and the dangers he had faced—all of it were far more powerful deterrents than whatever silly emotions he felt in the dead of night.

But this reunion...it was magical.

"Alright, alright, alright," Ford said, easing out from the group hug and squeezing past Father Jim. "Enough of the kumbaya guys and dolls, because it's crazier than a mule in heat out there! And my spidey senses tell me the sequel to the looney-toon Kirk Cameron after-school special from last century is unfolding before our eyes in ultra-definition color!"

The man motioned for Jin to follow him toward the front of the personal hydrocraft to a brightly colored panel of digital controls and sensors beneath a large windshield, half submerged beneath the glowing azure waters of the Mediterranean dappled in the full-on sun now shining above in a clear blue sky. Fires still raged across the horizon, the skyline collapsing under the destruction, while the faint yellow lighting of several personal submergence vehicles were spotted roaming below.

Alexander pulled back from the group and offered a grateful grin before it faded and the truth of Ford's words came crashing into him. "What the heck is going on out there?"

"You tell us, oh wise Master Zarruq," Ford said from the submarine's tiny bridge, turning back around and bowing with his hands pressed together.

Ignoring the man, Alexander turned to Father Jim. "Padre, what is this?" He gestured up toward the closed hatch above. "What just happened outside? Because surely you all saw what I saw, right, felt what I felt, even inside here? The darkness and crimson moon, the disappearing stars and fireballs falling to Earth, the earthquake and..."

He trailed off, swallowing hard and that blasted ache at the middle of his head returning. He felt faint, his stomach clenched with anxious dread at the meaning of all that had transpired. It was catching up to him now, the adrenaline high of the moment wearing out and reality settling deep into his bones.

Had the apocalypse truly arrived? Had the sixth seal to the Lamb's Scroll just been broken?

Was the Day of the Lord nigh, ushering in the next phase of the world's existence?

Father Jim grasped Alexander's shoulders, resting his large palms on either side and leaning close, face drawn and ashen and older than Alexander had remembered the man. He said, "You best sit down for this one, my boy. It's going to take some explaining."

"Yeah, strap in, homefry," Ford said, gesturing toward a row of four seats along one wall that faced another set. "And get us out of Dodge, Jin. Last thing we need is an Enforcer Stingray creepin' up on our asses."

"John Mark..." Father Jim said, fixing him with a look that told the man all he needed to know.

He frowned and nodded, leaning over Jin's shoulders at the controls and busying himself with operating the personal submergence vehicle. Engines engaged, the hydrocraft sank and dipped and propelled forward on command.

Alexander swallowed hard, a mass of flutters overtaking his stomach and head swimming with the claustrophobic realization he was quickly diving deep under several kilos of water, his worst nightmare. Hated the water. Avoided it at all cost, even refusing to travel throughout the Republic because of it. Yet there he was, being whisked away under the water to who knew where.

And who knew what. Because Ford and Father Jim meant the Ministerium. Which meant trouble.

He took one of the seats, wrapped in navy and feeling surprisingly plush. Who knew the Ministerium knew how to outfit a PSV with proper lumbar support?

Father Jim took a seat next to him, fixing him with tired eyes and an open mouth, seemingly searching for as many answers as he was. "First of all, Alex, how are you?"

Alexander took a breath and swallowed. "I'm fine."

"Are you?" There were those eyes again, probing this time. As if sizing him up for whatever was coming.

He cast his eyes down to the steel floor grating. He muttered, "I've been better..."

Father Jim placed an empathetic hand on his knee. "I understand discovering Martin Zarruq, your father, was not only alive and well but the chief architect behind Panligo and the latest destructive, persecuting designs against the Church was frightfully devastating. It was for me too, for all of us with the Ministerium. To have one of our former foremost prelates, a cardinal and former member of the Fidelium, no less, a faithkeeper—having been entrusted to guard the faith to not only abandon it but seek its destruction!"

The man's voice echoed with a straining rage Alexander had never before heard from the man. His face was red and eyes brimming with emotion. Apparently, the revelation had affected his former mentor as much as him. And why not? They had been close friends through both graduate school and serving together in ministry, his father having tapped Father Jim as the godfather to his only child and son. True, there had been a painful rift between the two after Father Jim basically moved for Martin's excommunication from Ichthus, stripping his father bare because of his apostasy. Yet this was at a whole new level. Because rather than merely seeking to progress the Christian faith, now Martin was seeking to destroy it. Replace it, even, with an abomination straight out of the Book of Revelation. Father Jim knew it; it showed.

The cardinal sighed. "Forgive me, son. But as you can imagine, we've been having a time of it since you went missing, what with the destruction of the Ministerium and the Republic designating Christians as Unfits and the Purge being waged against brothers and sisters in the faith across Solterra. And that's not even touching on the constant worry for your own safety!"

He raised his voice again, without rage but with the same strain. He had clearly been distraught over Alexander's absence.

"Forgive me for leaving, Padre. I just..." Alexander paused, swallowing hard as emotion overtook his throat. He cleared it, continuing: "I'm sorry. I really am. I just didn't know what to do with the news. And after all that had happened, all that I had seen, all that I had lost—my ministry, my parish, Zakaria! I just didn't know what to do."

Father Jim smiled and nodded. "I understand. I'm just

grateful you are safe, and that the Lord Almighty sought fit to return you to us by his good graces."

"How did you find me, anyhow?"

"That would be me," Ford said, turning around and leaning against the captain's chair with arms folded. "You're welcome by the way."

"But how? I made sure that I destroyed my DiviNet device, that I erased all traces of my identity, staying off the grid and lying low."

Ford scoffed. "As if any of that could keep a resourceful former Solterran Legion like me from discovering your whereabouts! Do have to give credit where credit is due, though. Did a bang-up job hiding out. Enough that the Republic sure left you alone. But word gets out about *mystiks* hiding out in Solterra's many armpits."

Alexander's eyes widened at the mention of the slur used for Ichthus ministers. "So I'd been discovered, then, by Solterra?"

"That's what we'd worried once there was word on the magnaroad from sources in southern Roma. Just happy we got to you before the Republic did."

He leaned forward, heart pounding now. "Were they coming for me?"

"Eventually. They always do."

Taking a measured breath, Alexander leaned back and offered a grateful nod. "So what has been transpiring in my absence? With Ichthus, with the Ministerium—with you all?"

"Oh, you know," Ford said, "just jumping phases back to the time of Jesus to retrieve his story for Ichthus in your absence."

Alexander sat up with a start. "Really?"

He laughed, passing a knowing glance to Lucy. "Long story, homefry." Ford looked to Father Jim now, who took over.

The cardinal shifted toward Alexander and fixed him with a serious gaze. "What have we been up to, you ask? Same as you, lad. Survival."

The word rattled inside him, compounded by the look Padre was giving him. A cross between a serious dread from all it meant for Ichthus, but also a hint of disappointment. It was the closest Father Jim came to chiding him for fleeing.

He turned away and nodded silently.

"What happened to the Ministerium headquarters in former Nicaea was the shot across the bow," Father Jim continued. "Similar destruction was wrought from Antakya to Alexandria, from millennia-old Catholic Orthodoxy cathedrals still servicing Ichthus congregations in Germania and Francia and Britannia, to those megachurch monstrosities of Evangelical Orthodoxy strewn across Noramericana and Louisiana all the way over to California and up the Pacific coast to Cascadia. Asiatica has been somewhat more immune to the Purge, as well as your homeland in Alkebulana, the Church in both the Asian and African continents knowing the full measure and might of authoritarian and radically extreme regimes stretching back generations. Brothers and sisters on those parts have been hiding out underground for generations, so they've been tougher to root out and purge from Solterra. It's been dreadful, Alex, simply dreadful..."

Father Jim shook his head with a moan, slumping back into his seat and resting a hand against his head. He went on, "And that's not even touching the surface of the internal strife caused by the likes of Cardinal Dominic Weiss and Josiah Abasi, Apollos Nicolai even, all of the wicked men and women inside the Church casting aside the once-for-all faith of God's holy people like some used garment, soiled in the waste of their adulterous affairs with heresy. Woe to them!" Father Jim exclaimed, pounding his fist into his knee. "Blemishes on

Ichthus, they are, scoffers who follow their own ungodly desires, dividing the Body of Christ and sowing seeds of discord —bringing swift destruction on themselves, even as they tear apart the Church!"

Guilt rose like bile from Alexander's gut, the truth of what Father Jim and Ford, Rebekah and Lucy and others had to face without his help a weight he didn't want to bear. But he had to, facing the fact he'd left his teammates, his family, high and dry.

Father Jim continued, "We've tried regrouping the Ministerium the past year, mostly thanks to John Mark's valiant efforts under Solterra's nose." Ford waved silently from the front. "We've made progress, even forming a Resistance front to the Republic's incursions against Ichthus of former Ministerium agents and everyday believers willing to risk it all for the Church's safety. Sasha has managed to get all of your video and audio recordings of the past up onto some node or something or other in DiviNet, accessible by the community of Ichthus across Solterra."

Alexander forced a smile. "That's good to hear. At least my trips through time were worth it..."

Padre chuckled Alexander's favorite belly laugh and slapped him on the back. "I'd say so, my boy! Your travels retrieving the Church's past has made a real difference in galvanizing the Resistance and informing everyday believers of their faith in Jesus Christ. Most of all, you'll recall Kareema Salam, the woman Ford and Lucy rescued from what used to be ancient Antioch, the woman you briefly met on the beach."

Alexander vaguely remembered the woman, but nodded Father Jim along anyway.

"Well, she has been using the map drawn on the Shroud of Turin you helped recover to locate her fellow members of the Order of Thaddeus Remnant. It's been a slow go of it with plodding progress, but with a dose of providential intervention we'll be able to reconstitute the Order to get us through these dark times—with you at the helm, I might add." Father Jim smiled and winked.

The prospect of Alexander assuming the role as Order Master sent a chill ratcheting up his spine. But he smiled and nodded anyway.

Glancing toward the polished chrome ceiling held up by those steel girders, he said, "What about up top, the signs of the..." He trailed off, not having the strength to voice what he feared he believed to be true.

"You mean the signs of the times?" Father Jim answered lowly. "The apocalypse?"

Alexander nodded quickly, fixing him with searching eyes. "What is it?"

"You tell us, homefry. We've been stuck down in this tin can hunting down your as—err...blessed baby bottom." He glanced at Father Jim, who frowned but didn't say a word. "Anyway, what the heck happened?"

Swallowing hard and rubbing his hands perspiring with the memory against his drying pants, Alexander recounted everything that had transpired—from the start of the earthquake to the dimming sun and on to the blood-red moon and fading, falling stars. Finishing, he looked to Ford and Jin behind him, then to Rebekah and Lucy, their faces registering the same shock and fear.

"'I watched as he opened the sixth seal,'" Father Jim intoned, quoting what Alexander had mentioned to Mateo from the Book of Revelation. "'There was a great earthquake. The sun turned black like sackcloth made of goat hair, the whole moon turned blood red, and the stars in the sky fell to earth, as figs drop from a fig tree when shaken by a strong wind.'"

"The Book of Revelation, chapter 6," Ford said, arms folded

and bobbing back and forth on the balls of his heels with a nervous energy.

Alexander nodded. "That's what I thought when it all went down. But I had always assumed it was figurative, symbolic language. After all, most of Revelation is, isn't it?"

"That's right, lad," Father Jim said, "'tis true. Yet the language is clearly prescient of some grand, cosmic catastrophe."

Ford scoffed. "I'd call the sun blotting out and moon turning red and the freakin' stars fallin' to earth more than prescient language of some grand, cosmic catastrophe!"

Alexander nodded. "The end of the world as we know it."

"And I don't feel fine, thank you very much!"

"Then why they hey-ho day are we still here?" asked Lucy, the petite blonde's lilt reflecting the same twang Ford carried from Noramericana.

"What is your meaning?" Rebekah asked in return, Alexander's heart leaping at the sound of her voice, her own tone and timbre lilting with echoes of his own homeland.

Lucy turned to her. "Meaning, dear sister, the Lord Jesus Christ was supposed to come back and beam us out of here, Star Trek style, before the apocalypse. If what you say is true, Alex and Cardinal Ferraro, that the sixth seal has been darn well near severed in two—then, well, what the hey-ho day happened?"

Father Jim went to answer when he was cut off by the blare of a warning.

It cried out from the digital panel of controls at the front. Something red and alarming and signaling some disturbance.

The whole hydrocraft seemed to seize with as much alarm, not understanding what it meant but understanding enough to be snapped to high-alert status themselves.

"What's the problem?" Alexander asked in ignorance, his heart picking up pace.

Ford spun back toward the controls and leaned over Jin's shoulders again, letting a curse slip under his breath.

"An Enforcer Stingray," he said, face white and drawn with worry.

"The Republic Legion..." Alexander muttered, his mouth going dry now at the truth of the matter.

It just got crazy serious.

Again.

CHAPTER 4

Ford's heart sank to the steel grating beneath; his bowels went with it. He eased into the captain's chair next to Jin and tapped the alarm, silencing the darn thing. Reminded him of a goat from childhood, an annoying critter that would follow him all across their family peanut farm, pestering him for a snack and snappin' at his backside if he didn't give up the goods.

He ran a worried hand across his close-cropped blond hair, the memory of that darn goat pretty well summarizing his annoyance but recognizing the threat was far worse than a missin' patch from his trousers.

Not good, Johnny Mark...

A cold dread swept through him and his mouth ran all sandpapery and coppery from the corresponding sudden surge of fight-or-flight adrenaline, the dreaded Grip wrapping its tentacles around him like those sea creatures he'd read about on DiviNet washing ashore during the Armageddon climate change decades ago. Boy, did he hate how he got when the pressure mounted, pressing in and tightening around his chest like a vice grip and flaring without warning.

Had stretched back to boyhood, having a rough time of keeping it together under pressure. And Pops had smacked him around plenty for it. Basic training with the Legion helped some, and he eventually managed to get it under control. Mostly thanks to bottles of moonshine his grandpappy had taught him to brew.

No moonshine was in reach now, and there was no way in hot Hades he'd let the Grip take hold bobbin' under the water like a rubber ducky.

If his years with the Republic Legion taught him anything, it was that wherever there was an Enforcer, the authoritarian law-and-order brigade of the Republic, that meant nothing good—whether for the polis, or Ichthus.

Or them.

Him especially, given he was a Defector.

Get it together, Ford. It's go time...

Alexander rushed up to his side. "What does that mean?"

Ford eyed the water, the midday sun bright and strong above as they floated several meters below the surface. A few PSV hydrocrafts, with their orange-glow headlamps, ran this way and that farther off into the darkened void that was the sea, a shroud hiding the threat that meant no uncertain doom for his Ministerium passengers.

He replied, "Remember when you asked if you'd been discovered by Solterra, cashing in on rumors of your whereabouts?"

"Yes..."

"Looks like the Republic has come to claim their *merca* credits, homefry."

"Has he spotted us?" Father Jim asked on a shaky breath from the seats. "Is it coming in for the kill, so to speak?"

"First off," Ford said, continuing to eye a part of the control panel that had turned into a radar display, "never utter the 'K' word while a hundred meters under the water, especially when the Legion is nigh. And second, no. Not yet anyway. We've got an early warning system on this puppy that's dialed into the Legion's monitoring systems through DiviNet."

"It can do that?" Alexander muttered over his shoulder.

"Not until I am outfitting the PSV with a special touch of Pavlovich love," Sasha said with a grin from back at his seat.

"Hold up..." Ford said.

"What is the matter, John Mark?" Father Jim said, coming up next to Alexander now.

"Looks like we've got more company than we bargained for." He pointed at the digital panel, two more pulsing red dots joining the one.

The original one stayed put while the other two began spreading out in both directions.

Not good, Johnny Mark...

"Bases loaded..." Ford mumbled, tapping the panel.

"What's that?" asked Alexander.

He twisted around and explained, "An Enforcer maneuver named after the old American baseball pastime from back home. Had been standard-op when I was in the service with Legion capture-and-command missions. A three-point spread that swoops in for the kill."

Alexander replied, "I thought you said never to use the 'K' word while a hundred meters under the water, especially when the Legion is nigh..."

"Look, there—" Ford pointed to the radar as the three points arrayed in a straight line began morphing into a triangle, the one original Stingray holding fast while the two wings started sweeping forward.

Toward their position.

"Hey, doc!" he exclaimed, gesturing toward Sasha. "See if you can work some of your technowizardry and confuse our new friends on the DiviNet side of things."

"I am already being on it, partner," Sasha said from his

seat, his tight blond curls bouncing as he clattered away on a laptop far more powerful than your average computer. Had been used to leverage the full power of DiviNet along with an algorithmic kernel to carry Ford and Alexander back through time. So it was a real powerhouse.

Ford watched the Stingrays continue their maneuvering into position, the one hydrocraft moving forward now as the two outer units zoomed forward to close the net. Didn't have long until their little yellow submarine was caught in their death trap.

With no hope of any escape.

Time to get to it.

He crossed himself on instinct. Which was weird, since he wasn't raised in the Catholic Orthodoxy tradition. But whatever. The maneuver was Christian, no matter how you sliced and diced the factions, and invoking the protection of the cross seemed about the only thing that made sense.

As well as his next move. Which was why he crossed himself.

"You really must have pissed off the Republic, homefry, for them to send three Stingrays to haul your backside to a reprogramming camp."

Ford grabbed hold of a dual-control stick that was divided in halves, both ends operating independently, and eying the radar for the right moment to act.

"Who's to say they're not coming to send your backside to a reprogramming camp!" Alexander said. "I seem to recall you sufficiently pissing them off a time or two, what with deserting them and all. Not to mention killing off their Purifiers and running away with the Order of Thaddeus Remnant they were interrogating."

Ford chuckled. "Suppose I have, haven't I. Either way,

they're coming in hot and heavy with a bone to pick with someone."

"Then what do we do about it?"

He held his breath as the red pulsing orbs on the radar slowly locked into position, two faint corresponding red orbs coming into view dead ahead now. Two headlamps looking like demonic peepers waiting to suck the life out of them.

Wait for it...

"John Mark," Father Jim said, "now seems as good a time as any to launch whatever plan you've been cooking up in that head of yours to whisk us away to safe harbor."

Wait for it...

Alexander chuckled nervously. "Yeah, mate. What's the plan?"

"The plan? I'll tell you the plan."

One end of Ford's mouth curled upward.

Now!

"The plan is to get the heck—"

The PSV suddenly dipped at his command, like an elevator falling down a shaft without its cable, sending everyone's stomachs into their throats and bracing themselves for the underwater plunge.

"—out of Dodge, homefry."

Ford cranked one end of the control stick down, pulling the hydrocraft deeper and deeper into the depths of the sea. He chuckled and added, "Oh, yeah, hold on by the way."

"John Mark..." Father Jim complained, sliding back into his seat and connecting his belt buckle in place. "A bit more warning next time before you take the plunge into the abyss!"

"Sorry about that. But no time to waste when you've got Enforcers on your ass."

"John Mark..."

Ford cleared his throat. "Sorry about that, chief."

The windshield darkened quickly into blackness as the PSV continued plunging deeper down under. The strong, midday sunlight filtering through the surface was gone now. The few other hydrocrafts he had spotted earlier roaming through designated hydrochannels, their headlights slicing through the seawater's depths, blinked dim the farther they fell.

"Where are we headed, Captain Nemo?" asked Lucy.

That bleating goat cut off any response, blaring up something fierce again as the triangle turned more into a funnel.

Heading straight for their position.

"Well, if there was any doubt the Stingrays were coming for us," Jin said, throwing up a pair of high-powered headlamps to illuminate the darkness, "that went out the window."

"Thanks, Captain Obvious..." Ford said, holding the controller steady as the cone of pursuing Enforcers narrowed into an arrow.

No doubt is right.

"Where are you taking us?" Alexander asked with a rushed panic.

"Spotted a volcanic ridgeline on the topographical mapping display a few klicks down below."

"Volcanic ridgeline?" Alexander settled into his seat and buckled in. "Is it safe?"

"Don't worry, homefry. Looks like it's been dormant for a century or two. Should be the perfect hideout until the minions of our Dear Leader lose interest."

"If we make it that far," Jin added, pointing at the radar. "They're gaining on us."

"This seems mighty crazy," Lucy said, voice showing clear strain from the moment. "Even for you, Johnny Mark."

"Thanks for the vote of confidence, sassafras," Ford said.

"Hope you know what you're doing..."

He turned around and flashed her his pearly whites. "Always—"

The PSV suddenly tilted with a rattling shudder, tipping to the left before dipping down with increased speed.

Sending Ford sailing into the control panel, his face smacking it with a thud. A dribble of blood seeped from his nose and down his throat, the coppery eruption reminding him that it was every bit as real as it had been when he was fighting for the Legion rounding up Unfits with the Purifier battalion and getting into firefights with Resistors.

Now he was the one resisting, and under the Legion gun with three Stingrays on his tail under several kilos of water!

"What the heck was that?" asked Alexander.

Ford answered, "The Republic, what else?"

"Are we hit?"

"No," Jin reassured. "Stunned with a high-level pulse wave that packs a punch."

"Which was their warning shot," Ford said, wiping another string of blood from his nose with the backside of his hand and getting hot under the collar from being under fire.

"What comes after the warning shot?" Alexander asked.

"You don't wanna know..."

"Well, can you do somethin' about it, hotshot?" Lucy asked. "Throw up some invisibility cloak and make the jump to hyperspace?"

Sasha shook his head, muttering, "You are watching too many old-school Hollywood sci-fi flicks, methinks."

She smacked him in the shoulder; he yelped. "I thought that's what you were supposed to be fixin' with that doodad of yours. Fiddlin' with the Legion's monitoring systems on DiviNet."

"It is not being so simple! I am just having broken through

the firewall and now I am having to parse through thousands of lines—"

Another shudder, another tilting dip that nearly sent the PSV on its head.

"More parsing, less talking, amigo," Ford said, yanking at the one side of the controller to stabilize their descent while trying to right the ship with the other. "Or we're liable for a date with Davy Jones real soon."

Sasha mumbled something in his Muscovia tongue before the clattering picked up pace.

Good lad.

Now for some fancy footwork to buy us some time...

There was a squeal from behind, then a shout from Lucy: "Mylanta..."

"Where is this water coming from?" asked Alexander.

Ford went to turn around when something caught his attention at his feet.

A puddle of water, quickly growing and spreading at the front.

Shucky ducky...

"Those damn Stingrays must've sprung a leak somewhere. Go find it would ya, Alex, and see what you can do."

"Me?"

"Well, I sure as hot Hades can't get to it with three Stingrays on our—"

"Alright, alright," he said, unbuckling himself.

"I'll go with you," Rebekah said, the pair rushing off to stem the stream threatening to sink their ship.

"And hold on!" Ford yelled, flexing his fingers around both sets of controls, two joysticks moving independently of one another to control the PSVs movement and up-down direction.

It's go time...

Not waiting for a reply, from either the pair in the back or the trio outside, Ford yanked the left stick left and pulled back on the right.

Sending their yellow submarine pivoting through the water and on a zooming course he hoped would throw the Republic off its game.

The cabin reacted as expected, startled protests thrown up but no broken bones. Same for the Stingrays outside, the cone suddenly spinning out like the tail of a Noramericanan tornado moving faster than its eye.

"Jin, cut the lights, would ya?" Ford commanded.

"Cut the lights?" Jin said. "Are you crazy? You'll be running blind here—"

"Just do it, alright! Because so will the Solterran knuckle-heads up on our tail. And if our Ukrainski friend can rustle up some DiviNet disrupting love, then we might have a chance."

"Would you be holding your horses, *bratishka?*" Sasha complained. "Still working on it."

"Well, work faster..." Ford muttered before yanking at the sticks again, throwing the hydrocraft to the right now and descending with a wicked slump that made even himself sick to his stomach.

Just as one of those pulse waves shuddered past, clipping their port-side fin and spinning it like a top.

The PSV threw up a collective yelp, another cough of water spreading through the main cabin and rising above the ankles now.

Double shucky ducky...

Ford yanked on the left stick to right the craft, then the other to straighten its bearing. "You guys making progress on that leak, homefry?" he shouted toward the back.

Another rush of belching water from the back, along with a muffled curse from Alexander, confirmed the worst of it.

They literally were on the run from the Republic and taking on water.

What else could go wrong?

A pair of red eyes suddenly sliced through the darkened abyss, spaced apart with charcoal skin and a pair of fins and a tail rising from the backside that took aim with menacing purpose.

Father Jim threw up a cry and started muttering a prayer, in Latin by the sound of it. Not a bad way to go, considering.

The radar confirmed the truth of it: one Enforcer Stingray coming at their twelve, with another hot on their tail!

The water suddenly glowed from behind. Ford knew the Stingray hydrocraft was getting ready for its ultimate weapon of PSV destruction.

The stinging raygun that would vaporize them into shattered pieces littering the Mediterranean floor in no time flat.

Yanking the stick again and throwing the other one forward, he zoomed past the hydrocraft by a hair just as it let loose its raygun.

A shot of fire blasted past the windshield, the heat of it boiling the water as it streaked past and striking something with a shattering explosion at their stern.

The second Stingray!

"Yee-haw!!" Ford exclaimed, laughing and pumping his fist in the air, one of the pulsing red lights on the radar blinking off with confirmation.

The others joined in as he fishtailed the PSV to throw off the other remaining Enforcer hydrocraft that took the downed fish's spot.

"Did we get one?" Alexander said, coming from behind out of breath.

"Not we. They!"

"The dunces smacked one of their own in the kisser with that fiery stingray thingy!" Lucy exclaimed.

Ford laughed. "The Legion isn't known for employing the best and brightest of the Republic."

"You would know..."

"Hey, watch it, sassafras. You're forgetting that I still got the controls." He dipped the PSV with a sudden jolt and weaved it left to right again, sending Lucy out of her seat to smack Ford's shoulder.

"I should give credit where credit is due, though," she went on. "That was some fancy footwork back there, setting the one Stingray up for the fall."

"Thanks, but we ain't out of the woods yet."

"We are being in luck now!" Sasha exclaimed with excitement.

"What's that, lad?" asked Father Jim.

"Mission is being complete."

A jolt of adrenaline-infused hope rose in Ford. He spun toward the man with a grin. "Lights out then? We got our invisibility cloak?"

"*Da.* I managed to find my way into their—"

"Don't need to know the details, doc," he said, spinning back to check the radar. And grinning at what he found.

The pair of fish that'd been forming behind them with precision for another run at their hide were starting to move with aimless drift, as if confused and blind and totally in the dark.

Which they were, thanks to the Ukrainski professor!

"Not sure how long my little trick will be holding," Sasha explained. "So you better hop to it before they go boom-boom again."

"Don't have to tell me twice..."

Punching through a series of options on the digital dashboard, Ford brought up a topographical map and searched for a spot in the ridgeline for safety.

And found just the spot.

"Hold on to your pants, folks. And goose those engines some, Jin. We're almost out of it..."

"Roger that."

Ford eased the one controller down as Jin thrust their PSV forward, the hydrocraft zooming down and through the darkness. When it was time, he threw on the headlamps to illuminate the seafloor below, a ridge of jagged rocks and waving sea plants shrouded in shadows and punctuated by the yellow light coming into view.

Then it opened up into a maw of darkness, the belly of the floor split like a chest cavity opened up for surgery, the depths below hiding secrets untold, stretching on for kilometers unknown.

"Dear Lord..." Alexander moaned. "You're not seriously contemplating taking us in there, are you?"

Ford smirked. "You scared, Master Zarruq?"

"I dare say we all are, John Mark," Father Jim said, standing behind him now.

Without answering, he told Jin to kill the thrusters and slipped the hydrocraft inside, coasting down through the crevice until bringing it to a rest underneath an outcropping that promised protection.

No one said a word; they dared not disturb the sanctity of the uncharted space. The minutes ticked by as they waited for word on their ruse, the radar falling dead under the weight of the volcanic rock's disrupting influence. When enough time had passed, Ford instructed Jin to give them a boost. He eased the PSV back out into the main crevice and up to the surface, the group holding their collective breath as they crested the lip back out into the open seafloor.

"Looks like we lost the Enforcers, sir," Jin finally said, pointing at the spinning radar, free and clear of any hostiles.

Ford clasped his shoulder and chuckled, heaving a breath and chuckling again. "Roger that. And good work. Why don't we hightail it outta here back to HQ and—"

"Wait a minute," Alexander said. "HQ?"

Ford turned around and grinned. "That's right, homefry."

"But I thought the Ministerium headquarters were leveled by the Republic."

"We got ourselves some new digs since you've been gone. Or rather, *several* new digs. We've sorta decentralized since Solterra rained on our parade."

Jin snorted a laugh. "And with Queller bombs, no less."

"Where?" asked Alexander.

"Actually, the nearest one isn't too far from here, my boy," Father Jim said. "Along the Mediterranean Ridge."

Alexander furrowed his brow with confusion. "The Mediterranean Ridge..." Then he widened his eyes, the truth of it coming into view. "Wait, you're not talking about a deep submergence outpost, are you?"

He looked from Father Jim to Ford, who was still grinning. "You bet your bottom dollar, homefry. A little home-away-from-home right there on the floor of the Great Sea, somewhere between the outer edges of Athenia and Byzantium."

Alexander slumped back into his seat as Jin brought the hydrocraft up to cruising speed, running a hand through his matted hair. "What the heck have I gotten myself back into..."

Ford leaned back in his chair with a smile and propped his feet up on the control panel. "You have no idea, partner."

CHAPTER 5

Sleep came fast and hard for Alexander, as it did for all on board the Ministerium PSV, everyone but Ford taking to different parts of the hydrocraft to snatch some rest during the undersea journey through the darkened depths of the Mediterranean to their new headquarters fighting for the Christian faith and what was left of the Church.

And in the midst of the apocalypse no less!

Boy, did he need the shut-eye, his body collapsing onto the charcoal couch of firm faux leather with a familiar heaviness he had carried with him for months—the bone weariness from the back-breaking work, the loneliness from being on the run, the anxiety from the fear of being caught and cancelled by the Republic. Add to that the apocalyptic chaos that unfolded on the beach and the near-death experience at the hands of those blasted Enforcer Stingrays—all of it had suddenly caught up with him. And now they were headed toward some bucket of bolts from last century that held Ichthus's last hope.

What did I get myself into...again?

The way Father Jim explained it, they were headed to a secret deep-sea submergence station, a so-called DS3, known only to a handful of people within the upper echelons of the

Ministerium's Resistance movement. Alexander was skeptical about the *secret* part, given what had happened to the Ministerium's previous headquarters at the hand of Solterra Quellers, yet another supposedly secretive outpost known only to a handful of people. Yet the mystery outpost was about the only option they had left at that point, relying on some decommissioned research station leftover from the early race to colonize the oceans a century ago under the auspices of the United Earth Oceanic Assembly.

While the former Asiatican nation of China won the space race to colonize the moon, the former United States of America had won the race to populate the seventy-one percent of Earth's surface with DS3 Atlantis. Of course, China followed up their lunar landing with their own DS3 version, called Matsu after the Taoist goddess of the seas—which led to a string of undersea conflicts that nearly derailed the utopian dream of colonizing the undersea world. The UEOA charter was ratified by all nations in 2045, serving as the national and transnational peace and trade accord governing stations, outposts, and the personal and commercial hydrocrafts now congesting the marina corridors like the magnacrafts on the rest of Earth's twenty-nine percent surface.

Although he had been intrigued as a child about stories of sea adventures and oceanic pioneering exploration, a real Wild West given the untamed nature of the underwater world and homestead leases offered for building out an empire embedded in the charter, Alexander wondered what would be awaiting him along the Mediterranean Ridge—and who. Because according to Father Jim, the outpost was staffed by an eclectic group of the Ichthus Resistance as they were now being called, given the Republic's open assault and designation of Christians as Unfits. Several survivors from across Ichthus had managed to get the outpost up and running over the past year after the Church was forced into hiding.

Never much cared for water, the claustrophobic anxiety of it all giving him palpitations even as he tried resting for the journey. So to say he was less than thrilled to be trading his former sea life on land as a wharf workhand for one under water as some Resistant soldier in the Lord's army was the understatement of the year!

A soft *slap* and then a louder *thud* shook him from his quiet contemplation.

Followed by an alarming *rap-rap-rap, rap-rap-rap*.

The rapid-fire slapping jolted Alexander upright in an instant, the rap echoing something fierce throughout the hull. He thought the bolts holding the hydrocraft together were popping clear off the bloomin' thing, it was so bad!

"Sorry about that!" Ford yelled from the front, the *rap-rap-rap* quieting some before picking up again. "Just a school of fish getting in our way, but we should be fine. This bucket of bolts has been through worse." He knocked on the windshield and gave a thumbs up.

"Bucket of bolts is right," Alexander moaned, easing back down for more shut-eye.

"Should reach the outpost in thirty. Catch whatever shut-eye you can get, because it's all hands on deck to sort through Ichthus's latest mess."

He closed his eyes to catch another catnap. "Can't come soon enough..."

"Aww, is big and bad Alexander Zarruq scared of a little water?"

He smiled, recognizing that voice with a lilt from his own lands back home.

"Who are you calling bad?" he said, a roll of knots from the hard faux-leather couch at the rear of the hydrocraft now biting into his back with pain. "You're pretty bad yourself from what I recall from our last experience together zooming through the elements toward no uncertain doom."

Rebekah giggled, taking a seat on a couch across from him. "What can I say? Zooming along the time-space continuum brings out the best in me."

"That is being the space-time continuum," Sasha mumbled down the way from a recliner made of the same tough faux charcoal leather.

She furrowed her brow and smiled at Alexander, whispering: "I stand corrected."

Wincing, he sat up and stretched. "Don't mind him. He's a rather particular individual, especially when his science is concerned and his pet time-travel project."

"I am hearing that, *bratishka*," Sasha muttered again.

"So the water, ehh?" Rebekah said, sliding next to him. "Not a fan?"

He shook his head. "It's that obvious?"

She smiled. "Just a little."

"Have never been much of a fan. But then the anxiety surrounding it went through the roof when my father jumped from that bridge back home, plummeting to his death in the river gorge. At least, that's what I thought had happened."

Alexander took a breath and ran a hand through his nappy hair, sniffing a ripeness to himself and not at all liking the feel of oily, gnarled hair. He needed a hot shower, and soon. A plate of hot food would be nice, too, and a week of sleep to recover.

Resting a hand on his leg, Rebekah asked, "How are you faring, with everything that's happened with your father, the revelations of him being alive and basically architecting the latest threat to Ichthus and the Ministerium?"

Alexander shrugged. "To be honest, I've been sort of numb

to it all, not allowing myself to think about it. To *feel* anything about it. Guess that's why I ran and hid out the past year."

"I understand the feeling. When I found out who my father was, the Minister of Peace and architect of one of the bloodiest authoritarian wars the world had ever seen, I did the same thing, actually."

"You did?" he said, turning toward her now.

"Sure. Ran and ran, then ran some more, with nowhere in particular to go. By then, I had escaped captivity as a child soldier—which was a whole other level of crazy, catching sight on OneWorld News of the man who had sold me to that godforsaken life!"

"I bet." He grinned a little now, mostly because he loved the way she rolled her *R*s, as she had with c-r-r-r-azy. But also because he could take a small measure of comfort from her knowing that she understood his plight—understood *him*, even just a smidge.

"Thankfully, was living with Mama Mara by this time, and had found Jesus Christ. Without him, I don't know what I would have done!"

"Gone c-r-r-r-azy?" Alexander said, mimicking her rolled *R*s.

To which she twisted up her face and put both hands on her hips in feigned disgust. "Are you mocking me, Master Zarruq?"

"Wha—what are you talking about? Wouldn't think about it."

One end of his mouth curled upward trying to suppress a giggle. Then it slipped. And so did Rebekah, shaking a finger at him while opening her mouth wide in laughter, showing him those wonderful white teeth of hers.

"I hope the bit of shut-eye did you some good, my boy," Father Jim said, sauntering over and sitting on the other side of

Alexander. He chuckled and patted his knee, adding: "Because soon you'll be back into the fray of things!"

Alexander smiled, saying nothing. He appreciated being rescued, and knew it was his duty to join the Ichthus Resistance, or the Christian Remnant, or whatever it was that was left of the Church. But wondered what Father Jim had in mind, what he and Ford and the others had been cooking up the past year—and whether he wanted any part of it. Yet voicing his doubts he did not.

"Any word on what the world suffered earlier today?" he said instead, nodding up toward the ceiling of the hydrocraft still humming with forward velocity.

The cardinal took a breath and frowned, shaking his head. "Not a word! A total blackout on DiviNet sites and the WeShare social media platforms. Even OneWorld News has been silent."

"That's changed, chief," Ford said, rushing up to the cardinal with a slate device, an image resting on the thin sapphire display. Max Bacchus himself, the propaganda-meister of Solterra Republic, wearing a powder-blue jacket with a shirt of a similar shade, ruffles poking out and hair matching with streaks of yellow.

"What's this?" Father Jim asked.

"The Republic's response to the full-on display of global cray-cray from sea to shining sea! It was just sent over. Very instructive, it is."

"How so?" asked Alexander, leaning toward the device and eager for news.

"Beats me. Just came as a flagged item through the secure channel from HQ." Ford punched the image and it began to play:

Bacchus laughed, his teeth displayed through a wide, jovial grin as the man snapped his head back in a full-on guffaw.

"Come now, surely you jest! The apocalypse, the end of the world, is that what people are saying?"

An unknown woman giggled and confirmed that was the word on the street.

"Oh, pish posh! It was nothing more than a bit of natural phenomenon that gave quite a show in one corner of the world. Nothing more. Just some sort of solar eclipse, if I heard right from the Ministry of Facts, with a meteor shower for an extra dose of flair. So if you were lucky enough to have witnessed the once in a lifetime phenomenon, then good on you!" The man giggled. "The end of the world...What will people think of next?"

Had to give the man credit. He played the part perfectly, spoon feeding the daily dose of Republic disinformation and alternative facts. Helped that the polis was more than willing to slurp it up, trading truth and transparency for peace, prosperity, and progress—*For Humanity!*

"In other news..." Bacchus said, taking a hand to his hair to smooth a stray lock back into place. "We have some exciting news out of Panligo!"

Alexander stiffened at the mention of Panligo, the memory of his father championing the new religious assembly rushing to the fore. Father Jim stood, grasping the slate device with a straining hold, waiting for the news.

The carnival barker pressed his lips together into a knowing smile, letting a few beats of anticipation tick by. Ever the propagandist! Then a clip of B-roll flashed up on the slate device, and Bacchus announced, "We have ourselves a Summus Sacerdos! I present to you our new Supreme Sacradi."

Alexander was forced to his feet alongside Father Jim with a gasp, the image of the new Panligo leader blazing across the screen.

It can't be...

Father Jim equally gasped at the sight, a tremor taking hold of his hand and nearly dropping the slate device at the reveal.

"Colonel Sanders!" Ford said.

"What was that, lad?" Father Jim muttered, brow furrowed and face fallen.

"The man Ford and I saw," Lucy answered, "on one of our missions to retrieve the Shroud of Turin before the Republic leveled the Ministerium. That official with the upper Solterran echelons."

Except Alexander knew him as someone entirely different.

There he was, a tall man with bronzed skin and wide shoulders and an aged gut, head flush with a mane of white hair, mouth adorned by a goatee and a mustache curled at both ends like handlebars—bearing a striking resemblance to Alexander.

Martin Zarruq. His father.

Alexander's head swam with a dizzying mixture of confusion and dumbfounded disbelief, his stomach clenching with anxious dread at the meaning of it all. His father, some sort of high priest of the newly constituted religious assembly of worldwide spiritualities?

"Bloody hell..." the cardinal muttered, the man seeming to forget himself with the tongue slip.

"Wait a darn second," Ford said. "The man said Summus Sacerdos. A Sacradi. As in some sacred, priestly type—a Panligo Pope, even?"

"In a way. The Summus Sacerdos designation was originally used for the pagan high priest of Rome's ancient religion, the most important position in the ancient imperial religion."

"And Sacradi?" said Lucy.

"As near as I can tell," Father Jim said, "it is a neologism. A mash up of two separate words meaning *community gods.*"

"With old man Zarruq as the head honcho," Ford said. "The high priest of his new Panligo community of the gods."

Father Jim nodded, going silent.

Alexander slumped into the couch, the full measure of the truth of his father's involvement in the pagan abomination realized.

Father Jim joined him, shutting off the slate device and handing it back to Ford, face fallen and drained of color. "Just like the Republic to appoint a Pope-like figure to their new cultic abomination! This raises the stakes to a whole new level, I fear."

And the stakes of Alexander's own involvement...

His head throbbed with the news, the reality quickly becoming a horror that he was now directly pitted against his father. Light versus dark. Good versus evil. Ichthus versus the Republic.

Father versus son.

Was he ready to face such a horror? Did he have a choice?

Yes, he realized. He did. Something Jesus said, in Matthew's Gospel, chapter 10, came rushing from memory: *'Anyone who loves their father or mother more than me is not worthy of me...Whoever does not take up their cross and follow me is not worthy of me. Whoever finds their life will lose it, and whoever loses their life for my sake will find it.'*

In the quiet of the moment, Alexander knew what he had to do. And without anyone knowing, he committed to whatever it took to follow Christ and save his Church.

Taking up his cross like thousands of the faithful before him.

"Then there was that bit of propaganda," Ford added, "from that fruitcake Max Bacchus about the magic show up top."

"Which was a total lie," the cardinal muttered. "Probably concocted by the Republic to shield the true nature of it all!"

"A lie? Which part?" asked Alexander.

"The only bit of intel we received from the field is that this was a worldwide phenomenon."

He stiffened and glanced at Rebekah, confusion mixed with worry flushing her face.

"What do you mean by worldwide phenomenon?" he wondered.

"Just what it sounds like, homefry," Ford answered. "The whole twilight-zone affair—from the darkened sun to the crimson moon to the fading and falling stars and earthquake— all of it was felt and seen across Solterra. But you wouldn't know that if you didn't have eyes around the world like we do. The Republic has put the kibosh on anything that might inform the polis of the imminent collapse of civilization."

"So one sector of Solterra would only think they themselves had experienced the unexpected cosmic display."

Father Jim nodded. "Precisely. The Patron simply hand-waved away the event as nothing more than a fluke of nature, as the OneWorld News report attested, rather than the *super*natural phenomenon that it was."

Alexander shifted and folded his arms, a worm of worry winding its way through him. "And that's what you think it was, Padre? Supernatural phenomenon. Something from—" He swallowed, the truth of it hard to voice. "From the Lord himself?"

"Yes, Cardinal Ferraro," Rebekah joined in, "what do you make of what happened? Was it the work of God?"

"Yeah, chief," Ford added, joining the conversation, "is this the end of the world as we know it, or what?"

The soft *beep-beep-beep* of an indicator alarm interrupted the discussion, bringing the group back to the moment. Something from the front.

Ford grinned. "Showtime." He headed back to join Jin at the controls.

Alexander looked at Rebekah, who shrugged. The pair went to the front to investigate.

Halfway there, Alexander caught his breath at what he saw through the darkened maw of ocean blackness outside, barely illuminated by a pair of headlights. For their lights were joined by dozens more.

Two rings of white lights indicating a large circular structure, with another thicker set at the center looking like windows peering out into the ocean depths. It was massive, the size of a sports stadium from back home. Getting closer, another set of orbs ringed by lights on the outer edges came into focus, then three more. Far smaller than the main hub, but giving the impressions of more pods connected by corridors. It was the largest underwater station Alexander had seen, and the prospects of him living inside for who knew how long did not thrill.

A string of blinking red lights guided them into the belly of the beast, where illuminated walls pressing in against their hydrocraft guided them forward until they emerged into a larger docking bay, a massive circular pool of parked personal submergence vehicles, larger and smaller hydrocrafts than their own, docked with mysterious purpose.

What is this place...

"Home sweet home, kiddos," Ford said, as if answering Alexander's question. The man eased their yellow PSV toward an open bay blinking green until a mechanical arm took over out front, drawing them into position.

A series of thuds and clangs resounded inside, causing Alexander not a small amount of anxiety. Soon the docking sequence was complete.

What awaited them out in the world above was anyone's guess.

CHAPTER 6
MEDITERRANEAN OUTPOST.

Ford's heart picked up pace as the yellow hydrocraft came to a shuddering halt, the water undulating in shades of white and yellow and green from lights mounted to walls of the docking bay. The arm outside the front windshield held the PSV securely between a pair of fish that looked like they'd seen better days, their dull-gray hulls visibly pockmarked from action and streaked by a palette of browns.

A *purr* sounded from the dashboard with an incoming call from up above. He punched the pulsing yellow circle, activating the call.

A woman with fair skin and a dark buzz cut greeted them, with piercing green eyes and a diamond stud accenting one side of her nose. Not what he expected, but he could deal.

"Greetings," she said. "You are being the Ministerium marauders, I presume?"

Ford nodded. "That we are, little missy."

Those eyes narrowed into a curious gaze, and her lips flattened into a smirk. "We shall see..." A vibration shuddered from up above as something latched around the hatch at the top of their fish, giving them the means of escape. She said, "You're cleared. We will be seeing you on the other side, cowboy."

Showtime...

Hopping out of his captain's chair, Ford shuffled to the red ladder stretching toward the hatch up top. Ever since he was a kid, he'd heard tales of exploration and adventure in the farthest stretches of the seas. People thought space would be the final frontier, and the near-Earth parts of it had been charted. But trekking across the galaxy to reach the farthest stars was for the birds, and darn near impossible anyway until recent advances in technology.

It was those stories of undersea adventure that had kept him going from Daddy's binge-drinking beatings. Kept him sane and near well kept him alive—the promise of wide-open plains of water and the freedom to make something of yourself, the comfort of anonymity and the prospect of escaping into a world the farthest thing from his dust bowl hellhole on that peanut farm south of the Mason-Dixon.

Never in a million Noramericana summers would he have dreamed he'd be pushing through a yellow hatch into one of the first research stations of the United Earth Oceanic Assembly! Yet there he was, crankin' the red airlock handle and flippin' the lid and pushing into one final interior hatch leading to the outside world—

Here goes nothin'...

—right before he popped his head up and a pair of strong, dark hands pulled him through and tossed him like a rag doll to a hard metal grating floor, water shimmering with those whites and yellows and greens underneath.

"What the hot Hades..." he moaned, a bell ringing in his head from the force of the drop. He went to all fours when he heard the distinct *chic-chic* of a weapon being cocked at the back of his head.

"Don't move..." a rumbly, rattly man said, sounding like he

smoked a carton of hashish a day and ruining his childhood dream. And it pissed Ford off.

A chorus of voices were raised behind him, but he didn't pay 'em much mind. All he cared about was the heat racin' up the back of his neck at being bamboozled. And right after his trip down nostalgia lane.

So he did something about it.

Springing to his feet, he spun around and pulled an alley-oop trick out of his old Purifier hat, disarming the man without even a shot being fired.

"What the—" the mystery man said, a big, burly thing with leathery skin and long dark dreadlocks spun up into a mean hive. Face was masked with a dark-gray strip of black cloth, and he wore some sort of uniform of the same, but no insignia that he could see.

"Too bad, so sad, partner," Ford said. "You've gotta—"

"John Mark! Put the gun down, if you please..."

It was the cardinal, pulled up top along with Alexander and Jin, the ladies, the Ukrainski doc. Pulled into a huddled group with weapons drawn on them by two chicks. One of which was the short, dark-haired Doberman he'd seen on the hydrocraft dashboard. The other looked like an exact replica, but with blond locks shaved just as close and blue eyes that were a bit hypnotic. Twins, by the looks of it.

Tweedle Dum and Tweedle Dee.

Just his luck.

Ford stood, lowering his weapon but ready to use it if he needed to. Didn't know what the hot Hades was going on. For all he knew, they'd walked into a trap. With no way out.

"Now, is that any way to treat a merry band of Ministerium marauders?" he said.

"The shibboleth," the original short-haired chick said.

"The whatchamacallit?"

"I believe our welcoming party is asking for the passcode," Father Jim said.

"Oh, is that all..."

Alexander came from behind the cardinal, tapping him on the shoulder. "It's a reference from the Book of Judges, chapter 12. Something to tell friend from foe."

Ford replied, "And how about open sesame?"

Short Blonde-Haired Chick suddenly raised a weapon at Ford, as did the burly dark-skinned man with a different gun and two others who looked like they'd been reared in Americana or Europa.

Which sent Alexander spreading his arms in front of Father Jim in protection and the others scurrying behind as well with muffled protests.

Ford dropped his weapon and raised his hands. "Was it something I said?"

Alexander chuckled. "Actually, it was. The wrong password. But I've got the right one."

"Then spit it out, homefry! No time like the present to save our backsides."

"*Sepio*," he said, raising his head high and withdrawing a round metal object from a pocket. That medallion he'd been gifted those many months ago from Theophilus, Master of the Order of Thaddeus, until he met his demise and passed the torch along to the kid.

Whispers rippled throughout the room at Alexander's mention of a word Ford had heard a time or two from Kareema. Something about a Christian version of the former American Navy SEALs, but stamped by the Holy Spirit.

Short Dark-Haired Chick stepped forward, wielding a staff outfitted with a wicked head that glowed purple and pointed in their direction, electrical tendrils racing around it. A shiver ran up Ford's spine at the familiar sight, something he had used a time or twelve with the Purifiers. Scythes, they were called. Its name pretty well told the whole story on its reason for being.

The woman took the medallion Alexander was holding out, flipping it over and sighing. Her face softened and she turned back toward her compadres, nodding and easing that wicked staff used to subdue unruly Unfits toward the floor.

Ford took in a measured breath, the tension easing from his shoulders and back and neck. Now they were getting somewhere, all thanks to Alexander's shibboleth, or whatever the hot Hades it was.

She handed it back to Alexander. "The Order of Thaddeus Master's medallion."

Alexander stuffed it back into a pocket and nodded. "That's right. I am him. And you all are part of the Ichthus Resistance, is that right?"

The woman nodded. "You are being correct. Nia, is my name."

"That's a mighty unusual one," Ford said.

She glanced at him, unsmiling. "It is being a shortened form of Junia. Junia Kaminski."

"Kaminski?" Sasha said, popping out from behind Father Jim, that moppy head of blond curls dancing with an extra skip in their step. "Are you being from Vostakana?"

"*Da*. Ukrainski."

Now he grinned like a little schoolboy, the man throwing up some Muscovia jibber-jabber. Love at first sight, by the looks of it.

"Can we get back to it, folks?" Ford said. "Or do you two need a room?"

"Junia," Father Jim said, coming back around from Alexander. "Named after the apostle commended to the ancient Church of Rome by the Apostle Paul?"

She smiled now and nodded. Then motioned toward the

other two who had engaged them. "These two are Phoebe and Titus, my twin sister and her husband."

"Named after the deaconess who bore Paul's letter to the same Christian community and the young man Paul left in charge of his church plant in Crete?"

"Correct, you are," Phoebe said, nodding to her husband with the dreads.

"How biblical..." Ford muttered. "How about we get the show on the road. Because I reckon the Republic won't be sitting on its laurels while we chew the cud." He stepped forward when Nia held out her staff, its head pulsing purple.

"This is being my station," she said, eyes narrowing and face hardening with resolve. "And we are going at my command."

"Alright, sassafras. No need to get your ushanka in a bunch."

"And you are being?" she asked.

"John Mark Ford, at your service." He bowed, then motioned toward the others. "You've already met Sasha Pavlovich."

Nia turned toward the man, brow raised. "*The* Sasha Pavlovich. The man who was inventing time travel?"

"Sister, you have no idea. The two gals behind him are Lucy and Rebekah. The distinguished fellow with silver hair is Cardinal James Ferraro."

"*Da.* Head of the Ministerium. We have been in contact."

"Very well. And this here is Alexander Zarruq. Our resident Master of the Order—"

The room suddenly shifted again, weapons drawn and that Scythe pointed now at the guy from Tripolitania.

"Whoa, whoa, whoa! What the hot Hades is this about?"

"You are being a *Zarruq?*" Nia said through gritted teeth.

Alexander's face fell, but the man kept it together. Had to give him credit for that.

"That is correct," he said.

"Any relation to our new Sacradi?" Titus said with raised weapon.

He hesitated, but replied, "The man is my father. Or at least was..."

"Do you realize what he has put us through? All of us!" Nia said, waving her one free arm around the room. The others nodded and grumbled in agreement.

Now Ford stepped forward and stepped up to the plate. "Lay off the guy, would ya? He thought the old man was dead. By suicide, none the less. Had not a clue what the psychopath was up to. We're here because we need help, because we're fixin' to do something about it. So are you game or what?"

Nia fixed him with those steely, slitted green eyes again, face hard and noticeably toned biceps gripping that Scythe with the purple head. She said something to her sister in that Muscovia tongue, then led the way out of the docking bay.

"Golly, that one's a ripe one, ain't she?" Lucy said, coming up to Ford's side.

He huffed a sigh and nodded, rushing after the lady who was plucking every last one of his nerves.

Nia and Phoebe led the way, followed by Ford and Alexander and Lucy, with Sasha trying to push past Father Jim and Rebekah toward the front—no doubt to strike back up again with his new Ukrainski chickadee—but the tight corridors of dull-gray steel wouldn't let him. Titus and the other two unknown Resistance men brought up the rear as they wound their way along several twists and turns and up along ramps through the deep submergence station, windows of darkened indigo water hiding the murky depths beyond and cold, hard steel shrouding the secrets of the Ministerium and Ichthus Resistance up ahead.

Stopping abruptly at a nondescript door, a zipper seam running the length of the closed entrance, Nia pressed a palm against a glass security device that glowed blue until flashing an approving green. A shudder echoed through the corridor and the seam unzipped before the doors retracted, revealing some sort of bridge, like something out of one of those Kindle bargain-bin sci-fi novels he read as a kid before Amazon was appropriated by Solterra.

It was roomy and dimly lit, warm lighting softening some of the cold harshness of the steel. It was also circular, the entire space ringed by windows looking out into the ocean depths curving toward a center point. Must be at the tippy-top of the station. Along the periphery were workstations manned by a smattering of men and women, all wearing the gray jumpsuits that had been standard-issue Ministerium garb at their former HQ. The one he had commanded but which had been destroyed. At the center was a circular table, edged by chairs.

"Nice digs," Ford said, planting his hands on his hips and sizing up the joint.

"It is being more than adequate," Nia said with a shrug, taking one of the seats and motioning toward the others. "Please, have a seat."

"What is it you've been doing here?" asked Alexander, sitting at the other end across from Nia, Ford and Father Jim sitting on either side. Lucy and Rebekah and Sasha joined them while Phoebe and Titus and the two other Johns joined Nia—consciously or not, forming two sides.

"Safeguarding Ichthus, that is being what!" Nia said, kicking up a leg and resting her foot on top of the table.

Ford raised a brow, eyeing the interesting show of classless bravado, asserting herself while leaning back in her oversized chair, its back jutting up higher than the rest. Clearly a tell that meant she believed she was the boss of the joint. What peeved him was that as chief of Ministerium operations, he technically outranked her, even with the newly formed Resistance. Although with HQ destroyed, and what was left of their Ministerium people dead or on the run, he wasn't even sure he had a show left for his operational dog and pony. Best to let her think she's in control and keep the yapper shut, then assert himself when the moment called for it.

Alexander continued, "What do you mean by that, safeguarding Ichthus? From what?"

She twisted up her face and smacked her staff on the tabletop with a thudding echo. "From the Republic, you moron! And from Zarruq, the other Zarruq. Your *bat'ko* who has been orchestrating the Church's destruction!"

Alexander shifted in his seat. He set a clenched fist on the table, head bowed but jaw clenched shut.

"Yeah, about that," Ford said, intervening before things got testier than they were. "Our friends topside said you've been doing a bang-up job secreting away Christians from the all-seeing Solterra eyes. Saving men, women, and children from no uncertain doom from the Republic's Purge." Figured slathering on a heaping scoop of attagirl would do the body good.

Nia nodded. "*Da.* That is being correct."

So much for modesty...

"The Purge has been more successful than we initially would have imagined," Titus intoned with that deep, baritone voice of his, a cord of dreadlocks coming loose and falling to his shoulder. Caressing it in one hand, he added: "And also less so, in unexpected ways."

"What do you mean by that, Titus?" asked Alexander.

The man slung his muscled arms up on the table with a thud, opening his hands to explain, "The all-out assault against the Church of Jesus Christ by Solterra over a year ago now was devastating. Leveling not only the Ministerium headquarters in former Nicaea, but also bringing the same destruction to Christian communities across Solterra. Church buildings across Europa stretching back to the Reformation and even the late Middle Ages were leveled. Megachurch monstrosities of steel and concrete were reduced to rubble in Americana and Noramericana. And what modest cathedrals dotted the landscapes of Alkebulana and Asiatica, they too were destroyed in a campaign to quell and purge the world of the obvious signs of Ichthus's presence."

The echo of the memory of those Queller bombing raids at the Ministerium's HQ gave Ford a shudder. They'd barely made it out alive at the hands of a platoon of Purifiers sent to cancel their backsides. Thank the Lord Almighty for the escape hatch—and the yellow submarine at the end of it!

"Entire worshipping communities were being smashed to smithereens," Nia added. "The fires of Solterra have driven us out of our towns and cities, like rats scurrying for hiding with rising floodwaters."

"Sending believers underground, you mean?" Alexander asked.

"Underground, under water, in caves and crevices across the Republic."

He nodded, his face falling and eyes going back to the surface of the table. Ford felt for the fella, given his own experience with dear ol' Dad. Only his had died in some backwoods border town between Americana and Noramericana before the Reckoning. At least he had that going for him. Couldn't imagine finding out he was in fact still alive; didn't know what he'd do if he went fixin' to embody Satan himself as some Grand Master of a Republic-endorsed cult.

Actually, he did know what he'd do. And that frightened him to pieces.

"And what is the unexpected part of the Purge?" Alexander asked, head raised and lookin' like he was back in the game. Good boy.

Titus smiled, a row of white teeth gleaming behind his flat black face, a gold tooth glinting in the light. "Not only has Ichthus survived, but we're thriving! Finding ways to embody Christ like never before outside the confines and trappings of ultramodernity. With its light shows and fog machines and highly amplified worship sets, with its buildings and programs and franchised churches showing some talking head on a screen."

Father Jim snorted. "The innovations of Evangelical Orthodoxy never cease to amaze me..."

"Not just Evangelical Orthodoxy, Cardinal Ferraro," Titus corrected. "All branches of Ichthus had taken to accommodating itself to culture post-Reckoning in order to claw back some semblance of power and status and respectability within the Republic and ultramodern culture."

Nia smirked. "That is not even touching on how Ichthus accommodated its beliefs to the paganism of Solterra."

"Which led to Panligo in the first place!" Father Jim added, "And the Church's current lot in life."

Titus leaned back. "Which hasn't been all bad, in my estimation."

"What are you playing at?" Alexander asked. "Ichthus has been reduced to rubble. What good can come from that?"

"Ichthus is not being reduced to rubble in the slightest!" Nia said, waving a hand in the air. "Her church buildings and infrastructure, perhaps. But not the Church itself."

"They are surviving and thriving in secret, yes," Titus said. "But also rediscovering what it means to be the Body of Christ through charitable acts of everyday kindness and bold, courageous witness to the good news of rescue in Jesus Christ alone. There is a movement afoot." The man smirked, smiling now, that golden tooth glinting with an ebullient joy that gave even Ford some hope. "A Resistance."

"And we are helping them," Nia added. "All of us in our network of survivors and Resistors to the pagan ways of Panligo and Solterra, combining the forces of the Ministerium leftovers and certain Remnants of Christian orders from ages past together with believers across the Republic living life in the everyday."

"Speaking of which," Ford said, clearing his throat and scooting to the edge of his seat. "Our friends up top also said you were in a position to be able to give us a helping hand down here."

"*Da*. That is being correct. But before I am agreeing to be doing that, I want you to be answering us one thing."

Ford leaned back. "Shoot, partner."

Her face grew grim, falling and jaw setting in place. Then her eyes went toward the glowing ceiling. "What is it that is happening up above?"

Ford snorted a laugh. "The end of the world, sister. What else?"

"I am being serious. We have been receiving reports from all across the Republic from our brothers and sisters in the faith, connecting with those left over from the Ministerium, and have seen the destruction that has been raining down from on high."

There was a quiver to her voice now, a quake that betrayed the earlier bravado. She was shaken. By the looks of it around the table, they all were.

Ford took a breath and gestured toward the cardinal. "Perhaps you should take this one, chief. A bit above my pay grade, I'm afraid."

Father Jim's face grew slack, and his eyes narrowed with an intensity that was unnerving. "What else, my dear, but the famed Day of the Lord?"

"The Day of the Lord?"

"He means the end of the world as we know it," Alexander answered. "The apocalypse."

A mixture of confusion and worry rippled through the room.

"What are you meaning by the apocalypse?" Nia exclaimed with a strained voice. "We are still being here, for God's sake!"

"Tell me about it, sister," Ford said. "That's what I wondered."

"Me too," Lucy added. "I voiced the same bewilderment, wondering if the sixth seal has been darn well near severed in two, then what the hey-ho day happened? Never got an answer."

"Interrupted by those blasted Stingrays."

"Stingrays?" Nia asked, brow raised with concern. "As in those crazy Solterra hydrocrafts that have been stalking the underwater church the past year?"

Ford waved a dismissive hand. "That's a whole other ball of ugly for another time."

"Padre," Alexander said, "Lucy's point is well taken, I believe. How is it possible that we have entered the apocalypse if Ichthus is still here?" He waved a hand around the room, adding: "If *we're* all still here?"

Ford chuckled. "Yeah, it's not like you're sayin' we've been left behind!"

The cardinal said nothing.

An anxious jitter suddenly ratcheted up his spine. He muttered, "Are you, chief?"

Father Jim took a breath and nodded. "I should probably explain my meaning." He raised a finger, pointing across the table and adding: "And what I mean, what I believe the Word of God itself means, is vitally important for the days ahead. For what I am about to share is a matter of truth and lies, belief and doubt—even life and death themselves."

He paused, fixing his gaze from one person to the next.

"It matters for the Republic, for Ichthus, for every person seated here this day."

Ford frowned and swallowed hard. Didn't have a clue what it all meant. Not what the Bible said, not what all the funk rainin' down from on high meant for the world and the Church. Not in the slightest. But they were about to find out.

And he didn't know if he was ready.

CHAPTER 7

Alexander glanced from Lucy to Rebekah to Ford. Their faces said it all: They weren't ready for what Father Jim was about to reveal.

Truth be told, neither was he.

The end of the world had always been something of a distant possibility, and much more of a theological idea, born first through his instruction in the Church and then his courses training to be a priest at Oxford. Perhaps had he and the others lived a generation ago, during the Great Reckoning when the world had been set on fire through cataclysmic climate change and the wars that nearly ended human civilization—living through that would have primed anyone to believe the end was near, and prompted Christians to anticipate Jesus Christ's second coming was one sleep away.

Now, post-Reckoning, with all the peace, progress, and prosperity the Republic offered, it was harder to believe the world as they knew it would end. Even with Solterra's Purge against Ichthus, labeling Christians as Unfits for reprogramming and destroying their churches—even then, Alexander had a hard time wrapping his mind around it all.

The coppery tang of adrenaline was heavy on his tongue

now, his heart thudding in his chest at the thought of what Father Jim would reveal. A tremor ran through a hand, and he clenched it. No time for that nonsense now. Time to keep his head in the game and get some answers.

"Padre," Alexander said before the man got into it, "do you think this is the end? That Jesus' second coming is near, that the Great Tribulation itself is around the corner?"

Father Jim leaned forward, placing his elbows on the table and making a tent with his hands at his nose. "While I cannot be entirely certain, and although every era of the world has had its share of apocalyptic-feeling events—be it the collapse of the Roman Empire to the Black Death of ancient Europa, from the two Great Wars on the same continent in the 20th century to the economic meltdowns and pandemics that popped up here and there through the 21st century and on until the events of the Great Reckoning just decades ago. And although every era has seen its share of Antichrist-like figures—be it Nero with the early Church to Pope Leo X, according to those rabble rousers of the Reformation, on to Hitler and Saddam Hussein of the 20th century and George Soros and Bill Gates of the 21st century—"

"Forgive me, cardinal," Nia interrupted, slinging another leg up on the tabletop in a way Alexander found disrespectful, "while I am appreciating all of the caveats and hedging, we are being rather pressed for time here. Can you be getting to it, hmm, and give it to us straight?"

Father Jim chuckled and put up a surrendering hand. "Point well taken. If you were to put a Neutralizer to my head, I would say—yes, I believe the return of Christ is at hand, that we are on the brink of what the Bible terms, the Day of the Lord."

The room went silent at his honesty. And given Padre's hedges, and knowing he was not one who was given to flights of fancy, especially apocalyptic ones, Alexander guessed the man was surer of the truth of what he voiced than of anything he'd ever said in his entire life.

"Excuse me, Father," Rebekah said, raising her hand. Alexander thought that was cute, as if she were sitting in one of his classes back at Oxford. In many ways, they were all being schooled in the nature of the end times by no better a professor.

"Yes, dear, what is it?" Father Jim said.

She cleared her throat. "What is this Day of the Lord you speak of?"

"An important theme from the Prophets in the Hebrew Scriptures that portends a coming day when the Lord Yahweh would come to act in judgment against the wickedness and sin and unrighteousness of the world whilst also extending mercy and salvation." Father Jim tilted his head back and closed his eyes, reciting from memory:

> *Let all who live in the land tremble,*
> *for the day of the Lord is coming.*
> *It is close at hand—*
> *a day of darkness and gloom,*
> *a day of clouds and blackness.*
> *Like dawn spreading across the mountains*
> *a large and mighty army comes,*
> *such as never was in ancient times*
> *nor ever will be in ages to come.*
> *The day of the Lord is great;*
> *it is dreadful.*
> *Who can endure it?*

Ford swallowed. "How ominous..."

Alexander leaned over and whispered, "I think you mean, how apocalyptic."

Rebekah sat up straight in her seat. "That is from the prophetic Book of Joel, chapter 2, isn't that right?"

The cardinal nodded. "Indeed. And in light of Christ's first coming, we understand the Day of the Lord to include his death on the cross, the event fulfilling the Messianic promises of judgment and mercy in the present through his crucifixion, where judgment was passed on the sins of the world through him and mercy extended to those who trust in his work by faith. But then it also anticipates a future event, where God's ultimate judgment will be passed on the last day when Christ returns a second time in glory with his holy ones."

"And you are believing that day has come?" asked Nia from the other end of the table.

He took a breath, glancing at Alexander, then nodded. "I do. At least it is the beginning of the end. The birthing pains of the coming full judgment through the Great Tribulation."

Alexander took a breath, a flutter of anxiety and dread and anticipation beginning to well within his stomach and bloom through his body and head. The apocalypse, the Day of the Lord, the end times, coming to bear upon the Republic, across Solterra.

For real?

He had a hard time believing it to be true. Probably because he didn't want it to be true. Especially because the cardinal had signaled that believers themselves would experience at least part of this judgment unleashed from the outstretched arm of the Lord alongside the rest of Solterra. Something that needed clarity, which Father Jim could provide.

He cleared his throat and scooted to the edge of his seat. "But again, you were about to explain why we're all still here before we were so rudely interrupted by those Enforcer Stingrays—"

Ford snorted a chuckle. "Yeah, don't you love it when the Republic drops in and messes up your Bible study?"

The room joined in with a knowing laugh. For the Republic had wrought far worse across Solterra.

Alexander appreciated the lighter moment, laughing as well. Then continued, "What I'm asking, Padre, is if the apocalypse is nigh, if Christ's return will then follow this…this Great Tribulation, as you put it—then why hasn't he raptured all of us sitting here beforehand?"

Father Jim shifted in his seat, leaning back and furrowing his brow, like the good old days back at university when he prepared to launch into an hour-long lecture. Alexander couldn't help but smile at the memory, knowing what they were all in for once Padre got started.

The man said, "That is precisely what I wanted to talk to you all about, Alex. So thanks for reorienting the discussion straight away."

Alexander smiled and nodded, his head feeling a bit dizzy now with an anxious anticipation at what Padre was about to reveal.

"Over a century ago," Father Jim began, "there was a popular novel series that promised a glimpse of the apocalypse in a fictitious, yet biblical way what would happen if all true Christians were suddenly raptured to heaven, a secret snatching and transporting of believers from this world into the next, leaving the world behind to face God's judgments during the so-called Great Tribulation."

"Sort of a beam-me-up end-times belief?" asked Ford.

"That's right."

"How rather escapist theologically."

"And Western," Alexander added.

Father Jim nodded. "Exactly, my boy! It was a precisely Western, even Americanan response to the existential anxieties of the world and the possibilities of the genuine Day of the Lord prophetically revealed in the Bible and all the end-times details surrounding that day."

"What was being the problem, exactly?" asked Nia.

"The problem, Junia, is that there is absolutely no biblical evidence that this so-called pre-Tribulation framework for understanding the end of the world as we know it is the truth of the matter! No Bible text explicitly teaches that Ichthus will be removed from the world before the Great Tribulation of God's judgment."

"Really?" Ford said. "My meemaw seemed to be dialed in pretty tightly into that pre-Tribulation framework, as you put it. Was pretty well raised on that flavor of Ichthus myself." He laughed, running a hand across his close-cropped hair. "And when the Second Civil War reared its head back in the former U.S. of A., we pretty well thought Jesus' return was right around the corner!"

"And where were you being raised?" Nia asked.

"Noramericana."

"Which I believe was being the point the cardinal was making before, about it being a thoroughly Western, Americana belief."

He went to respond, but shut his mouth. Alexander chuckled to himself at the woman, leaving the man speechless. No small feat.

"To be fair," Lucy added, "Ford here isn't the only one who was reared in this understanding of the end of the world. My own meemaw and grandpappy and parents themselves taught that Christians would escape the worst of the world's suffering and persecution when the Antichrist makes his appearance. And especially would be snatched up before the Lord Almighty doled out his just desserts on the world."

"Thank you, Luciana Jane," Ford said with an air of vindication, nodding and folding his arms. He turned back to Padre and said, "Are you sure that this pre-Trib framework for the end times isn't in the Bible, chief?"

Father Jim leaned back and crossed his arms. "You think otherwise, John Mark? Try to find one single verse to support it in its entirety, go on!"

He opened his mouth to speak, then closed it, tilting his head and looking off as if in thought, eventually saying: "Yeah, I got bupkis."

Father Jim nodded. "That's what I thought."

"So what's the alternative, Padre?" Alexander asked with intrigue, yet regretting the possible answer. "If Christians aren't —well, beamed up, so to speak, before the return of Christ, then what's the alternative?"

The man leaned in closer, as if letting him in on a secret. "The alternative, my boy, is this: What if *everybody* is left behind?"

"Everybody?"

"Including Ichthus, the remnant of the Church?" asked Ford.

"That's right." Padre went on, "Or to put it more baldly, what if no one can or should expect to escape before the Great Tribulation, the era of God's judgment? That would mean Christians would only escape, if you can call it that, in the way Christians have always escaped from persecution."

"And what way is that?" Lucy asked.

"Why, by dying, Ms. Jane."

"Dying?" Alexander exclaimed, not at all liking where Father Jim was taking the conversation.

"That's one helluva way to escape..." Ford muttered before his eyes went wide and he bowed his head at the slip of the tongue.

Alexander had to agree with the man, though. He hadn't

been catechized in a deep framework of the end times like Ford had, with Christians exiting the world before it was judged. But it all seemed much, the idea that the Church would experience the unleashing of the Four Horses, and the trumpets announcing doom, and the bowls of wrath!

"The notion of escaping the Great Tribulation is certainly appealing," Father Jim went on. "Especially for those in the last few centuries in the former European and American nations who had enjoyed relative peace and safety from any sort of persecuting fires. Oh, they might have had their freedoms of speech curtailed or lost employment opportunities for their belief. Perhaps were shunned by family or friends, dropped off the holiday card list once it was known they were a Christian. But persecution in those nations, during those times, wasn't persecution; it was an inconvenience."

The cardinal shifted in his seat again, leaning toward the table and pressing his palms on its surface. He continued quieter now, more solemn, even: "And yet, untold numbers of our brothers and sisters of Ichthus from around the world have long been experiencing what we would consider tribulation, especially outside the traditional West, in former Europa and the Americas. Martyrdom, suffering from wars, facing plagues and drought, their children kidnapped for their parents' faith. The issue shouldn't be whether we would like to escape tribulation—whether from Republic Quellers destroying our Ministerium headquarters with rockets or meteors crashing into our beach at the breaking of the sixth seal. The issue is whether the Bible teaches that the Church will experience the effects of the unfolding of God's judgment."

"And does it?" Ford said on a nervous breath.

"Paul's second letter to the Thessalonians makes this clear." The man spoke from memory: "'*The coming of the lawless one will be in accordance with how Satan works. He will use all sorts of displays of power through signs and wonders that serve the lie, and all the ways that wickedness deceives those who are perishing. They perish because they refused to love the truth and so be saved. For this reason God sends them a powerful delusion so that they will believe the lie.'"* He added: "Two things are clear here about two things that must happen before Christ finally returns in all his glory: apostasy and the revelation of the lawless one."

Ford asked, "The lawless one? Who's that?"

Alexander wondered the same thing. Until it dawned on him. "You're speaking of the Antichrist, aren't you?"

The cardinal nodded. "And the Book of Revelation seems to suggest this person storms upon the stage of history to make his stand against King Jesus upon the commencement of the Great Tribulation. At some point anyway."

"So apostasy, apocalypse, and Antichrist..." Alexander said in contemplation. "That's the order before the return of Christ?"

"Something to that effect, my boy. After the man of lawlessness, the Antichrist is revealed, with signs and deceptive wonders to entice the world into its idolatrous abominations, including trying to drag away members of Ichthus into its den of copulation with the whore of Babylon—it is then that Jesus will come to gather his people, his saints and give them rest from affliction, all the while destroying the Antichrist and his followers."

Nia suddenly pulled her legs off from the table and slid to the edge of her seat. "But how are you saying that Ichthus themselves will be experiencing the kinds of apocalyptic mayhem that the Book of Revelation says the world will be experiencing, with all the seals and trumpets and bowls?"

"Didn't think I'd say this," Ford muttered, "but I'm with her."

"Take Paul's first letter to the Thessalonians, chapter 4," Father Jim said, sliding to the table as well. Again, he quoted from memory:

> *According to the Lord's word, we tell you that*
> *we who are still alive, who are left until the*
> *coming of the Lord, will certainly not*
> *precede those who have fallen asleep. For*
> *the Lord himself will come down from*
> *heaven, with a loud command, with the*
> *voice of the archangel and with the trumpet*
> *call of God, and the dead in Christ will rise*
> *first. After that, we who are still alive and*
> *are left will be caught up together with them*
> *in the clouds to meet the Lord in the air.*
> *And so we will be with the Lord forever.*

"Paul does not teach some sort of secret call to believers here," the man went on, "one that the world itself cannot hear. No, instead he speaks of a shout and God's trumpet, the antithesis of some sort of secret signal reserved for a few. And such calls were typically battle cries in the ancient world when combined with trumpets. No, my brothers and sisters, what the Apostle is speaking of here is certainly not any secret coming or secret rapture. The rest of Scripture doesn't depict Jesus' coming as secretive, either. Instead, it will be a very public viewing. And according to the rest of the Bible, following a time of great calamity."

"The Great Tribulation," Alexander added, a growing sense of dread churning in his belly that the past twenty-four hours portended much more than a meteor shower to come.

Father Jim nodded. "That's right. The New Testament seems to suggest a period of final, particularly intense affliction

—birth pangs, if you will, at the very end of the age. Nevertheless, it also speaks of prior events as merely the beginning of birth pangs, which have been occurring since Christ's resurrection and ascension, even in the first century. However, Jesus said that those initial birth pangs are not the end themselves. This is what is meant by the seals of Revelation, actually. They depict the generalized judgment of God through wars and human violence, economic downfalls and depressions, plagues and famine, and the persecution and martyrdom of the saints. It is not until the blowing of the final trumpets that the true judgment of God is unleashed upon the world, the content of the final, seventh seal."

"And all of this we will experience, without escape?" asked Alexander.

"That's correct. At least, that is one interpretation of the apocalyptic prophesies of Scripture. Which seems to be proving true, given what unfolded half a day ago above the water's surface."

Ford scoffed. "Where's the hope in that?"

Father Jim turned to him. "Hope? The hope given us in the Bible isn't that we will escape, but instead that we will be resurrected when Jesus returns when he brings to end the cosmic age, finally establishing his ultimate rule and reign and recreating our world anew. Although the hope of escapist theology is that the last generation of believers before Christ's return are resurrected before the Great Tribulation, appealing to those who believe they belong to that last generation, such belief has not proven itself relevant in the two millennia since Jesus' first coming. Remarkably, it never showed up in the history of the Church until merely three centuries ago!"

"Where'd it come from then?"

"It was based on a system of beliefs first developed around 1830, by one John Nelson Darby, where he devised a theory of a secret pre-Tribulational rapture. However, no such talk is anywhere in Paul's letters, or the Gospels and the Book of Revelation for that matter. One has to wonder that if the theory of a secret rapture is so secret that it is not even explicit in the Bible, why then should anyone believe such a thing? And no one did until around 1830."

"Then why did they?" asked Alexander.

Padre explained, "Many Christians latched onto Darby's view for the wrong reasons, believing they were the last generation and that they would escape severe persecution. Which made sense in the 19th and 20th centuries, given the chaos that unfolded through the Great Wars and plagues and economic meltdowns. Such beliefs were held firmly clear through the 20th and 21st centuries as more chaos unfolded on the world, with wars and rumors of wars, recessions and depressions ravaging the world's economies, plagues of unknown origin skipping around the world unabated. The only problem is that the earliest Church fathers in the second century were premillennial and post-Tribulational."

"Meaning?" Nia asked.

Alexander answered, "That they believed Jesus would return before reigning on Earth and establishing his kingdom, but only after the Great Tribulation. Isn't that right, Padre?"

Father Jim nodded. "Precisely. These earliest believers thought they themselves were in the midst of the Great Tribulation or about to go through it. Which was understandable, given the waves of Roman persecution throughout the Empire. Saint Irenaeus taught this view, writing about *'the resurrection of the just, which takes place after the coming of Antichrist, and the destruction of all nations under his rule.'* Revelation 12 supports this, suggesting that tribulation is a normal experience for believers in this age. And then in chapter 7, John the Seer offers revelation insight that the great multitude of believers before the throne of God '*are they who have come out of the great tribulation; they have washed their robes and made them white in the blood of the Lamb.*'"

"Meaning these are Christian martyrs who have persevered," Alexander said, "who remained faithful to Christ through the Great Tribulation we've been speaking of?"

The man nodded but said nothing, letting the insights from the Word of God settle in the room. A minute later, he added, "Yes indeed, the spirit of lawlessness has been among us for a long time, and so has tribulation. And the Church of Jesus Christ should not expect to escape either before Christ's final, glorious return."

Alexander bowed his head to consider this. It didn't sit right, as truthful as it might be. The idea that they—*he!*—would suffer through the furnace fires of Solterra's persecution and the Lord's destructive judgment started ratcheting his anxiety anew. Was he ready for such tribulation? Would he last, persevere, remain faithful? He wasn't sure.

Which scared the hell out of him...

The door to the command center opened suddenly, and a man rushed to Nia's side, whispering something in her ear. Her eyes went big, and she stood.

Ford joined her. "What is it?"

"We are having a visitor."

"Who? What visitor?"

"One of the Remnant."

Now Alexander startled. The last time that word was used was to describe someone from the Order of Thaddeus.

"What Remnant?" he asked.

"From some lost Ichthus order," Nia said, walking toward the door.

Alexander glanced at Father Jim, whose eyes went large.

"And what does this mysterious visitor bear?" the cardinal asked.

Nia stopped and turned around. "News."

"What kind of news?" Alexander asked.

"The kind that can get us all killed." Then the woman left, leaving the others behind.

CHAPTER 8

FORD WASTED no time chasing after Nia, a woman who seemed to style herself as some sort of rogue She-Ra Amazonian woman who didn't answer to anyone but herself. A part of him understood that, respected it even, given his own penchant for going rogue. Defecting from the Republic Legion was proof of that. But the other part was ticked to high heaven that she was stepping on his operational turf when it came to ensuring Ichthus's survival. Yet he also knew they all had bigger fish to fry than his ego.

Let it go, Ford. Not worth it...

Probably so. But there was a mighty fierce battle going on in his head to reassert himself. So he took a breath and eased it out through parted lips as he caught up to the woman taking a left at a T-junction.

Their shuffling, heavy rubber military boots echoed through the steel-lined corridor bathed in blue. Some sort of tank ran the length of one side of the corridor, lights casting undulating azure within and inside the passageway winding down and through the deep submergence station with every change in water ripples. The same metallic, oily, fishy smell from their initial docking followed them with every step, reminding him why he never signed up for Solterra's Classis navy fleet.

He finally caught up to Nia, reaching her side. He went to ask where the fire was when something caught his attention. Glancing its way, he gave a startled cry and jolted with a skip to the right, banging his head with a cry on a steel pipe running along the bulkhead. He cursed himself silently, then stiffened with composure before shuffling back to her side.

Nia and the other dude laughed and exchanged something in that blasted Muscovia tongue. "I am seeing you have met our resident dolphin, Galileo," she said, coming up to another bend in the hallway, the tank following alongside one wall and the dolphin swimming to join in the pursuit.

"Dolphin? What are you, Doctor Dolittle?" Ford complained, wincing as he rubbed a hand against a growing goose egg at the back of his head. "Got any ducks or fish in this joint, maybe a gorilla or giraffe or fox?"

She threw him a confused glance and shook her head. "I am not knowing about this Doctor Dolittle person, but Galileo was part of the original research team in the station from several years ago."

Ford glanced at the tank still running alongside them, the gray aquatic mammal bobbing up and down and throwing the guy a glance, its mouth widening to reveal a ridge of sharp teeth, some sort of chirp escaping it. Didn't know whether it was a smile or a grimace, whether he was cussing him out or giving him a hidey-ho. Ford hustled back to Nia's side for comfort anyhow.

Nia continued, "He was being found when Ichthus...shall we say, commandeered the facility over a year ago. As far as we can tell, he was taking part in the research at the station until the team left elsewhere."

"You found him, what, like abandoned or something?"

"*Da*. Jacob, here," she said, gesturing to the man on her other side who had brought news of the newcomer, "was bringing Galileo back to health, the poor thing nearly having starved to death."

Ford gave the fish another sideways glance, its beady eye seeming to follow him along the way, warming up to the fella some knowing he was orphaned. Then he disappeared, finning down his own T-junction and out of sight.

"Hey, where'd the little fella go?"

Nia glanced at the tank as they came up to a solid steel door, another zipper snaking down the middle with a security device standing at its side. "There is being a whole network of watery passages for Galileo throughout the station. Probably was getting weirded by your sideways glances."

"Gee, thanks."

"Besides, we are being here." She slapped her hand against the palm-reading device, the familiar blue pulsing before giving a positive green reply.

"Where's here?" asked Ford.

A shudder of gears inside the wall gave him his answer, the zipper unrolling and doors parting to reveal what appeared to be a medical facility deep inside the station, the distinct scent of alcohol and cleaning agents and blood rushing to greet them.

Several beds were lined along the perimeter of the brightly lit space, separated by glass walls and doors. One stood open with a man lying in a bed underneath a white sheet, his feet protruding underneath but his face shrouded by thick bandaging stained crimson on one side of his head. He was attended by another man in a white coat, presumably a physician.

"Come," Nia simply said, rushing over to the man. Ford went to follow, but glanced behind as the others in the group finally reached them.

Alexander rushed to his side, saying, "She said Remnant. Someone from the Remnant had arrived. You don't suppose she meant the leftovers from the Order of Thaddeus, do you?"

Ford shrugged, then slapped a hand on his shoulder. "Only one way to find out, Master Zarruq."

He led his teammates inside, eyeing a surgical table in a larger room at the back of the sprawling space with a massive disc of lights hanging above and various equipment and monitors stationed around it. Other than that, the place was empty with no other patients but the mystery man talking in hushed tones with Nia.

Time to get some answers, and pronto.

"I am just being happy you made it out alive," Ford heard Nia say to the man as he walked up.

He had olive skin with blood crusted underneath his large nose. One eye was blackened, and the fella was struggling to rise to propped arms, one of which was bandaged with a white bulge at the forearm, a line of red seeping through. Poor guy had been through the wringer, that's for sure. For what, exactly, was all the more mysterious.

"*Nyet, nyet, nyet,*" Nia complained, pressing a hand to the man's shoulder. "You should be lying still and saving your energy, *bratishka.*"

The man went to reply when he and the others arrived at the foot of his bed.

"Mind if we join the party?" Ford asked with a grin.

The man in the bed snapped his head toward the incomers, fixing Ford in particular with searching, probing eyes, narrowing as if trying to discern something about the man and saying nothing.

Then they instantly snapped open, going wide with horror before he sucked in a startled breath and a string of foreign words flew out of his mouth, riding on a wild gallop along a quivering, frightened voice, one hand struggling to point a shaking finger at Ford while using the other to push himself back with a scramble.

Ford frowned. "Was it something I said?"

Nia began trying to calm him with a string of her own Muscovian words, Jacob and the doctor putting firm hands on the man to keep him from falling.

"What is going on, Junia?" Father Jim asked, edging to her side. "What's he saying?"

Nia threw Ford a glance, her face going hard and draining of color. "Simeon is saying something about the Carpathians, along the Black Sea. Something about you and some Purifier raid on a monastery he was part of."

Now Ford's eyes went wide; his heart sank and his bowels went with it. For he knew exactly what the man was referring to.

The Buzau monastery. Two hundred klicks west of the Black Sea and nestled at the base of the Carpathian Mountain range that formed the spine to Vostakana.

Father Jim glanced his way. "What's the man going on about? Who is this Simeon fellow? And why the hysterics after glimpsing you?"

Ford went to answer but couldn't; the words wouldn't come. His mouth gawped for an explanation he knew he had, but he dreaded voicing.

The man's hysterics seemed to suddenly lessen some now, the doctor holding a syringe after presumably stuffing his veins with a sedative and Jacob speaking to him with calming words in the same tongue.

Nia pushed past Father Jim and pressed a firm finger into Ford's chest, jabbing it into his sternum like a woodpecker. "What in *peklo* is Simeon talking about?" she said through gritted teeth.

"Uh-oh," Sasha said from behind. "Now the *moloda zhinka* is getting angry, invoking the biblical underworld." He added with a whisper: "Better be watching out, cowboy."

"Answer me!"

"It was an early mission," Ford stammered on loose lips while his brain tried throttling the confession. "Near the front end of my career."

Nia twisted up her face with confusion. "Mission? Career?" She turned toward the man named Simeon, then back again, her face steely with slitted eyes and a clenched jaw. "Purifier?"

Ford swallowed hard, glancing at Father Jim who nodded him onward. He took a deep breath and sighed, running a nervous hand across his close-cropped blond hair. Time to atone, again; he feared it would always be like this.

"That's right. I was a Purifier. And apparently Simeon, here, got swept up in one of my earlier raids. At a monastery devoted to Saint Andrew, the apostle who apparently evangelized much of Vostokana back in the day."

"Simeon escaped from a reprogramming camp," she growled, fixing him with those She-Ra eyes that looked like she was ready to rip his heart out. "Spent years under the torturous thumb of the Republic, being labeled an Unfit as a despised monk with Byzantine Orthodoxy before it was being Solterra policy across the world for all Ichthus!"

"I know," Ford said quietly. Moving to the foot of the bed, he added: "And for what it's worth, I'm sorry, partner. Truly."

"John Mark, here," Father Jim said, putting a staying hand on Nia's shoulder, making her flinch, "was led to faith in Christ by a kindhearted monk with the Benedictine order a few years ago. He defected and deprogrammed from the murderous pogroms of persecution wrought by the Republic. To great danger to his own life, might I add. He has since reformed his ways and joined the Ministerium as chief of operations, given his...well, skills in those areas."

"Simeon is telling me of those skills in those areas," she growled again.

"And we can adjudicate the fallout later," he said with a firm voice, "but now is not the time. From what it seemed, Simeon came bearing news."

Nia went to reply when she snapped her mouth closed and nodded. "He has, having escaped the Supermaxx in Canadia, but not before retrieving news and intel on the Purge and Panligo."

Ford sucked in a startled breath, exclaiming: "He busted out of Canadia?"

"And with an armful of intel on the Republic?" Alexander said.

She nodded. "*Da.*"

"But I thought you said he was a Remnant. Which I took him as being of the Order of Thaddeus."

"That is being correct. After escaping the Supermaxx, he found refuge with the Order of Thaddeus."

"Is that where the man suffered his injuries?" asked Father Jim. "From his escape?"

"*Nyet.* These were more recent. After escaping months ago, a pair of brothers found him on the brink of death. Nursing him back to health, he was initiated into the Order, where he was sent on mission to bring the plans to the Ministerium. But he did not arrive in time. Solterra initiated its Purge, and he was nearly captured and killed by another wave of Purifiers infiltrating his city of refuge. It was in that escape that he suffered his wounds before commandeering the hydrocraft that brought him here through the Resistance."

Alexander brushed past Ford to Simeon's bedside, resting a hand on the man's leg. "Do you know who I am?"

Simeon's eyes carried a glazed-over look about him, brought on by the sedative, and he shook his head.

"I am Alexander Zarruq. Master of the Order of Thaddeus."

The man brightened at this revelation, a smile stretching from ear to ear.

He smiled back. "Thank you for your service."

"Alright, we can glad-hand our comrade later," Ford said. "What I want to know is, what are these plans of his?"

Alexander threw him a frown but nodded. "Yes, the plans. And where are they?"

Nia held up a microchip. The tiny thing shined with slick crimson.

Ford glanced at Simeon's arm, the bandage bearing the crimson line making more sense.

"Did you wrench that thing from the guy's arm?"

"*Da*," she said. "It was the only way he was able to be keeping it safe."

"And what is it that he was keeping safe?" Alexander asked, giving a nervous glance to Ford before looking back at Simeon with the same eyes.

Ford understood the feeling.

Nia nodded to Simeon and said something in that Muscovia tongue of hers. Which seemed to give the guy permission to speak freely. And freely he did.

The man motioned to Jacob and the doctor to help him up. Each grabbing an arm, they propped him up against the bed's backboard. He winced with pain, face twisting up as they moved him, but he held firm. Shame flooded Ford at the sight, knowing he had been responsible, as well as fearing he would never escape who he had been before he defected and decided to follow Jesus.

"The Purge," Simeon started, voice hoarse and strained

with a Semitic lilt to it, "has been one of the most systemic pogroms launched against any religious group since the Nazi's sought to purge Europa of the Hebrew people. *My* people. Or former people, until I embraced Jesus as my Messiah." He changed positions, wincing again, then continued: "At any rate, you are probably aware of the destruction of the artifices of Ichthus, Cardinal Ferraro. The cathedrals and churches and ministries."

Father Jim nodded. "That I am, having been informed by Ministerium agents still in the field. At least, what little made it through to us after our headquarters were obliterated."

"Well, the destruction is far worse than that."

"How so, partner?" asked Ford.

Simeon threw him a skeptical glance before landing back on Father Jim, jaw clenching and nose flaring for angry breaths.

"Go on, lad," the cardinal instructed. "After all, John Mark is still the chief of operations for the Ministerium. Which I should probably mention includes this station."

One end of Ford's mouth began to curl upward with satisfaction, but he held it together. Neither the time nor the place. Nia, on the other hand...she looked madder than a wet hen at the idea. A beautiful sight to behold.

"Very well," Simeon said. Then he looked to Ford and answered, "Ichthus isn't merely being destroyed, its buildings and relics, the trappings of its worship. Rather, the people, men and women and children even, are being hunted. Rounded up by outfitted Quellers that stun their targets with some sort of weapon."

"Quellers, you say?" Ford said, face twisted up in amusement. "Sorry, partner, but those bad boys are the B52 bombers of the 22nd century, delivering payloads that destroy, certainly, but not civilian targets the way you're describing."

"You're wrong," the man said, narrowing his eyes and

clenching his jaw. "Saw them myself, letting loose something that leveled an entire community of Christians gathering for worship." His eyes fell, and his lower lip quivered. "One I myself had been amongst until I left to retrieve a packet of intel from an asset in the city. When I returned, the Queller had neutralized the believers, right before a platoon of Enforcer Purifiers descended upon them like the vermin they are! It's how I got my injuries, escaping their clutches."

Ford took in a measured breath, bringing a hand to his chin. A Queller outfitted with some newfangled technology that neutralized the polis at the press of a button? That was something they would definitely have to follow up on.

"Anything on the apocalyptic front?" he asked. "What's been going on above the past twenty-four hours that the Republic seems dead set on suppressing?"

Simeon shrugged. "Only what I saw myself before plunging underwater with my PSV. I checked a node on the Order's secure socket on DiviNet, the same story told across Solterra of the darkened sun and discolored moon and fallen, fading stars. There were whisperings of the end times, wondering what it all meant for the Church, and whether the Rapture was nigh or had already happened, with references to obscure theologians and interpretations of the Book of Revelation. But nothing concrete, only confusion."

Ford glanced at Alexander and Father Jim. "Confusion...definitely know the feeling. But what of this intel. Did you make contact with your asset?"

"*Da*. And he delivered the packet." He motioned toward Nia, who held up the microchip again. "It's all there, on that chip."

"Then maybe we should take a gander at what you retrieved, partner." Nodding toward Nia, he added, "You got any equipment in this here station of yours that can decode this microchip?"

"I am able to be helping!" a voice exclaimed from behind.

There was a sudden shuffle and a small medical cart toppled over, plastic containers and some expensive-looking equipment crashing to the floor.

"*Der'mo...*" Sasha muttered, scrambling to pick up the pieces. The doctor mumbled something to himself before coming around to clean up his mess.

"What was that, doc?" asked Ford.

Sasha stepped back and furrowed his brow, his mouth open and hands gesturing like he didn't know whether to help or step away. He chose the latter and threw a schoolboy smile toward Nia, holding out his hand. "Hand the microchip over. I am able to be helping decode the chip, no matter what equipment you are having or not. Whatever you are needing, I'm here to help!"

Ford folded his arms and rolled his eyes, but couldn't help but chuckle. It was puppy love at first Ukrainski sight. But he had no chance. Life was a high school cafeteria all the way down. And jock chicks like Nia wouldn't give the nerd the time of day.

Although he seemed to catch Nia blushing while dipping her head and trying to hide a smile, brushing a hand past her ear to push back a non-existent lock of hair. A bashful tick left-over before She-Ra buzzed her hair short that meant the guy might have a fighting chance.

Go, doc!

With an outstretched hand, Sasha added, "I was seeing some mighty fine computing power in the bunker we were coming from. So hand it over, *mon cheri.*"

An end of Nia's mouth curled upward as she pinched the microchip between her thumb and forefinger. She carefully set it in Sasha's hand.

He closed it and smiled, then darted off.

She called after the man, but it was no use. He was out the door and skipping down the hall. "How is he knowing where to go?"

Ford said, "Where there's a will to impress a chickadee, there's a way."

She blushed and turned away.

Looking at Simeon, he asked, "Did you take a gander at the intel, partner? Do you know what that microchip says?"

He shook his head. "I was not able to access the chip itself, but my contact reviewed with me its contents."

"And?"

"As I said before, the Republic's Purge plans. I only wish we had been able to get them to the Ministerium sooner. But the others might be as useful."

"Which are?" Alexander asked now.

"The plans for Panligo."

"Again, which are?" Ford said.

"Not sure entirely," Simeon said, shifting and wincing again. "But the asset made reference to Arius and the Council of Nicaea."

Father Jim startled. "Arius and the Council of Nicaea, you say?"

"That's right."

The cardinal turned to Ford. "We need to access the contents on that chip, straight away."

"Then I'd say the doc's clock has run out of sand."

"Mixing metaphors there a bit, aren't you?" Alexander said.

Ford frowned and went to the door. "Let's see what Sasha's found. And hope it lends Ichthus a helping hand."

"And doesn't slit its throat."

That too...

CHAPTER 9

SOON THE TEAM was winding its way back through the maze of steel-lined corridors in search of Sasha, that dreadful stench of oil now combined with spicy meat and garlic and onions turning Alexander's stomach as they hustled forward. It was then he realized he was hungry. Famished, actually, his stomach grumbling and turning over on itself at not having had a meal since yesterday morning before the world crashed and burned.

He glanced at the tank edging the corridors for the dolphin that had touched off a memory—a sweet and sour memory, to be sure.

It was one from childhood, well before his mother's death and even further back before his father's apostasy. Martin had been newly installed in the parish church of Tripolitania, the one Alexander would eventually take over. After a flurry of activity unpacking boxes and moving into their new parsonage, followed by countless dinners from well-meaning parishioners welcoming them to the church, then several weeks of meetings and leading Sunday morning services, the young family needed a weekend to relax and acclimate to their new rhythm. His mother found a small cottage on a beach up the coast in Kemet, former Egypt. So his father arranged for a pair of elders to tend to the Sunday worship activities while they basked in the sun and baked fish, spending time together laughing and collecting sea glass along the Mediterranean. It was then that they came across the memory sparked by the tank following them along the maze of steel corridors hundreds of kilometers under the Great Sea.

A bottlenose dolphin stranded on the seashore. The poor thing was alive, but barely, wrapped in a fishing net either discarded or lost at sea. It was Alexander who spotted him first, and the trio spent the rest of their mini vacation seeing that the dolphin got the care it needed.

After carefully untangling it from netting, they loaded the dolphin in their car and drove it to the nearest veterinarian. When they wouldn't help, Father drove farther into the nearest city, not stopping until he found help while Alexander and his mother kept the poor thing wet with a towel and bucket of water. When they finally did manage to find help, a marine biologist Martin tracked down through contacts in the Ministerium, the man stayed with the poor thing through the night, sending Alexander and his mother home and sparing no expense to spare its life.

The next morning, Father returned to their rental weary but joyful that the aquatic mammal had made it through the night. The marine biologist assured him it would live, mostly because of the Zarruqs' care. When Alexander asked him why they went through the trouble, Martin responded: "Because the Word of God teaches us in the Book of Proverbs that *'The righteous care for the needs of their animals.'* And although the dolphin didn't belong to us, it was ours for the moment, entrusted to our care by the providential hand of God."

"Sort of like Jesus' Parable of the Good Samaritan?"

Alexander had asked, referencing Christ's teachings on neighbor-love.

Martin tousled his hair and grinned. "Sort of like that, yes. While the Creator gave mankind dominion over creatures, he also called upon them to steward, guard, and care for them. And so going through all the trouble, as you asked, son, was an act of obedience, and a response to the Creator's righteousness. I believe it is what Jesus himself would have done—through whom and by whom and for whom all things were created. Even bottlenose dolphins and curious little boys!"

Alexander smiled at the memory before it faded into a deep sadness for how sour things had turned with his father—and with Ichthus.

Oh, Father...what happened to you?

A loud-cursing Ukrainski professor echoed down to them from the open door to the command center up ahead, snapping Alexander back to the task at hand. The one that would hopefully bring clarity to all that his father was planning.

"What the blazes is the doc going on about?" Ford muttered as they reached the door.

"...expecting me to be working under these conditions!" Sasha shouted.

Alexander pushed past Ford to find a very irritated Doctor Pavlovich, the preeminent theoretical physicist who discovered time travel. Hunched over a workstation and pounding on a keyboard, his overgrown, tightly curled blond hair bounced with every punch and his face twisted up with reddened irritation. A pair of station workers wisely looked on from a distance, continuing to receive his tongue lashing. He was slinging a string of Muscovia at the poor men now, gesturing wildly at the monitor.

"What the devil is going on here?" asked Father Jim as the

rest of the group filed inside the steel circular room bathed in that warm dim yellow light.

"What is going on here," Sasha said, turning around, "is that I am not having the necessary equipment and algorithmic software that I am needing!"

Ford mumbled, "This from the guy who said he could decode the chip no matter what equipment this bucket of bolts had?"

Sasha spun around and pointed a not-happy finger. "I am hearing that, cowboy!"

Alexander stepped forward with raised hands. "Slow down, Sasha. What's the problem? Spell it out so we can help."

He took a deep breath and sighed, then spun around to the workstation. "I was finding a laser conduit accentuator that I finagled into a connection between the computer and the microchip."

"*Dobre,*" Nia said, coming up behind. "What is being the problem?"

"The problem is being," he said, pointing at the monitor, "that it is not working! And I am not being able to find any input terminal to program the damn thing, even if I am being able to make the connection! No one thought to upgrade these computers to the latest DiviNet version, methinks."

She huffed and hustled over to the workstation. Bending low and eying the equipment Sasha had set up, she mumbled something before saying: "That is because you are needing to attach the fibroptic cable here," she said, adjusting the hardware setup. "Then input the following string into the terminal utility like so..." She reached around Sasha and clacked away at the keyboard before bringing up a window that listed a string of files in neat rows.

While Sasha scrunched up his brow and strained toward the monitor, Nia stepped back with a satisfied grin.

"*Khorosho!*" Which Alexander took for the French version of 'Voila!'.

Ford leaned over and muttered, "She schooled him."

Alexander smiled and shushed him, but suspected Sasha was more intrigued than embarrassed that Nia showed him up, thrilled with a beautiful young Ukrainski lady to pursue. And one who knew her way around a hacked DiviNet workstation.

Sasha frowned, his cheeks growing rosy. "I would have been getting there eventually..." he muttered, taking over the keyboard and entering another series of inputs that brought the files to a larger broadcaster displayed at the center of one wall between two windows peering out into the Mediterranean depths.

"This intelligence was retrieved at great risk to the Resistance agent who handed it off to Simeon," Nia explained, taking steps toward the display and folding her arms as Sasha cycled through the various files. "We should all be grateful for his sacrifice."

"What is this Resistance you speak of?" asked Alexander, joining her at her side. "You've mentioned it before, and it carried with it undertones of those who resisted totalitarian regimes of the 20th century."

"*Da.* That is precisely its meaning!"

"It is what's left of the Ministerium, my boy," Father Jim answered as well. "The last of those agents who were able to go underground before..."

The man trailed off, but Alexander understood the rest: Before they were cancelled or reprogrammed at some Republic black-site camp.

"That," Nia added, "combined with the everyday efforts of average Christian men and women to support one another against the tyrannical rule of the Republic."

"Violently?" Alexander asked with hesitation.

She looked to Padre, who said nothing. Nia simply said, "Not as a default."

"The Remnant, on the other hand, homefry," Ford said, "is a whole other story."

He turned toward the man, brow furrowed with curiosity. "What do you mean?"

"Apparently your underground minions of the Order of Thaddeus, the remaining faith-defenders that've been burrowed and scattered across the world, have been resurrecting an old project."

"And what's that?" asked Alexander.

"SEPIO, they are calling it," Nia added.

His eyes got big with recognition. The shibboleth given to him by the former Order Master, Theophilus, shortly before he passed. Before Alexander could respond, Sasha interjected with an announcement.

"I am finding something," the professor said.

"What's up, doc?" Ford said, coming up to the man before Nia could.

"A video file."

"What sort of video?"

Sasha clacked away and pointed at the screen. "An encrypted text file is describing it as the meeting between Lucius Severus and Martin Zarruq."

Nia muttered something under her breath in her native tongue, then added: "The Patron and Sacradi."

All eyes seemed to spin on a dime toward Alexander, time seeming to slow as well as the force of the revelation hit the room. His father and the Republic Regis, the man who basically served as the Emperor of Solterra.

Ford grinned and let out a *yee-haw!* "A convo between the titular heads of the Republic government and religion? Hot damn, that's great news!"

"John Mark..." Father Jim said, throwing Ford a sideways glance.

He cleared his throat. "Sorry, chief. What's the convo about?"

"Best rip the bandage off the wound and get to it," Father Jim said.

Before Alexander could prepare himself, his father and Severus were seen on the screen, the audio cutting to the Patron mid-sentence.

"...going far better than I could have hoped."

The picture was grainy, with a sort of fishy-eye view that suggested the camera was hidden somewhere. It was also bright, what looked like white marble veined with faint gray lining the floor and walls. Corinthian columns soared toward the ceiling edged by gilt lines circling the white pillars like candy canes. Even the furniture pieces were edged in gold leafing, adding to the sense of brightness. If Alexander were to guess, they were somewhere at the Capitolium, perhaps in the Patron's very own quarters. Which meant his father was in the heart of Solterra power.

His father spoke before Alexander could register any feeling about it all: "Soon even the Resistance itself will be crushed and we can unfold the next phase of our plans."

"You believe Ichthus will fade that easily?" asked Severus.

"I do. Especially when we reveal the truth of their religion, how Jesus became God—how the Church *made* him a deity."

"What the hey-ho day is the man talkin' about?" Lucy asked.

"Hold on..." Father Jim said, pointing to the broadcaster.

"If you perpetuate a big enough idea," Martin continued, "whether true or not, and tell it frequently enough, it will not only be believed—it will be *worshipped*."

"And how do you propose we go about this...reprogramming effort of Ichthus's faithful? After all, belief runs deep in them. The kind that will drive them to their deaths."

"Which I am not necessarily opposed to."

Walking to one of those gilded couches, the Patron slumped down and snapped his fingers. "But one we've ruled out. At least for now, given their entanglements in the highest levels of the Republic."

A man from off-camera appeared, dressed in a white robe. He handed Severus a crystal goblet of something crimson.

Severus took a long sip and continued, "We cannot simply exterminate some of the most productive members of our society, you know. So how do you propose solving our dilemma?"

Martin sat in a chair across from him. "That's a political question, and an economic one."

Severus laughed. "How convenient. No, you're not getting off that easily. You suggested you had a solution, a religious one! After all, it's why I pushed for your position as Sacradi, resurrecting the ancient designation of the ancient Roman religion for what we envision is to come."

Alexander's father crossed a leg. "The solution is one Ichthus itself has been employing."

"And what is that?"

"Retrieving history. But in our case, reclaiming it for our own purposes."

"What the hot Hades is that man yapping on about?" asked Ford.

"Not sure..." Alexander said.

His father added: "Only this time we shall reclaim that history as our own, under our terms. Something I've taken care of as we speak."

Suddenly he was very sure what he meant.

Alexander sucked in a startled breath, a cold dread flooding his veins at what his father meant. "Retrieving the past..." he whispered, running a worried hand through his thick hair.

"What was that, my boy?" Father Jim asked. "Pause it, would you?" Sasha obliged.

He turned to him, eyes wide. "Padre, what happened to the time travel devices?"

Father Jim furrowed his brow. "Safe and sound in our personal submergence vehicle, why?"

"You're sure? Positive?"

"Absolutely," Ford answered. "We secured those puppies after you took off on the beach a year ago. Have been carting them around with us ever since."

"Even making some modifications to them when we were going ashore," Sasha added proudly. "The most important of which is putting the device on autopilot."

"Autopilot?" Alexander asked.

"*Da.* I am no longer needing to help jump time travelers to the past. An AI-driven algorithmic kernel inside Ichthus's node on DiviNet now controls the devices."

Alexander nodded, sighing with relief and heart returning to normal a bit knowing the devices were secure. Thought Father had run off with one of them or something, or perhaps one of his Enforcer goons.

If not that, then what was the man getting at?

He turned back to Father Jim. "You mentioned when you rescued me that the visual and aural material I retrieved from the past had been put up on some sort of portal, for Ichthus's viewing?"

The cardinal nodded. "That's right. Has been a real boon for keeping people committed to the faith, helping them persevere and gain some sense of Church history."

"Any chance something's happened to it? That Solterra has disrupted it somehow?"

"I don't see why it could have. No way the Republic could have known about the operation!"

"Like they didn't know about the Ministerium?" asked Ford, making a good point about its destruction despite its secrecy.

"Give me one second..." Sasha began clacking away at the workstation. Until he stood up and cursed loudly: *"Der'mo!"*

Everyone huddled around Sasha for a look. Seeing the same bad news.

A white screen with the spinning globe of Solterra's insignia, the Pangea supercontinent of unified land masses bunched together and framed by olive branches. Along with a message: *This DiviNet Portal Has Been Seized by Order of Solterra Republic!* It went on to condemn the propaganda by certified Unfits.

"Shucky ducky," Ford said. Alexander had to agree.

Father Jim added, "I suppose that settles Martin's grand plans against the Ministerium."

"Perhaps it is," Nia said, "but what is the rest of the video recording saying?"

Sasha resumed the recording, the bright room animating again.

"Even if the heretics of Ichthus," Martin Zarruq went on, "threaten us with ten thousand deaths, they will not prevail. Though I would certainly like to see them try!"

Severus shook his head. "Don't underestimate the Resistance, Martin. Especially the Order Remnant. They have been surprisingly resourceful."

"Granted. But we shall co-opt the former heretic and turn its rejected teaching into the mark of Panligo doctrine. For although Jesus didn't claim the mantle of divinity himself, his followers made him such! And there is one man who can help us reorient the perspective of those dreadful

Christians while also unifying the rest of the faiths as well around his teaching, making room for the other so-called great spiritual teachers."

"What's he yapping on about now?" asked Ford.

Alexander quieted him down as the Regis replied: "And what will Panligo say and teach on the subject? How will it leverage this heretic's teachings?"

"That the Son is not unbegotten," the Sacradi said, "nor a part of an unbegotten entity in any way, nor from anything in existence. Before he was begotten or created or defined or established as the supposed Son of God, he did not exist. For not only was he made, being born as a man, he was created—the Christ of faith as much as the Christ of history."

Ford whistled. "Some certified crazy right there."

"Quiet!" Father Jim snapped. "There is a ring of familiarity to all of this..."

"But I and my colleagues," Martin went on, "not to mention my kinship with those who were martyred as heretics from times past, were maligned because we have said the Son has a beginning, but God has no beginning. It is really quite simple: For it is clear to all that which is created did not exist before it came into being."

"What came into being has a beginning," Severus added. "That is a basic tenet of human existence."

"Precisely! I was personally persecuted within the upper echelons of the Ministerium for saying that Jesus the Christ came from nonbeing, rising to prominence thanks to the Zeitgeist, due to a confluence of events within history marching forward in the backwater Roman province of Judea. We said this since he is not a portion of God nor of anything in existence. Instead, he was manufactured by his followers as something more than he was not, the decisive Council bestowing upon him his deity by those in power at the expense of the purer understanding of his consciousness, my kinship, my spiritual ancestors."

Father Jim sucked in a sudden breath. "My God…"

"What's the matter, Padre?" asked Alexander.

The man stepped closer to the broadcaster. Before he could answer, the full-scale image of Alexander's father continued: "Others have recognized what Panligo will teach: the Universe as the cause of all that happens, is absolutely alone without beginning, imbuing all with divine power, Jesus included. He was created apart from time by the confluence of historical realities in the Universe's march. He is neither eternal nor co-eternal nor co-unbegotten with the Universe, nor does he have his being together with this divine principle, as some speak of relations. Therefore, the Universe and its principle of divine power stands before Jesus' existence."

The feed suddenly went fritzy, the picture blurring and growing fuzzy before cutting out entirely.

Alexander walked up to Father Jim, placing a hand on his shoulder. "Padre, what is it?"

The man turned to him, eyes wide and face white. "The Republic has let slip the dogs of war. Again."

CHAPTER 10

Father Jim was already several paces ahead by the time Alexander went back into the hallway, the whisper of Padre's cassock echoing back to him through the station's network of gun-metal gray corridors. He was heading somewhere fast, the revelations from the video of his father talking with Severus clearly shaking the man and sending him on a hunt.

"What do you suppose that was about, homefry?" Ford said, coming up behind him.

Nia joined him on the other side. "*Da.* What is it the cardinal is thinking about?"

Alexander shook his head. "Not sure. But something clearly rattled the man." He swallowed hard, adding: "Something my father said seems to have set him off."

"And running," Ford said.

Nia pushed past and started forward. "We should be running after the cardinal then."

Alexander chased after her and Father Jim, followed closely by Ford and then the others. His heart picked up pace as they raced through the corridor. Pipes ran along the bulkhead hiding wires and carrying fluids throughout the station, the now familiar tanks following them along one wall with

Galileo finning through the water bathed blue. A coppery taste was heavy on his tongue now, the traces of the initial adrenaline rush from seeing his father and listening to the conversation with the Patron—compounded by another jolt at yet another mystery wondering what Father had said that had sent the cardinal running who knew where through the station.

They would soon find out.

"Here we are," Father Jim muttered, stopping at the familiar military-grade steel door, entry pad and biometric scanner affixed to the right on the wall.

"Padre," Alexander whispered as the cardinal went through the now-familiar routine. "What is it? What's the matter?"

There was a *ping* of success and an audible unlocking of the door, the zipper lock unsnaking and doors parting. Without answering, the cardinal shoved inside.

Alexander hesitated, but followed his direction, as did Ford and Nia close behind with the others trailing. They emerged into another dim room of the familiar sanitized, boring metal gray and steel. However, this one was different.

It wasn't a large room, about the size of a modest two-stall magnacar garage, for those who could afford it. The walls carried metal shelving that were lined by books, from top to bottom, with a small metal table anchored at the center and a couch against one wall. Made sense, given the station was a research center. And yet...

Alexander stepped closer to one of the walls. It was clear these books didn't belong. Titles ranged from *Against Heresies* by the early Church father Irenaeus to Saint Augustine's *City of God*, from the Medieval theologian Thomas Aquinas's *Summa Theologica* to the *Institutes on the Christian Faith* by the great Reformer John Calvin—which was an odd pairing!—on to *Church Dogmatics* by Karl Barth and N.T. Wright's *Jesus and the Victory of God,* two of the greatest theologians of the 20th and 21st centuries.

He didn't spot any more recent titles. Then again, he was distracted by the unexpected sight. Only problem was, it didn't at all smell like he expected it. Fresh, sanitized air with the traces of that oil and metallic smell from the main station flooded his senses. Not the old library scent of dank must and pulpy paper and sweet ink, as one would expect from such books stuffed in a confined space. And he was pretty sure he knew why.

Ford whistled, craning his neck for a look around. "Digs are a bit cramped here compared to the last one, don't ya think, chief?"

Father Jim ignored him and began searching the shelves, a man on a mission who was looking desperate for answers.

"What is this place?" asked Nia, following Ford's moves.

Alexander turned to her. "You don't know?"

Ford scoffed and crossed his arms. "Thought you were in command of this ship. Wouldn't let nothing like this slip under my nose."

She stepped up to him and narrowed her eyes. "Only in recent months, cowboy. The Ministerium was setting up shop in these parts months before I was being brought on board."

"Then you're in for quite the surprise, sister."

"And why is that?"

"Because these are the Vatican Archives,"Alexander explained. "Well, some of it anyway. Though you can access the rest if you want."

Nia snapped her head toward him with wide eyes. "That is being impossible. The Archives drowned in the sea when the waters were rising from climate change. OneWorld News said so."

Ford said, "That's what the Ministerium *wanted* OneWorld News to report."

Alexander added, "And some of the precious manuscripts and documents and codices of the Church's past did unfortunately sink to the bottom of the Mediterranean when the seas rose after the cataclysmic climate change events of the past half a century."

"Nice alliteration there, partner," Ford said with a wink.

He frowned. "Apparently Ichthus transferred the most important and vast majority of them into safe harbor, where they're accessed now at the drop of a command."

"And now it appears from anywhere in the world."

"But that is still being impossible!" Nia exclaimed. "The Republic was banning books."

She was right. After the Reckoning, real books were hard to come by. Deforestation for paper production was a strict no-no that carried significant monetary and hard-labor penalties. So digital was the way the biblio-world went. Alexander was one of many who suspected the Republic outlawed paper production for reasons other than merely environmental protection: Information was much easier to control when it was in ones and zeros rather than ink and parchment. Who needed book burnings when they could be evaporated with a simple command input from the Patron or an AI algorithmic command line?

Ford grinned. "That's the beauty of this here set up."

Alexander added, "It's all been uploaded into the Ministerium cloud."

"Digital?" Nia said with surprise. "It is looking real to me."

She eyed the space some more, walking up to a wall as Father Jim scurried around her, continuing his frantic search for something, raising a finger and muttering to himself before moving to another panel.

"It was programmed to look that way, apparently," Alexander said.

Nia startled. "Programmed?"

Before he could explain, Father Jim announced, "Qoheleth, bring up everything you can from the writings of Arius. Might as well throw in Athanasius and the Nicene Council as well."

Alexander smiled at the call word, *Qoheleth*. The purported author of the Book of Ecclesiastes. Thought it was just as clever now as the first time he heard it.

"Granted," a male Britannia-sounding voice echoed. The room instantly transformed into a selection of spine-out titles neatly arrayed across one of the walls.

Ford whistled. "Some fine Ichthus ingenuity, that there is."

"What are those being?" asked Nia, taking a hesitant step to a wall.

Alexander shrugged. "Books, what else?"

The cardinal continued ignoring them, muttering to himself as he walked over to the metal table at the center of the room. He retrieved a familiar sapphire slate before heading for the shelves of digital titles arrayed on one panel.

Alexander nodded toward the digital wall arrayed with titles. "Go ahead, touch it."

Nia furrowed her brow in confusion, then brought a hand up to the surface. Hesitating a moment, she touched the smooth-as-glass surface, her face scrunching up in confusion at what happened next. Alexander himself recalled being startled by the feeling. The image instantly rippled with red, blue, and green perturbation, like a stone dropped in a pond until it evened back out into the faux library of books.

"I don't understand," she said. "What is being the point of this?"

"The point, my dear," Father Jim finally said, "is to offer the

Ministerium instant access to a billion-book digital archive from the storehouses of the Church's knowledge."

"So we are being able to retrieve any book we want?"

He nodded. "That's right. The digital archives have preserved knowledge of all sorts during these dark times. Not just that which had been contained in the Vatican Archives before it sank beneath the sea, but all books from every corner of the world. As you'll recall, it was the Church that preserved knowledge through the so-called Dark Ages—a misnomer if there ever was one! The Renaissance was only made possible by the studious and judicious care with which Christians sought, discovered, and preserved the wisdom that God himself ordained his creatures to possess."

"Fascinating..." Nia marveled.

"This room, like the one from the old Ministerium HQ, which has been replicated across our very own sector of DiviNet thanks to Sasha, here—" Father Jim patted Sasha on the back, who grinned and puffed out his chest with pride. "Just like the original, this one gives us access to nearly the entire storehouse of knowledge across the full spectrum of humanity. Using machine learning algorithms, the Archives not only catalogues but cross-checks the vault of knowledge with other bits and bobs of information and sources. And Solterra thinks we're just a bunch of rubes stuck in the Stone Age." Father Jim huffed and shook his head, fiddling with the sapphire slate. "At any rate, it's quite simple, really. You walk over to the shelves and search for your book. When you find it, simply tap once, then again for it to be instantly delivered to the device. It's quite magical, really. Now, observe and be amazed..."

He brought the sapphire tablet near a particular set of tomes that lined the wall on the middle shelf, the others surrounding it instantly dimmed while three remained brightly lit. Father Jim touched the middle volume, and the others joined the other books in dimmed darkness. He tapped it again, and it shone with an almost golden brilliance, a faint halo of rainbow light ringing it.

"There we go," the cardinal announced.

"What did you find?" asked Alexander, craning over his shoulder.

Father Jim cleared his throat and read aloud:

We are not able to listen to these kinds of impieties, even if the heretics threaten us with ten thousand deaths. But what do we say and think and what have we previously taught and do we presently teach? That the Son is not unbegotten, nor a part of an unbegotten entity in any way, nor from anything in existence, but that he is subsisting in will and intention before time and before the ages, full of grace and truth, God, the only-begotten, unchangeable. Before he was begotten, or created, or defined, or established, he did not exist. We are persecuted because we have said the Son has a beginning but God has no beginning, and for saying he came from non-being. But we said this since he is not a portion of God nor of anything in existence. That is why we are persecuted; you know the rest.

"What the hot Hades is that nonsense about?" Ford asked, face twisted up with confusion.

"And who the hey-ho day was spouting the nonsense?" Lucy asked, wearing the same face.

Father Jim answered, "The nonsense the man was spouting, John Mark, was on the doctrine of Jesus Christ's nature.

And the one spouting it, Luciana Jane, was none other than Arius of Alexandria."

"Who is this Arius fellow being?" asked Nia.

Alexander answered, "Not is, *was*. And one of the greatest heretics that stormed the stage of the ancient Church, if I recall correctly."

Father Jim nodded. "You do recall correctly. Although I'm not surprised, given your top-notch education," he added with a wink.

He smiled. "That I did, thanks to a fine teacher."

"At any rate, the man was a bishop birthed from the cradle of your people's country, actually, who—"

"From Tripolitania?" Alexander exclaimed. "*The heretic from my ancestor's lands...*" he whispered, recalling what Father had said.

"He was indeed a Libyan presbyter serving the Church of North Africa and across those lands decades before taking up residence in Alexandria where he breathed the toxic fumes of his heretical, unorthodox teachings, exchanging the truth of Jesus Christ for a lie built on philosophical speculation and humanistic dogma."

"Tell us what you really think, chief..." Ford said.

"If I recall," Alexander added, "he was also one of the chief architects of the teachings that led to the Council of Nicaea."

"Right you are again," Father Jim said.

"And what, pray tell," Nia said, "was the man teaching that was being so problematic?"

"That there was a time when Jesus, God the Son, was not," Alexander answered.

"Meaning?"

"Meaning, that Jesus was not in the same sense eternally God as God the Father is."

The woman crossed her arms and furrowed her brow. "I am not understanding your meaning."

"You and me both, sister," Ford agreed.

"Arianism is a non-Trinitarian Christological doctrine," Father Jim added, "which asserts the belief that Jesus Christ as the Son of God was created by God the Father at a certain point in time, so that the Son of God became a creature distinct from the Father and is therefore subordinate to him and of a different substance, while also being God as Son."

Ford stared dumbly. "Yeah, for those of us not raised in the Church and not attending any fancy-shmancy Ichthus training schools, you're gonna have to ease the cookies down to the lower shelf on this one. Because that was crazier than a one-legged mule."

Alexander explained, "What Padre means is, Arius challenged the prevailing orthodox view of Christian beliefs that taught Jesus Christ, the Son of God come in the flesh, was himself God in the same way the Father was—existing from eternity past without having been created."

"Recall the creed that sits at the heart of Ichthus's faith," Padre said. He cleared his throat, then recited from memory:

> *We believe in one God, the Father, the*
> *Almighty, maker of heaven and earth, of all*
> *that is, seen and unseen.*
> *We believe in one Lord, Jesus Christ, the only*
> *Son of God, eternally begotten of the Father,*
> *God from God, Light from Light, true God*
> *from true God, begotten, not made, of one*
> *Being with the Father. Through him all*
> *things were made. For us and for our salva-*
> *tion he came down from heaven: by the*
> *power of the Holy Spirit he became incar-*

> *nate from the Virgin Mary, and was made man. For our sake he was crucified under Pontius Pilate; he suffered death and was buried. On the third day he rose again in accordance with the Scriptures; he ascended into heaven and is seated at the right hand of the Father. He will come again in glory to judge the living and the dead, and his kingdom will have no end.*
>
> *We believe in the Holy Spirit, the Lord, the giver of life, who proceeds from the Father and the Son. With the Father and the Son he is worshiped and glorified. He has spoken through the Prophets. We believe in one holy catholic and apostolic Church. We acknowledge one baptism for the forgiveness of sins. We look for the resurrection of the dead, and the life of the world to come. Amen.*

"Ahh, yes," Nia said. "I am recognizing that as the Nicene Creed."

"Very good, young lady. You are correct. Christianity's central creed, litigated precisely because of Arius's false teachings concerning Jesus Christ."

"Which part?" asked Ford, brow still furrowed with confusion.

Alexander answered, reciting: "'*We believe in one God, the Father Almighty, maker of all things visible and invisible; and in one Lord Jesus Christ, the Son of God, Light of Light, very God of very God, begotten, not made, being of one substance with the Father.*' As the Council concluded, begotten, not made, and being of the same essential being as the Father were crucial to the Church's understanding of right beliefs when it came to Jesus' personhood."

"And crucial to the gospel, I might add," said Father Jim. "God's revolutionary story of rescue in Jesus Christ is entirely dependent upon whether Jesus Christ really is God, or merely a man, a wise prophet. Ever since those days, and really from the beginning of Ichthus's teachings concerning Jesus, there has been confusion about who Jesus is and what he came to do. Both outside and inside the Church."

"How so?" Ford asked.

A cold dread began to spread over Alexander. For the reason why this was all so devastating was beginning to become clearer. Which had massive implications for Ichthus if his father was tapping the heretic to help the Panligo and Solterra cause.

Father Jim went to answer when a shudder ratcheted through the floor—ricocheting through the walls before thundering up above.

Ford turned wide-eyed to Nia. "What the hot Hades was that?"

*W*HAT THE HOT *Hades is right...*

Alexander braced himself against one of the wall panels, the red and blue and green nanopixels flaring up with perturbation under his weight. Felt like before back in Roma, but something told him it was worse.

Which threw up all kinds of bad, biblical implications.

The apocalyptic kind.

Another groan from the deep submergence station interrupted any reply from Nia, the rumbling continuing much like what happened the day before. An earthquake of such magnitude that it cut down into the heart of the sea and ratcheted through the underwater building anchored to part of the seafloor.

Father Jim cried out, losing his balance and toppling from the quake. The sapphire slate slipped from his hand and clanged to the steel floor as the man banged into the table, his feet slipping out from under him and forehead banging against a corner. A gash instantly split, blood spilling down his face.

Lucy and Rebekah raced to his side, the pair tending to his wound.

"You both should be coming with me," Nia said, snapping

her fingers and pointing to Ford and Alexander. When they both hesitated, she added with exclamation: "*Zaraz!*"

Alexander understood her meaning—hop to it!—but looked to Rebekah, who was pressing a torn piece of her shirt against Father Jim's head. "Go on," she said, "Lucy and I have this."

He nodded and followed after Nia and Ford.

The quaking continued its relentless assault on the station, the water inside the tank running alongside the steel corridors sloshing something fierce. They braced themselves against the walls, the hardened metal feeling as though it would buckle. And praying that it wouldn't.

"We need to be getting to the control room!" Nia said. "*Zaraz!*"

Ford said, "Sorry to break it to you, sister—" A foot slipped, sending him stumbling to the floor. He let a curse slip, then added: "No control room is going to matter much with the tilt-a-whirl the Universe has thrown at us!"

"Or God Almighty from above..." Alexander muttered.

They kept at it, weaving through the wavering corridors, the groans and creaks and thuds echoing through the station with menacing intent.

"Here, we are reaching the control room," Nia announced, slapping her hand against the security keypad and shoving through the door after it unzipped and departed.

Inside was chaos.

Equipment had toppled, smashing and coming apart. Water was leaking across the floor, the sea having broken inside from somewhere. One crew member was putting out an electrical fire still flaring up from a control board. Another was tending to a woman who had a gash similar to Father Jim's.

Nia didn't let it deter her, jumping to take command of the chaotic situation.

"Engage the seafloor release sequence!" she shouted to no

one in particular, walking to a center console bright with blinking warnings and a string of assessments streaming across its screens.

"Seafloor release sequence?" Alexander said, glancing at Ford and wondering if what he thought she meant was really what she meant.

Ford joined Nia at the center, who was already fast at work. He said, "Are you saying what I think you're saying, sister?"

Another shudder rattled through the station, a pipe at the bulkhead bursting from the strain and sending a firehose of water cascading into the room already reeling from the chaos.

Nia didn't answer the man. Instead, she pressed a blinking indicator light on the console display, then another until a warning chime sounded and the quaking began to instantly lessen.

Alexander heaved a breath when the convulsions ceased altogether, the tension of the moment sending his pulse soaring and the solution adding to the confusion.

"The station will be continuing to shake some after what I am doing," Nia said, "as the seismic waves are passing through the water. But we are coming out of the woods, as you Amerikanskis are saying."

"*Nor*–amerikanskis, you mean," Ford said. "You're forgetting we fought a second war of secession. Succeeding this time, might I add, along with the rest of country splintering in quintuplets."

She muttered something in her foreign tongue, continuing to fiddle with the console.

"What just happened?" Alexander asked on a still-shaking breath, coming to Nia's side.

"I am releasing the station from the seafloor. A temporary

solution until we are figuring out what is happening and how we are solving it."

"Releasing the station from the seafloor?" Ford exclaimed.

"*Da*," was all Nia replied.

"Well, is it safe?"

She shrugged. "It is emergency measure until we are figuring—"

"You already said that! I asked if it was safe."

"We'll find out soon."

Ford threw his hands behind his head. "Just great..."

"It has never been done before, as far as I know. Station was being designed to float in the event of such an earthquake affecting the seafloor."

"Not an apocalyptic one sent by the Lord Almighty himself to smite our asses!"

"Ford..." Alexander said, heart pulsing in his ears now at the turn. But he was right. This wasn't good.

"Do not be worrying so much, cowboy!" Nia said, shifting back to the console display and pointing to what looked like an image of the station, white ovals at four ends showing a hundred percent. She pointed at the display. "Those are ballasts that are meant to be keeping the station afloat."

"Meant to be?" Ford said, raising a brow. "What happens if they don't?"

She sighed, putting her hands on her hips. "Then we'll be sinking to the floor and be facing a whole other set of deep-doo-doo problems."

A *purr* from the console interrupted any further discussion.

"What's that?" Alexander said in a rush. "Are the ballasts failing? Are we going to sink?"

"*Nyet*. It is message. Several, in fact. Looks like a combination of the Resistance and Remnant." She opened the first one and started playing an attached media file.

Static filled the video and audio until it normalized. An Anglo was speaking with a rush into a handheld device on shaking hands mid-sentence: "...started happening out of nowhere. Right here, in Noramericana!"

Ford stiffened, and a wheeze of surprise escaped him. "My homeland..."

"The rumbling that jostled Solterra has returned, and crazier than ever. Has to be a 7 or 8 on the Richter Scale, given how violent the shaking is."

The man was in a house, and the jostling of lamps and falling objects and cracking walls were heard. The man himself was surprisingly calm for the convulsions wracking his home.

He continued, "I know the Republic denies it being a worldwide phenomenon, but I know better. We know better, us in the Resistance Alliance who have been exchanging stories of similar apocalyptic events. Well, it's back. And worse."

The picture swung around to a door. It opened, and a new view emerged: a pastoral landscape. An old John Deere tractor with faded green and yellow paint was anchored at one end of a parched lot, a few rusted farming attachments scattered near it beside flat fields under a wide, cloudless blue sky. Except what was happening shouldn't have been happening.

Thunder was rumbling, and purple-white tendrils of lightning were streaking across the sky. The kind that would fascinate Alexander as a boy and keep him up for hours on end in the middle of the night when fierce storms rolled across the Mediterranean. He'd sit under their family parish porch in his jammies and watch as spidery legs of purple and white danced across the sky. Exactly as they were doing—except there was no fierce thunderstorm with whipping winds and sheeting rain.

The feed suddenly cut. And that was the rest of the file.

"What the hot Hades was that..." Ford muttered, barely above a whisper.

Alexander didn't voice what he thought was the answer; didn't dare. But something about it all rang true, connecting to a part of John the Seer's revelations about the apocalypse.

Nia said nothing, opening the next file and finding a variation on the same theme: a quaking rumble, thunderous skies and a lightning show to rival those childhood memories in a clear sky. Every message sent to the station, presumably from the Resistance, was a replica of this theme.

Then it hit him. From the recesses of his memory of Scripture, which had surely been resurrected and fortified the past day after Solterra came crashing into the end of the world as they knew it.

He bit his lip and sucked in a worried breath, his heart picking up pace beyond what it was already galloping, worried that his inclinations were proving true right before their eyes. Regardless of his disbelief, or rather his unwillingness to believe, he could hardly deny what Solterra was witnessing, from the thundering to the lightning to the quaking.

Recalling the passage from Revelation, chapter 8, he muttered, "*'There came peals of thunder, rumblings, flashes of lightning and an earthquake...'*"

"What was that, homefry?" asked Ford.

"Huh?" he said, turning to the man with wide eyes, mouth a coppery dry from the revelation.

"You were mumbling to yourself like a crazy person."

Nia turned to him, demanding: "What is it that you are knowing?"

Alexander swallowed, then quoted: "*'Then the angel took the censer, filled it with fire from the altar, and hurled it on the earth; and there came peals of thunder, rumblings, flashes of lightning and an earthquake.'*"

"What is this you are speaking?" Nia said, face twisting with confusion.

"It's from the Book of Revelation."

Ford's eyes widened before glancing at Nia. He whispered on a worried breath, "So it's the apocalypse then?"

Alexander hesitated, gathering his words. "Presumably. It's from chapter 8, after Jesus himself opens the seventh seal—"

"The seventh?" Ford exclaimed with interruption. "That's after the sixth!"

Nia frowned. "That is generally how it is working..."

"As I was saying..." Alexander went on. "Jesus opens the seventh seal, and after a period of silence in heaven—well, then seven angels were spotted standing before God, and they were given seven trumpets."

Nia folded her arms. "And what is it that they are doing?"

"It's something to do with the apocalypse. We best ask Father Jim for further explanation. However, what I recall is that in the passage another angel, carrying a golden censer, stood at the altar."

"And what is this angel doing?"

"Offering the prayers of God's people, the martyrs in particular, before God's throne. And that's when it happened."

"What happened, homefry?" asked Ford, a tremble in his voice now.

Alexander swallowed. "The angel filled the censer with fire from the altar and hurled it to the earth. Then came peals of thunder, flashes of lightning, and the rumblings of an earthquake."

Nia let a startled sigh escape. "Just like what we were just experiencing."

He nodded.

Ford leaned against the console display, bringing a hand to his head, as if rubbing away a headache. "So that's it then," he said quietly. "The worm has turned."

Silence engulfed them as the station resumed some semblance of normalcy, the quaking having stopped and the crew having gotten the command center back under control. Whether from the ballasts or the end to the events of the seventh seal's opening, it wasn't clear. What was, based on the flood of incoming intel from the Resistance in the field, was that Ford was right: The worm had turned. The Day of the Lord had indeed arrived. And both Solterra and Ichthus were caught in the middle of its unfolding judgments.

Nia went back to the messages, opening the latest incoming transmission—when she gave a startled cry.

"*Apokalipsys!*"

No translation was necessary for that one. The Ukrainski woman was plain enough.

Apocalypse.

Alexander found it amusing that the word for the end of the world was pretty much universal across Solterra. Same in Germania, Athenia, even in the language of his Alkebulanan homeland. And now Muscovia of Ukrainski. Perhaps that was because every civilization from the dawn of time had some sort of apocalyptic lore at the end of their core worldview. A final reckoning for humanity that would either end in the world's destruction, or end in its final cleansing.

Regardless, something had just popped in from the Resistance that apparently made it all the more real for Nia. He leaned in for a closer look.

Ford said, "Pretty sure we already established that we're neck deep in the end of the world as we know it, but thanks for playing."

Nia grabbed his arm and yanked him toward the screen. "No, you idiot! It is being worse than we are imagining it!"

She pointed at the screen and ran a finger back down a message that had popped on the screen, reading it a second time. *"Bozhe moy!"* she exclaimed, then clattered away at a keyboard.

"Muscovia is not my forte," Ford said, sidling up as she brought up another video. "But that don't sound so good."

What started playing sucked the wind out of Alexander's lungs, and sent his pulse plunging in despair. And head swimming for a carton of narcowafers to take him far, far away from the reality that was now fully gripping the Republic.

There was no audio for the video; didn't need any. The visuals told all that needed to be told.

The rolling image could have been mistaken for a black and white pastoral scene from the 19th century, the picture speckled with debris and the landscape flat. Except there were erect posts scattered about, all bearing arms going this way and that, naked and blushing with the indignity of having been stripped of their clothes on top of what else must have rolled through.

The trio stood silent before the revelation, the only sound in Alexander's ears was the thudding of his heartbeat at the slow-motion dawning of what they were looking at, disbelief rising on a tide of bile up his throat.

As a teenager, he had seen photos of the events leading up to the Great Reckoning, the period before the formation of Solterra Republic that could arguably be called World War III. Entire cities—not to mention countries—had been laid to waste by hydrogen bombs wielded without discrimination by all the great powers of the day. A thousand times more deadly than the atomic bombs that came to define the 20th century, they leveled cities to heaping piles of rubble, charring the country-side and leaving behind nothing but smoldering twigs erect at wicked, naked angles in charcoal dirt. Ash and soot saturated the air for miles and for weeks, so that the sun itself was blotted from view.

What they saw was worse.

According to the label on the video file, it was drone footage of the Amazon, the largest forest in the world, spanning over five million kilometers and home to the longest river in the world snaking through its dense foliage. Except there were no longer any trees. No dense greenery, no charred trunk remains left behind, no emergent growth singed at the forest floor. It was a blank canvas of blackness, like cooled lava —wavy and pockmarked with craters still smoldering with ruin.

Even the famous river was nearly nonexistent, the remaining riverbed not more than a Tripolitanian creek bed, the contrails of its former life still rising in the air on heads of steam. Old black-and-white pictures of Nagasaki and Hiroshima, the infamous cities that had been obliterated by the atomic bombs of the former U.S. came close to imaging what the world looked like, but in more sepia tones thanks to the shrouded sun.

The picture changed, another view from another part of Solterra flashing on the console. This time it was ground level, from Cascadia, a temperate rainforest in the Pacific Northwest of the North American continent. Same burned-up destruction, same cloud of rising ash, the person holding the recording device crunching along similar blackened ground. The view changed again, this time with loss of buildings and other dwellings it seemed. Then again, panning to the same sad, terrifying incineration.

Bile rose to the surface at the sight of so much destruction, Alexander's stomach clenching with painful dread and head throbbing with horrifying tremble. His bowels went watery, his legs wobbled as if they would give way then and there. For a frightening possibility came rising to the surface along with that bile.

Which he knew deep down was much more of a *probability.*

"The first trumpet..." he muttered to himself, finally coming to grips with the truth of it all.

"What was it you are saying?" Nia snapped.

"Yeah, homefry," Ford added. "You've gotta stop this muttering business. Totally puts a crimp in our—"

"I said it's the first trumpet!" Alexander took a breath and ran a hand through his hair. "Sorry, but it is like I said before. From the Book of Revelation, chapter 8: *'The first angel blew his trumpet, and there came hail and fire, mixed with blood, and they were hurled to the earth; and a third of the earth was burned up, and a third of the trees were burned up, and all green grass was burned up.'*"

He pointed at the screen, the video cycling back through the charred desolation. "This is that. The first trumpet has been blown. This is it. We are living through the end times!"

Ford folded his arms, face flat and stoic. "The worm really has turned then. All official like."

Nia matched him, saying grimly: "The apocalypse is officially being now."

Alexander turned to leave. "We need to get back to Father Jim. He'll know what to do."

"My God..." Ford suddenly cried out, slumping to his knees.

Alexander turned back, furrowing his brow with confusion. "What's the matter?"

"It's..." The man trailed off, swallowing hard and doubling over, placing both hands on his knees and panting for more breath.

Nia leaned in closer for a better look, matching Alexander's confusion. "I am not under—"

"Springer Mountain," Ford interrupted, bringing his hands

up to his head, face pained and drained of color. "A rising ridge at the northern border of Noramericana that starts the two-thousand-plus mile trek along the Appalachian Trail to Mount Katahdin in north Americana."

Alexander couldn't imagine it, but his stomach sank further. He knew what that meant.

Nia scoffed. "Who cares? Why is this being so dread—"

"It's my homeland!" Ford cried out, face twisted with anguish. "My people. My family..."

And all of it had been obliterated. A third of Solterra, if the prophecies concerning the end of the world were unfolding.

Ford looked to Alexander, moistened eyes pleading for answers. He had very few. But he knew who did.

"Come on. We should go check on Father Jim. He'll know what to do."

For Ford, for Ichthus. For Solterra even.

Martin Zarruq closed his eyes, tipped his head back, and stroked one end of his white handlebar mustache, his heart thudding expectantly in his chest even as his pulse raced into the gilded ceremonial vial resting on the white marble table. A reed protruded from his arm, carefully channeling his life force out of his body and into a rising pool of crimson at the bottom. A pleasurable sigh escaped him, both from the exhumation of his life force and at the anticipation rising inside at what it would bring.

He settled into the plush, gilded chair at the glass table and heaved another pleasurable sigh, the vast, bright room of white marble veined with faint gray lining the floor and walls agreeing with another echoing reply. Easing his eyes open, one end of his mouth curled upward at the view of a ceiling vaulted by soaring Corinthian columns edged by gilt lines circling the white pillars like candy canes. High above, crystals clung to the corners and seams of the ceiling like clusters of grapes, a sort of celestial crown molding that refracted the light from the day with rainbow brilliance, although dimming now under the threat of rain.

"Like Heaven..."

He smiled knowingly at the tongue slip.

No, like the Republic of Heaven.

Martin had personally overseen the construction of the hall, patterning it after another that had been destroyed by an ancient enemy over a century ago. The Order of Thaddeus. He sourced the best materials the Universe had to offer, ones that had unfortunately gone by the wayside in ultramodern Solterra, with all of its gleaming glass and polished chrome. He shuddered at the thought, more beholden to the ancient, alchemic metals and stones to festoon his temple. But as brilliant as the gilded columns and refracting crystals were, the real center of attention was the mural of celestial beings locked in arms with recognizable figures peering down at him, witnessing his moment of self-pleasure.

The full range of scenery from across Solterra's religious landscape was depicted, beginning with the Bible. From the Garden of Eden to Abraham sacrificing Isaac on Mount Moriah, Moses parting the Red Sea to the birth of Jesus, his feeding of the five thousand miracle to his crucifixion. But then it continued on in a way the in-the-know observer would have found confusing, depicting neither Christ's resurrection nor ascension.

Of course Martin had it designed that way, adding still other familiar religious depictions that would have seemed out of place in what one might have assumed was a place of Christian worship. There was Muhammad's First Revelation, the event described in Islam where the prophet was visited by the angel Jibrīl and revealed to him the beginnings of what would later become the Qur'an. And then another: a familiar depiction of Siddhartha Gautama, Buddha, sitting cross-legged in a crimson sash, one hand raised with enlightenment. All combining into the tapestry of the movement he was building for the Republic to unify the polis into a singular religious affection.

With him as the head, the High Priest.

The Summus Sacerdos, the Greatest Priest.

The air seemed to hum with agreement as his blood continued pouring out, readying him for his offering to the Universe, the man continuing to stroke the mustache end in sync with his heart beating his blood into the sacred vessel. Even the furniture pieces, edged in gold leafing and adding to the sense of brightness, seemed to glow especially bright in the presence of his act of letting.

His tongue tingled now with anticipation as the ceremonial vial filled, desire welling with a climactic groan within his belly for what would come next, down below in the bowels of Panligo's sanctum, the climax to his reappearing after having risen from the dead and back into public life.

Alexander must have been overcome with confusion mixed with anger, rage even. After all, he'd fooled the boy just as much as he'd fooled the fool, James Ferraro. That man and his Ministerium who had run him out those years ago. The man who was dreadfully stuck in his regressive beliefs, refusing to face the facts that the new ultramodern era required—no, *demanded* new, progressive answers to the world's age-old questions. Yet the man refused to do anything about it! Refused to thank *him* for doing something about it.

Martin tightened his fist, rage swelling at the thought of Father Ferraro besting him by excommunicating him from the Ministerium, from Ichthus even. Then he took a breath, relaxing his body again after tensing from what had been a low point in his illustrious career pointing people to the truths embedded deep within the Universe.

No matter. Things have a way of working themselves out; the Universe has a way of course correcting. For which he was eternally grateful. Or at least presently so, given what he was up against.

The man snapped open his eyes, his head feeling suddenly faint. He eyed the gilded vial and startled. The thing was nearly filled to the brim! No wonder he was feeling it, a goodly amount of the crimson liquid having been let from his arm during his absentminded contemplation.

Grasping the slender stem with his thumb and forefinger, Martin pulled the long end from his arm, the centimeter worth stuck inside his vein sliding out easily. Blood seeped from the hole in his arm, but he left it. It also collected at the end of the reed, that quickening stirring again.

He dropped his jaw with lustful hunger and pressed the bloodied end against his tongue. The coppery sensation of old-world pennies sent an instant jolt of orgasmic delight through every nerve ending in his mouth. He sucked at the reed, his life force slowly sapping into his mouth like a straw. His skin rippled with goose pimples at the amplified coppery taste compounded by the salty scent, his head growing dizzy again.

Then he set the slender stem on his desk. Mustn't get too greedy. Soon he would have his fill, and so would the others.

A rapping against the door of polished chrome at the far end of the vast room of white marble stole his attention, cutting off his moment of secret pleasure.

Martin carefully sealed the gilded vial with a cork and set it aside, then stood and called out for the intruder to enter. The door slid open. In strode Dominic Weiss and Apollos Nicolai, the men who he was leaning on to unfold his grand plans for Panligo.

For Ichthus...

"Come along, then," he said, motioning them toward the far end.

He sauntered over to the grouping of chairs, his crimson

silk robe swishing and bare feet slapping against the cold, hard marble with each step. He met the men at the same cluster of couches at one end that he and Lucius Severus had sat at days ago when he stopped by to assess progress on bringing the Republic's plans to fruition.

He only hoped these men would please him as much as he tried to please the Patron with the designs of his own plans for the future. Failure was not an option.

"Care for a drink?" he asked, stopping at a long mahogany table, bottles of wine and liquor arrayed on top.

"Yes, Cardinal—"

His head snapped toward the sound of his previous title. The one he'd held before his demise in the Ministerium.

It was Apollos, eyes wide and searching for help from Dominic.

The man gave a curt smile and offered a short bow. Weiss said, "Yes, *Sacradi*, that would be splendid. Whatever you are imbibing should suit us, isn't that right?"

"Ye—yes, Sacradi," Apollos stammered. "Whatever you are imbibing should suit us."

Martin frowned, annoyed already at the intrusion before the ceremony, but doubly so after the insult.

He returned to the table and opened a bottle of Barlo red wine bottled in 2085. A good year. The year Alexander was born, actually. It was also the year he was ordained into ministry with the Church. Seemed like an apropos offering, considering the consecration that would soon take place. Pouring three glasses, he joined the men seated on a cream couch rimed in gilt.

Passing out the two glasses, he raised his own. "*Ad bonum vitae!*"

"To the good life, indeed," Dominic said, raising his glass before taking a sip. Apollos did the same.

"Now, please tell me you come bearing good tidings of great joy."

Weiss grinned, glancing at Apollos. "We do. The most excellent tidings, actually."

Surprised, Martin leaned back and took hold of one end of his mustache. "Do tell."

"Our engineers believe they finally have a working prototype that can be used."

He threw back a swig of wine and drilled him with irritation. "*Believe?*"

Dominic threw back a swig of his own, matching his stare. "You have to understand, the device left behind in the Ministerium rubble was only half finished. We wouldn't have even known what to do with it had it not been for the agent left behind in that jail cell of theirs."

"That Tara Rodriguez woman?"

"That's right. She proved to be quite useful in exposing Ichthus's various side projects."

"Side projects?" Martin exclaimed, throwing back another mouthful. "Project 65 seems to be much more than a side project!"

"With your son at the center of it all..." Apollos said from the side, filling his own mouth with wine after seemingly understanding his slip.

"Yes, well, be that as it may, we need our weapon operational before the day is out, am I clear? The Patron is eager to unfold this second phase of the Purge, and I assured him all would be ready soon."

"We're already readying the...weapon, as you put it, for use very soon."

Martin sat forward with interest. "Really?"

"Yes, sir," Apollos said with a knowing grin. "We are being more than ready to come through for you and the Patron."

One end of his mouth curled upward at that German accent and those perfectly coiffed locks of his. He could see why Dominic fancied the young man.

A chime rang out on the other side of the hall from near his glass desk, its echo clear as the bell inside that vintage wooden Howard Miller grandfather clock from pre-Reckoning. It was a bit ironic he cherished such antique treasures, given his penchant for progressing his ancient faith forward into ultra-modern realms. Be that as it may, he understood some things were worth holding onto, even from the past.

Dominic turned toward the chime. "It sounds like the hour of your christening is nigh."

Martin downed the glass and set it on a table, then stood; the others joined him. "It is. When do you plan to use the weapon?"

"A day, maybe two more if we can finalize the—"

"I don't need to know the details. Just get it done. We need the minority voice of reason tucked in the Church's past to rise above those in power who shaped Ichthus's doctrines. Notify me the minute you're back with the results."

"Yes, Sacradi. Although, I imagine you'll know sooner than us if all goes according to plan..."

He nodded, then waved them off, bidding them goodbye.

The men left, and Martin sauntered back for the gilded vial. He grasped it with both hands, a bloody fingerprint left behind on the large cork plugging the mouth shining crimson.

The hour is nigh, indeed...

Rumbling thunder in the distance brought him back to the moment, desire beginning to churn in his belly from the weight and pleasure of what was to come. He took the vial and went to a panel on a blank wall that disguised what was below. Pressing his hand against the device, it pulsed blue before flashing green.

The wall shuddered before revealing a stairwell that stretched downward.

On toward destiny.

The floor felt cold under Martin's bare feet as he slowly descended the stone stairway of his sanctum, earth and stone, mold and must mixing with delight. He had always had a certain fascination with the elemental, the earthen, believing as his Alkebulanan ancestors did that there was a life force that permeated all things, binding them together in divinity.

That One is all, and all is One.

He brought that principle of universal divinity to bear on Panligo, leveraging the insights of the Solterran faiths that expressed that universal force, binding them together—to bind together the world faiths.

Only one thing was standing in the way: the Christian claim that Jesus himself was God. Was divine, the Absolute Principle that stood above all others.

Still the largest religion in the world, Christianity and its singular claims posed a unique problem for the Republic, for him even as the new Pope of Panligo. Claims he intimately understood, having been at one point a high-profile cardinal in the Church.

Luckily for him, he would deal with both in one swift blow.

Thunder rumbled as Martin continued his descent, LED lights along the base of the stairwell wall lighting his way to the chamber below. The wind howled now as a mixture of rain and heavy, wet snow beat against the thick, interlocking stones of the ancient castle, a violent reflection of the nature of what was about to take place below the legendary, rebuilt heart of Panligo, one that had been beaten for centuries.

Originally built in the seventeenth century, it later became the central headquarters of the German SS and central command for Heinrich Himmler. Though it had become a sort of museum and youth hostel post-WWII, the estate had been acquired by a former Grand Master of Nous over a century ago —before his unfortunate demise and much of the headquarters were destroyed by a rival that eventually became an ally.

The stuff of legends that man was, Rudolph Borg, the one who had reactivated the enemy of the Church stretching back to its founding, transforming the castle and the alt-spiritual Nous organization into his own needs: a nerve center of spiritual enlightenment and war. Bless the Universe he had the foresight to train his successor in the ways of Nous, ironically a twin to a Master of the Order of Thaddeus. What they preserved for decades through the past century paved the way for a new, rising, finalizing force that would finally eliminate the Christians, the Church.

The Christ, even!

Martin continued his descent, the red silk robe swishing with every step. Reaching the bottom, he kept on toward the chamber, but he stopped when he reached a statue.

Bird-Man Thoth, the ancient Egyptian god of wisdom. Of revelation. Of *gnostikos*, the divine knowledge. It was a perfect replica of the colossal statue artifact discovered near the mortuary temple of Amenhotep III in Luxor a decade ago, surviving the original destruction of the Nous compound. Universe only knows how, but it stood as a testament to the enduring legacy of the entity that had made Panligo possible. Measuring eleven-and-a-half feet tall and made of pure, red granite culled from ancient quarries in Egypt, the statue stood towering over Martin, reminding him of his ancient calling and setting his face like flint against Ichthus.

He focused his attention on the ancient face, the ibis head peering down at him with a mask of pure gold, with a black onyx beak, flanked by indigo ribbons, and the Atef crown of white and red feathers stretching upward. It was truly a testimony to the enduring legacy of the ancient cult.

Thoth's roles in Egyptian mythology were varied. The god served as a mediating power between good and evil, as a scribe of the gods, and weighed the lives of the dead. The ancient Egyptians regarded Thoth as One, self-begotten and self-produced, like the Übermensch of his own ancient Germanic ancestors. The Egyptians credited him as the author of all works of science and religion, philosophy and magic. His power was unlimited and unrivaled by all other gods. The ancients even declared him the inventor of every work of every branch of knowledge.

Human and divine.

"'You know all that is hidden under the heavenly vault,'" Martin intoned, bowing his head reverently before the stone effigy as he quoted from the mystical sayings surrounding the god. *"'Now, that which has been hidden shall be revealed.'* And it shall be mine," he finished, clenching his fist with resolve.

Lightning flashed behind him through the windows up the stairwell, illuminating the god of knowledge in flickering white light. A few seconds later, thunder rumbled in the distance, bringing Martin out of his trance. He stiffened with purpose and continued down the darkly lit hallway, striding forth to meet his gathered brothers.

A glowing light up ahead pulled him onward, orange and warm. Voices, low and incoherent, were chanting the ancient mantra he knew by heart. A bleating screech sliced through the noise, and he quickened his pace. He reached the heavy, golden door standing ajar and pushed it open. The voices stopped as he entered. Facing him were seventeen Bird-Men, all wearing the face of Thoth.

The god of divine knowledge.

"Brothers," Martin said, striding toward them. The Bird-Men nodded in silent unison, welcoming their Grand Master.

He stepped into the circular cavern, high and domed. Made out of quarried stone, the room was illuminated by eight windows that flickered every so often with the storm's light. Thirteen torches displayed around the room offered a soft glow to provide the remaining light. They hung above thirteen small, stone seats upon which bare-chested Bird-Men sat with ornamented shoulder drapes of gold and indigo beadwork, all wearing masks of pure gold, flanked by ribbons of indigo, with beaks of black onyx.

Martin scanned the room, then lifted his head toward the high dome, smiling reverently at the symbol adorning its center: a swastika, made infamous by the radicals of the 20th century. Far from a modern symbol of fascist oppression, it was an ancient religious one, taking the form of the familiar equilateral cross with its four legs bent at ninety degrees. Considered to be a sacred symbol of such spiritualities as Hinduism, Buddhism, and Jainism, it dated back to before the second century BC. Small terracotta pots and ancient coins from Crete were found to have borne the symbol. And it had been used as a decorative element in various cultures stretching back to at least the Neolithic period. For Martin, the symbol held all the divine promises of these pre-modern cultures for such a time as this.

Directly beneath the dome, in the middle of the room, was the crown jewel of the crypt: the ceremonial basin. It acted as a baptismal pool for the rite of passage into the upper echelon of the ancient order of divine knowledge and power.

Tonight, it would be used for a very different purpose, a sacred purpose.

He strode farther into the chamber, the cool, dank air making the silver hairs on the back of his neck stand upright in delight. Seats were arrayed around the outer rim of the room for the Thirteen, the coterie of high-ranking associates representing the Wheel of the Year and the perfection of the earthly and heavenly alignment of seasons. Five more lined the front of the chamber, holding the Council of Five. The seats of the Pentacle, of Man.

Of God.

Martin breathed in deeply and moved toward a throne-like chair in the middle of the arrayed seats. His chair. He took his place among the Council at the center reserved for the Grand Master. To his right was the ceremonial ibis dress. It mirrored the statue of Thoth he had just passed, white and red plumes, gold mask and all. He smiled and placed the headdress upon his head, then affixed the gold mask to his face, along with an intricately beaded gold and indigo sash hanging at his shoulders.

A small, muffled bleat was heard from the center of the ceremonial basin. He spun toward it and peered through his gold mask, over the onyx beak, to the four-legged victim tied and muzzled in the center of the floor. It strained violently against its restraints, nibbling at the muzzle keeping his mouth tightly closed, as if it anticipated what was impending.

The snapping of the torch flames provided the only sound in the chamber as Martin strolled toward the center, his garment swishing in sync. He untied the animal and undid the muzzle. A bleating, mournful cry instantly escaped its lips.

Out from under his robe, Martin removed a jewel-encrusted athame knife passed down from Grand Master to Grand Master from each successive generation to use in ceremonies such as this one. In one swift swipe, he sliced the blade across the goat's throat. The bleating stopped as blood spilled from its neck onto the cold, hard stone floor. The animal twitched in his tight grip, then went limp, its life force draining into the baptismal pool.

He withdrew the golden vial from the robe and uncorked it, pouring the contents of his life force into the pool, his blood mixing with that of the goat. The animal was a symbol of purity and preciousness, and the regenerative nature of the Universe, ancient civilizations lionizing the goat as a god of nature—Pan.

The rest of the room silently looked on as their Grand Master performed the necessary sacrificial ceremony in anticipation of the greater good that was to come.

One fueled by fire, now cleansed by blood.

CHAPTER 13

MEDITERRANEAN OUTPOST.

Alexander led the charge back to the renewed Archives room in the bowels of the deep submergence station, feeling more familiar with the underwater facility now and feeling a surprising rise in duty to resume the mantle he had accepted over a year ago now.

Master of the Order of Thaddeus, ancient defender and contender of the Christian faith, of the Church, of Ichthus—the Christian remnant during these last days.

Weaving through the corridors of steel, the tank of blue iridescent water having calmed now that they were floating and the dolphin Galileo following their movements again, it surprised Alexander to feel such duty returning, given how he had left things.

After what happened on that beach all those many months ago, the return of his father, compounded by the man's betrayal of him personally and of Ichthus and the faith—no way was he coming back to lead the charge to contend for the once-for-all faith of God's holy people, or join the Resistance, or whatever. He was through with it all. Done fighting for the faith. Let someone else traipse through time retrieving the memory of Ichthus and what she believed. That's what he had felt back then running across the wet sand toward that town in the fading evening light, leaving his friends behind. And his responsibilities to his faith.

But now...with the dawn of the apocalypse rising?

Something about witnessing the devastation wrought across Solterra, knowing the real lives of real people were coming under what appeared to be a ratcheting up of God's judgment, and then seeing one of his own friends beside himself with worry and agony at realizing his very own homeland and family were experiencing the same devastation—all of it seemed to trigger something inside, activating Alexander to...

Well, to do what wasn't all that clear at that point in all the crazy as he rounded the final bend. Mostly since what came next wasn't all that clear as he made for the Archives of the Church's most sacred creeds and theological treatises and history.

What was the Church to do at the onset of the apocalypse? What were average Christians to do when Jesus Christ split open the seventh seal, that holy hush of trembling, suspenseful anticipation welling up within the hosts of heaven before the seven angels with their seven trumpets of judgment were let loose upon the Republic?

What was he to do, Alexander Zarruq?

He reached the door but realized he couldn't gain entry. Ford came up to his side, his face blotchy and eyes rimmed with grief. Nia came up to the door bearing one of the powerhouse workstation portables under one arm.

Alexander ran through that question—the one about what he was going to do about the end times—for what seemed like a hundred cycles as he waited for the door to open. The time it took for Nia to slap her hand on the security device, to wait for the pulsing blue to change to green, and finally for the door to unlock cranked up the anxiety around the options that seemed to dwindle down to two.

Fight or flee.

Contend for the faith, for the Republic's very soul even. Or shrink back to what was left of that seaside wharf at the edge of Roma, scrubbing those blasted barnacles off those blasted hydrocrafts the rest of his life.

The door unlocked and opened. Nia pushed through, followed by Ford.

Soon he would know his answer.

The Archives was relatively intact, considering the shaking they'd all experienced. Aside from a crack running at one corner of the digital panels on the far-left wall, the place was in order and relatively calm. Father Jim was seated at the steel center table, Rebekah and Lucy still tending to the man who had a piece of bloodied cloth pressed against his head. Even Sasha was calm, lying on the couch behind the table with his hands behind his head.

He sat up when they entered, then asked in a rush, "Is it being over? Are we being safe?"

So much for calm. Although who could blame him, especially if the apocalypse truly was upon Solterra?

"Yeah, about that..." Ford said.

"*Da i nyet*," Nia said, going on to explain how she had activated the emergency measures to keep the station stable, for now.

"That is being the *da* part."

Sasha sat up straighter. "And what is being the *nyet* part?"

Ford looked to Alexander. "Care to do the honors, Master Zarruq?"

Alexander took a breath and nodded, then launched into a review of what they had seen. From the drone footage of the Amazon laid waste, charred beyond recognition, to the thunderous roars and phantasmic lightning show, to what looked like craters from meteors of fire being hurled to the earth, the montage of other sites across Solterra all confirming the truth that the destruction was widespread—including Ford's Noramericana homeland. Looked like much of Earth's vegetation had been decimated.

The room was silent for it all until Father Jim drew in a stabilizing breath and tilted his head back contemplatively. He closed his eyes and said lowly, "*'Then the angel took the censer, filled it with fire from the altar, and hurled it on the earth; and there came peals of thunder, rumblings, flashes of lightning and an earthquake.'*"

Ford swallowed and glanced at Alexander. "That's what our resident Order Master had quoted. From the Book of Revelation, isn't that right?"

"Indeed. Chapter 8. The unfolding of the next stage of God's judgment upon the world."

"With Ichthus squarely within the same crosshairs."

The cardinal winced as he adjusted the cloth at his head. "No, that is not correct, John Mark."

"It ain't?"

"The Church is not in any way shape or form in the crosshairs, so to speak, of God's wrath!"

Nia said, "But you were saying earlier that we were meant to experience the Great Tribulation!"

"Not experience it, as the unregenerate do, as judgment for their wickedness and under the wrathful hand of the Lord. But live through it, *endure* and *persevere* through it. The previous chapter before the trumpets presaging the Great Tribulation, chapter 7, makes this clear."

"In what way?" asked Alexander.

"We find two multitudes representing Ichthus from two vantage points of the coming apocalypse. The 144,000 from all the tribes of Israel representing the Church who are sealed by the Lord Almighty that they might be protected from the plagues expressing God's wrath upon the rising Antichrist and his followers. Then there is Ichthus on the other side of the Tribulation, those who have washed their robes in the blood of the lamb, the believers who have suffered persecution and martyrdom under the mighty hand of the Antichrist, yet are victorious. So no, the end times are not meant for the Church, but they will live through them, and in complete victory."

"And that's what you think is happening?" Alexander said. "We are now in fact living through the end times—the Church is, Ichthus?"

"And us fine folks?" Ford said, throwing Alexander a glance.

"I don't know how else to interpret it!" Father Jim exclaimed, his voice rising and all at once cracking and shaking, betraying a level of fear and concern he had not openly confessed. "Consider the manner in which the world quaked and trembled the past day. With the day-lit sky fading into darkness and the moon turning blood red—fitting the apocalyptic description of Revelation 6:12 to a T."

"Which was only ever thought to be just that," Alexander responded, "apocalyptic language."

"Apparently such language was far more accurate to the truth of the matter, my boy. And then for the world to witness the cataclysmic decimation of a third of the world's vegetation—it fits perfectly!"

"We are not having confirmation of that yet," Nia corrected, a command to her voice that signaled she wasn't interested in speculation. "Cataclysmic decimation, *da*. But how much or widespread isn't being for certain. We are needing more information from the field."

Ford complained, "Which we're not going to get stuck in this tin can 20,000 leagues under the sea!"

Alexander nodded. "You're right. We should probably think about heading back up to the surface soon. Or at least connecting with the Resistance somehow through secure Ministerium channels on DiviNet."

Father Jim waved a dismissive hand, wincing again. "Be that as it may, given what we already know, what we have witnessed with our own eyes and the communication already sent our way from the Resistance, I cannot imagine what has transpired across the Republic the past day is anything else besides the unfolding of that dreadful yet glorious day when the Lord Almighty finally comes to do what he promised from the beginning."

"And what is that being?" asked Nia, her voice less hardened than before, arms at her side now and head cocked and ready for some sort of revelation.

"Why, to judge the world, unfold his wrath upon wicked humanity, and recreate the world as he intended it to be at the start of this whole bloody human affair before we vandalized it all to hell!"

The woman went to the table and slung her portable workstation on top. "I am thinking we are needing some sort of confirmation. Mr. Ford—" she said, motioning toward the man.

He raised a brow and glanced at Alexander, mouthing *'Mister?'*

Alexander smiled, a chuckle slipping through as the man sauntered over.

"What can I do you for, little missy?"

"You and the cardinal were in continued communication with Ministerium contacts in the last several months, *da?*"

"*Da.* I mean, yes."

"How were you getting in touch with them?"

Ford looked to Sasha. "The good doc over yonder set up a secure nodule, or something or other."

Sasha shook his head and hopped to his feet. "It is being *node*, not nodule."

"Whatever. Node, then. But what about your own contacts? The Resistance that sent in all the intel from earlier?"

Nia said something to Sasha and stepped aside as he came up to the computer. He hunched over its keyboard and started clacking away.

She said, "It is not being easy to reach the Resistance. They are being underground and scattered about. I am thinking it is easier to be reaching Ministerium agents who are being more accustomed to answering the call of duty from afar."

Ford said to Sasha, "Well, what are you able to finagle there, doc?"

Alexander watched the man work, a series of windows filled with correspondence and images coming in and out, much the same as they had seen before.

He said, "We've seen much of this already. Not much more can be gleaned from images and video files. Anyone we can connect with?"

Sasha straightened and brought a hand to his chin. "There is not much activity on the comm channel, I am being afraid. Other than—" He hunched back over, clacking again on the keyboard. "I am finding one person. Somewhere in the province of Georgia, in Nor—"

"Georgia?!" Ford exclaimed, shuffling over and shoving Sasha out of the way.

The man gave a startled cry, tripping over his feet and falling to the floor. Father Jim protested, so did Nia.

Ford ignored them. "It's a distress call..." He went to press it when Nia swatted his hand away.

He spun toward her with irritation. "Hey! What the hot Hades—"

"I am not so sure that is being a good idea," she said, folding her arms and staring him down.

"Why not?"

"Because we are not sure what the Republic is doing right now under these extreme circumstances. They are having to be thinking something is up. They may even be blaming Ichthus for all the trouble."

Ford scoffed. "Should be blaming the Lord Almighty, is who they should be blaming!"

"I am not disagreeing," Nia said, crossing herself and mumbling something in her Muscovia tongue. "At any rate, Solterra could be monitoring our Ministerium communications."

"And when has that stopped us before?"

"Perhaps she's right, Ford," Alexander said. "Maybe we take this one with a bit more caution."

"I ain't runnin' scared down no beach just because the Republic might be on my tail."

That one stung, a clear reference to him abandoning them those many months ago.

"Besides," Ford went on, "we agreed we need actual eyes and ears on the ground, telling us what the hot Hades is going on!"

"I have to agree with John Mark here," Lucy said.

"Thank you! Now can I help our brother out—or sister, as the case may be—and answer the damn comm call?"

Father Jim cleared his throat and threw him a reproachful eye at the language.

He took a breath and dipped his head. "Sorry. But can I see why someone from Noramericana is using our secure line to try to get ahold of the few remaining Ministerium homies this side of the Atlantic?"

The cardinal glanced at Nia, then at Alexander, who gave a subtle nod of approval. He did the same.

Ford punched the alert to the blinking incoming call. "Glad we ran that one by committee when the world is—"

He stopped mid-sentence, the scene on the workstation monitor taking all of their breaths away.

"Fire..." Alexander said, barely above a whisper, finishing the sentence and horrified at what he saw.

Inferno more like it, devilish tails of orange and crimson in the near distance rising and falling in swirling waves, smoke thick and bitter billowing high into the sky. Looked like a small city was being consumed by the blaze, older buildings of stone and wood along with ultramodern ones of gleaming glass and polished chrome eaten alive by the hungry flames of fire. Beyond was the now familiar scene of leveled trees and consumed hillsides, blackened by fiery consumption.

The angle was odd, high and through a wall of windows, but the image was clear.

Noramericana was on fire. Still.

"Hello?" Ford said, a thud sounding off-camera followed by the fuzz of distortion in the audio and video. He cleared his throat then asked again: "Hello, anyone there?"

Suddenly the picture swung up toward the ceiling of some flat then swooped down with a jiggly jerk, a face coming into view. It brightened and mouth widened into a smile.

"About time you answered my—"

The picture cut out with distorting fuzz, followed by a hiss of the audio.

Ford hit the workstation screen. Sasha complained and took over until the picture came back online.

"Sorry about that," the mystery man continued. "It's been a right wicked morning, as you all know. Just thankful I finally got through!" Dark hair, dark skin, he talked with a thicker twang than John Mark, pegging him from deep in the former American South. Maybe originally from Louisiana, which was unusual for black folk to live that far south of the Mason-Dixon after the Second Civil War. After all, it was partly fought to reclaim the glory of the Lost Cause from the original war centuries ago.

"Actually, we are not knowing," Nia said, coming over Ford's shoulders.

"And who might you be, little missy? In fact, who'r all y'all?"

"John Mark Ford," the man answered, "chief of operations with the Ministerium. Or, what's left of it. This is Junia Kaminski, chief over at a deep submergence station in the Mediterranean with the Resistance. I've got James Ferraro here as well, the head honcho himself."

"Nice to meet y'all. And boy am I glad to see you, Ford. Ryder Reeves, here. Went underground when .... was unleashed on Ichthus those many months ago, keeping a low ... then when everything hit the fan across Solterra yesterday, and then more earlier in the day, well I very well nearly threw in the towel and—" The distorting fuzz and audio hiss was back, getting worse as the man tried explaining his lot in life.

Ford glanced at Alexander, worry written on his face.

The picture came back. "Sorry about that. Everything's been spotty with DiviNet after it all started."

"What can you tell us about what's been going down?" Ford asked.

"See for yourself." Reeves took the device to a balcony and turned the picture toward the fiery maw and billowing smoke below. He came back on: "As you can see, all hell's broken loose, sir. Which is sorta obvious. What's worse are the Enforcers that showed up to quarantine the area."

"Enforcers?" Ford exclaimed, bending toward the screen.

"Yep. Caught sight of some Purifiers as well wandering down below. My guess is they're fixin' to round us all up and reprogram us who lived to tell the tale of the apocalypse raining down on us. That, and blame Ichthus for it all to begin with."

Alexander stepped to Ford's side. "Why do you say that?"

"And who might you be?"

Ford answered, "Alexander Zarruq. Master of the Order of Thaddeus."

Reeves's dark eyes got as round as Alexander's father's tea saucers. He exclaimed, "Master of the Order of Thadd—"

Ford let a curse slip as the feed cut out again. Several seconds ticked by before it came back.

"—trying to talk to you!"

"Ryder, my man, you cut out. Sounded like someone wanted to talk with Alexander."

"You got that right!" Reeves laughed and whistled, surely excited.

Why was the mystery.

Alexander went to ask when he saw it.

A split second before it happened, just as the man opened his mouth to share more.

Balls of fire falling from the sky and slamming into the earth, consuming the world below. A broiling inferno rolling over what was left until it boiled up the apartment several stories up and cut out the feed completely.

The fate of Reeves unknown.

CHAPTER 14

THE ROOM FELL silent for several minutes after the feed cut to black, the HVAC hum of the station the only soundtrack after the continued unfolding of God's wrath seemed to consume their only lead on the ground.

Ford assumed what they had seen on those communiques from the field from hours ago was the worst of it—whatever *it* was. Seeing it all unfold live, right there in ultra-definition TV though...

That was crazier than a one-armed octopus!

And frighteningly scary, knowing that his homeland had been part of heaven's judgment, God raining down the funk on his people. His family, even.

A tremor grabbed hold of his hand. He clenched it into a fist and glanced at Nia then to Alexander, not wanting anyone to see his show of weakness. His chest began thumping away and the air was heavy in his chest. He took a breath and closed his eyes, counting backwards from a hundred. No way he'd let the Grip get ahold of him while the world burned.

Who knew walking into 2125 would bring the end of the world as he knew it. The apocalypse, of all things!

Crazier than a one-armed octopus, yessiree.

And scarier than his toothless meemaw gumming in to plant a wet kiss on his cheeks!

Growing up, he'd been schooled in the finer points of the end times, Meemaw and Ma both drilling into him the Left Behind theology Father Jim had dismissed. It was meant to scare him straight, keep him on the straight and narrow with the threat of the impending rapture, with Jesus snatching people from Earth to Heaven and leaving the rest to suffer seven years of hell. Didn't take, but now that he was living it, and now that his own family could be in the crosshairs...

No more of this standing around business. Enough jibber-jabbering. Enough getting caught with their pants down around the ankles at the mercy of the Republic and the apocalyptic doom.

It was go time.

Suddenly, there was a rush of pesky questions rising to the surface: What was Ichthus to do about it all, about the apocalypse? What were average Christians to do now that the seventh seal was opened and the seven trumpets of judgment were about to be let loose? What was he himself supposed to do about it, the guy who had persecuted the Church and enabled the Republic to throw its own version of the Book of Revelation at 'em?

He didn't know the answers—to any of the big fat question marks. But he aimed to find out.

On the double.

Ford clenched his jaw with resolve and turned to Nia. "How many underwater ponies you got stabled in this joint?"

She squinted one eye at him with skepticism. "We are having four PSVs."

"Including our own yellow submarine?"

"*Nyet.* That is being extra."

He grinned. "That should be enough."

"Enough for what?" asked Alexander.

"For answers."

"Where are you getting these answers?" Nia asked.

Ford pointed at the portable workstation. "Back there."

The room fell silent for a beat, as if trying to work out the haywire plan he was hatching.

"Wait a minute..." Alexander finally said, the lightbulb clicking on. "You mean Noramericana, don't you?"

"Yessiree, Bob."

"Golly," Lucy said. "After what we all just witnessed?"

Father Jim said, "I'm not so sure about this plan of yours, John Mark."

Ford ran a frustrated hand across his close-cropped hair. You and me both, chief, he wanted to say. Instead, he launched into his defense.

He folded his arms. "Think about it. All we've got to go on are the videos sent from a handful of former Ministerium members of the Resistance and some good ol' boy who seemed dialed into the Order Remnant. In fact, the lad seemed like there was more to share. And given part of our mission the past year has been trying to hunt down and root out the remaining faith-defenders, I'd say it's imperative we figure out what went down back in Noramericana." He paused, catching his breath and throat catching as he added: "Back home."

"I suppose the man does have a point," the cardinal said.

"We need boots on the ground," Ford continued. "To see for ourselves what this whole apocalypse is anyway—and what the hot Hades the Republic is trying to cover up."

"Literally," Lucy quipped.

"Righto. The way I figure it, if we can get a visual we might leverage it for the Ichthus Resistance. Maybe record it and get it up on DiviNet like we did with all that time-travel footage. And if there's a pocket of the Remnant hunkered down nearby as well, then maybe they're the break we need to get the Church back in the ring with Panligo—with the Republic even."

He looked to Alexander, knowing the man was part of the decision tree, given his role in the Ministerium as Order Master.

Alexander seemed to consider this, then nodded. "Makes sense to me."

"I suppose there's some sense in it as well," Father Jim added.

Nia sighed. "And I am having some contacts in some of the more backwater outposts along the way that could be of use. Because there is no way you are being able to cross the Atlantic in any of the hydrocrafts we are docking."

"And there's no way," Lucy added, "that we're making the journey in one of those deep submergence vehicles that carts people across the Atlantic."

Ford raised a brow. "We?"

She gave him a punch in the shoulder. "No way are you traipsin' halfway across the world without your new sidekick after all we've been through!"

"Wouldn't think of it."

"I might be persuaded to join as well," Nia said. "For the sake of Ichthus, of course."

"I am being persuaded too!" Sasha added, jumping to his feet and joining the small group.

"Splendid!" Ford laughed and clapped his hands together, finding a surprising eagerness to get back into the fray of it all—against the Republic even, with their Enforcers and Purifiers, the Stingrays and Trackers, the Quellers and Neutralizers, and all the rest.

Perhaps *because* of the Republic with their Enforcers and

Purifiers, the Stingrays and Trackers, the Quellers and Neutralizers, and all the rest! Getting even had been a flaw.

"Sounds like we're all operating from the same playbook. Any more questions before we get to it?"

"I've got one more thing," Alexander said.

"And what's that?"

"For Padre," he said, turning to Father Jim.

The man raised his head. "Yes, Alex, what is it?"

"Earlier, before the blasted station started shaking and, well, everything else that went down—earlier you were answering John Mark's questions about the confusion surrounding Jesus, both inside and outside Ichthus. Seems especially important now given what we've witnessed, what the world is experiencing, and what we promised that agent."

"Indeed, it is vitally important."

Ford went to complain about the rabbit trail now that they'd gotten their marching orders, eager to get to it. But then he thought better of it. There might be something to that side of it, the side he didn't quite get about that Arius fella.

So he took a breath. "Yeah, care to elaborate, chief?"

Father Jim took the sapphire slate resting on the metal table, then stood. "I have been having a think about the latter which is directly tied to the former."

"What do you mean by that? You think the apocalypse is somehow connected to questions around Jesus' identity and that Arius fella?"

He smiled. "Perhaps you should sit down for this one." He sauntered to one of the panels still showcasing a number of tomes from the Ministerium Archives.

"You were wondering, John Mark," Father Jim said across the room, "about why there has been confusion about who Jesus is and what he came to do, both outside and inside the Church. Isn't that right?"

Ford nodded. "Yeah, something like that. Outside I can understand, but why inside Ichthus? Seems to me we should be the ones with the clearest impression, given he's the guy behind our faith and all."

The cardinal laughed. "You would think that's right, wouldn't you."

"Again, how so?" asked Ford, folding his arms with impatience and trying to move it along.

"Have a think about it. Outside the Church, Jesus is viewed as one religious teacher among many. There's Buddha, Muhammed, Krishna. And then Jesus of Nazareth."

"A sort of Gandhi on steroids, right?" Alexander offered.

Ford snorted a laugh; not a bad visual. "Gandhi on steroids. That fella from the Indian province of Asiatica way back when. Nice."

"But it's true, isn't it?" Father Jim said. "Which of course makes sense in our ultramodern polytheistic world. It's always been this way, really. The one true God and Lord standing amongst the other so-called gods and lords, as the Apostle Paul says. So this confusion about the person of Jesus outside the Church is understandable. And to some extent it makes sense that people inside the Church would be confused as well, because throughout Church history there's been confusion."

"But what is being so confusing about Jesus, about who he is?" asked Nia.

"More or less, the confusion has boiled down to his nature," Alexander offered. "Who he is as God, which also has implications for the nature of his work as well—his death on the cross, paying the price for our rebellion in our place, and whatnot."

Father Jim nodded. "Impressive, Master Zarruq. You're right."

Ford leaned over and whispered, "Teacher's pet."

Alexander frowned and smacked his arm. Ford yelped with a grin.

"Early on," the cardinal continued, "some people couldn't wrap their minds around the idea that the Creator would stoop so low as to become a creature—bearing all the trappings of creatureliness. Like hunger and sleep and—"

"Constipation and smelly armpits?" Ford added. The room moaned collectively. "What?"

Father Jim returned with a frown. "Something like that. Remember what the Book of Hebrews makes clear: God did in fact take upon himself flesh and blood. John wrote in his Gospel that *'God became flesh and moved into the neighborhood,'* as one Bible translation puts it."

"In other words, God became a real live human being," Alexander said. "That God, well, Jesus was really human."

"That's exactly right."

The cardinal returned to his seat. The man set the tablet down on the metal table, wrapping one arm around his waist, propping an elbow on his hand and raising the other to his chin. Ford imagined he was assuming a pose he'd honed from Oxford. He just hoped the man wasn't in lecture mode, because school definitely wasn't his strong suit!

"I am getting confused," Nia said.

"You and me both, sister," Ford muttered.

She smiled and went on, "So Jesus was being a real live human. This is seeming pretty basic to me, so what is this having to do with this Arius character? I thought what he was teaching was something about his divinity."

Father Jim nodded. "I was getting to that, Junia. Because as with the confusion over Jesus' humanity, early in the Church's history there was confusion over Jesus' deity. Some believed Jesus the man was adopted by the Father to become the Son of

God—that there was a time when Jesus was not God, and only later became God."

Alexander added, "Which is the heresy we call Arianism, named after the Alexandrian priest."

"Exactly. To clarify what I said earlier, putting the cookies on the lower shelf as you requested, John Mark..." The cardinal threw Ford a wink; the man smiled and nodded. "What I meant to say was that the false teacher Arius maintained that the Son of God was created by the Father and was therefore neither coeternal with him, nor cosubstantial. Meaning, Jesus neither existed from the beginning of time nor was he of one substance with God the Father."

"Because in essence," Alexander said, "what Arius was saying is, Jesus wasn't really God, isn't that right?"

Father Jim nodded. "If Jesus was created and later adopted, then he was a creature and not co-equal with the Father. And frankly, it matters because there is a sort of new kind of Arianism today, perpetuated by progressive Christians who would seek to reimagine a new kind of Christianity for our multi-faith world. This Jesus is said to be divine, not God. A sort of Gandhi by nature of his moral example and life illustrating the universal human ideal of love—only on steroids, as you put it, Master Zarruq," he said with a chuckle. "Like Arius' Jesus, this one isn't the real Jesus either. It is fake."

Ford nodded, then frowned. "Yeah, I don't follow, chief."

Father Jim offered a huff, as if exasperated. Before he could respond, Alexander intervened. "Maybe this would help."

The cardinal nodded and offered a hand. "By all means, Master Zarruq."

"Central to the Christian faith are the three words *Jesus is God*."

"Yeah, sure. I get that," Ford said. "That's basic."

"Basic, yes. But you won't find certain progressive Christians voicing those three important words, much less non-Christians. Instead, they'll say things like Jesus is *the very movement of God in flesh and blood*' or Jesus is *the divine in flesh and blood.*'"

"But he is being God in the flesh and blood, isn't he?" Nia said. "You said it yourself. Or the Book of Hebrews is, saying that Jesus was sharing in our flesh and blood."

Alexander nodded. "True, but notice that, like Arius, these kinds of Christians insist that Jesus is *divine*. While this language seems right, it isn't. It's code language for Jesus being this really good guy who lived the best possible life—who lived *divinely*."

"A Gandhi on steroids," Ford said.

"That's exactly right, John Mark," Father Jim said. "The Jesus you find in progressive Christian theology is described as a teacher and a liver of divine goodness, peace, and love. For them, Jesus the man simply showed the world what it means to be human, what it means to live a meaningful existence on this earth that's heavenly, rather than hellish. He is made out to be nothing more than a guru. Certainly not God."

"But, again, isn't this all being true?" asked Nia.

"To some extent," Alexander added. "However, to speak of Jesus' divinity is not the same as speaking of his *deity*."

Father Jim hummed with approval. "A very apropos and crucial distinction, Alexander. You will hardly find progressive Christians giving a positive statement of Jesus' deity. Saying Jesus is God would mean all other so-called gods are not. Instead, as Alexander here said, they will insist that Jesus gives us *the highest, deepest, and most mature view of the character of the living God.*' Yet again, their Jesus isn't God but merely a *person* who shows us the divine. The result is that Jesus is left merely as a person who exhibits the divine. He is the image of God; he resembles and is *like* God. This kind of Jesus embodied and modeled God through his ethics, not his nature."

"My head is hurting..." Ford moaned. This was way above his pay grade, and he wanted to get to it. Get back home, to his people to see what the hot Hades was going down! "And why does this matter, anyhow?"

"Why it all matters," the cardinal went on, "especially since these teachings were being spouted by the very titular head of the Republic's new pagan religion Panligo, is that Arius was the reason for the Council of Nicaea, and the reason why hundreds of bishops throughout the Church put pen to paper to craft the Creed sitting at the heart of Christianity, reminding Ichthus what we believe about Jesus' nature for nearly two millennia. That he was very God as much as very human."

"Which means the teachings of this Arius fella aren't anything new."

"Now you're catching on, John Mark! In fact..." Father Jim brought up the slate device and started flipping through some of the icons of books he had pulled. "Ahh! Listen to this."

He cleared his throat, then read aloud:

Since you think properly, pray that everyone will think that way. For it is clear to all that *the thing which is made did not exist before it came into being; but rather what came into being has a beginning to its existence.*

"That that Arius fella?" asked Ford.

The cardinal nodded. "Precisely."

"I don't get his meaning."

"This was a nascent articulation of his belief that Jesus Christ, Son of God, second person of the Trinity, did not exist before he was born, but rather came into being in the person of Jesus. And here is a more developed version."

Again, Father Jim read aloud:

And God, being the cause of all that happens, is absolutely alone without beginning; but the Son, begotten apart from time by the Father, and created and founded before the ages, was not in existence before his generation, but was begotten apart from time before all things, and he alone came into existence from the Father. For he is neither eternal nor co-eternal nor co-unbegotten with the Father, nor does he have his being together with the Father, as some speak of relations, introducing two unbegotten beginnings. But God is before all things as monad and beginning of all. Therefore he is also before the Son, who thus has his being from God.

Alexander whistled. "That pretty much puts an exclamation point on the end of it."

"Indeed," Father Jim said, Rebekah and Lucy nodding along.

Irritation flooded Ford, and humiliation. Never was good in school, and never was good with no religious and no Christian mumbo-jumbo. Probably why he didn't take to it until later in life.

"Again, the idea that the Son of God, Jesus Christ," Alexander explained, "was a separate being from God the Father."

Father Jim exclaimed, "Yes! Which has radical implications for the gospel, given that if Jesus wasn't God himself, but merely a man, then we're all still dead in our sins! His death would have done nothing for us. Even Emperor Constantine knew that!"

"Emperor who?" asked Ford.

Alexander replied, "The man who was basically responsible for gifting us Ichthus's cornerstone creed."

"You are speaking of the Nicene Creed, *da*?" Nia asked.

"Precisely, my dear!" Father Jim affirmed. "And listen to what the Emperor had to say about our fellow Arius." He said aloud:

The great and victorious Constantine Augustus to the bishops and laity: Since Arius is an imitator of the wicked and the ungodly, it is only right that he should suffer the same dishonor as they.

If any writing composed by Arius should be found, it should be handed over to the flames, so that not only will the wickedness of his teaching be obliterated, but nothing will be left even to remind anyone of him. And I hereby make a public order, that if someone should be discovered to have hidden a writing composed by Arius, and not to have immediately brought it forward and destroyed it by fire, his penalty shall be death. God will watch over you, beloved.

Ford smirked. "Sounds like our Dear Leader, the Patron himself, with all the post-Reckoning book burnings and whatnot."

"And for good reason!" the cardinal exclaimed. "Let's be clear. For Arius, Jesus was the *moral* Son of God, not the *metaphysical* Son of God. Rather than God himself becoming a human being, Jesus was viewed as a man who merely embodied the deepest meaning of life, as even some contemporary teachers would say. I'd say that was reason enough for the good Emperor Constantine to send his teachings to the flames!"

"Touché, chief."

"And cue that wackadoodle guru's Super Soul Sunday theme music," Lucy chuckled.

"Oh, yeah. Oprastein. That guy with the perpetual smile and spray-on tan with that popular Sunday morning DiviNet religious show?"

Lucy added, "That'd be the one. A cross between the non-denominational, mega-church evangelicalism of the 21st century and New Age spiritualism of the 20th century."

"And quite the feat to pull off, I reckon," Ford said.

"God's crazy love through Jesus' life, death, and resurrection," Alexander interjected, "you're saying that's what is at stake, Padre?"

"Indeed," the cardinal said. "Which impacts the real lives of real people and their real eternal destinies. And given the onset of the final days, the apocalypse if you will, that isn't something we should stand to let be fiddled with."

Ford shifted loudly, folding his arms and leaning back. Enough talk. Time to get to it.

"That's all fine and dandy, and I'm always one for a good Sunday school lesson in the finer points of Christianity, given I was a pagan and whatnot, but this ain't addin' up to a hill of beans in the real world outside these steel walls and up above that seawater if we don't do something about it all."

"I absolutely agree with you, John Mark," Father Jim said.

"Then what are we gonna do about it?" He knew he sounded worked up, but the doctrine download made his head hurt, and he knew a world outside was hurting for far more tangible action than just some words.

The cardinal raised a finger and returned to the slate device. "Indulge me for just a few more readings..."

Ford tried not to moan, but one slipped. Father Jim didn't notice, as he was readying to read anyhow. He said aloud:

The effects of that envious spirit which so troubled the peace of the churches of God in Alexandria continued to cause Constantine no little disturbance of mind. For in fact, in every city bishops were engaged in obstinate conflict with bishops, and people rising against people, causing in him sorrow of spirit; for he deeply deplored the folly that had been exhibited by the deranged Arians.

"That sounds like a copy of Eusebius's *Life of Constantine*," Alexander said.

"I trained you well," the cardinal said with a wink. "But one more...Ahh! There you are." Again, he read aloud:

As if to bring a divine array against this enemy, he assembled a general council and invited bishops from all quarters, expressing his honorable estimation. When they were assembled, it appeared evident that the proceeding was the work of God. For those who had been most widely separated, not only in sentiment but also personally, as well as by country, place, and nation, were brought together, forming as it were a vast garland of priests, composed of a variety of the choicest flowers.

Alexander twisted up his face in confusion. "Wait a minute...'he assembled a general council and invited bishops from all quarters, expressing his honorable estimation.'"

He looked to Ford, then back to Father Jim again, eyes wide and nose flaring like someone had just dumped a carton of the heebee jeebees on the fella.

"I don't get it," Ford said. "What's the matter?"

"You're talking about the Council of Nicaea," Alexander answered, "aren't you?"

The cardinal grinned, a twinkle in his eyes that led Ford to believe they had their answer to what was next on the horizon.

He confirmed it: "And that's our next move, Master Zarruq. While John Mark and his merry band head off to Noramericana, I'm sending you back in time to retrieve the memory of, I dare say, the most pivotal moment in the Church's history."

Alex didn't look too happy about it, but now they were getting somewhere. Finally!

Noramericana or bust, baby...

CHAPTER 15

MEDITERRANEAN SEA.

ALEXANDER AWOKE WITH A START, the plasticky sensation under his hands unfamiliar and confusing, slippery and firm with barely any purchase as he felt for a solid ground for his scramble toward consciousness. Same for the low hum, a sound that seemed to penetrate even his chest, combined with a pressure in his head that left him unsettled.

He snapped open his eyes, a dim dark blue greeting him along with the static scent of heavily sanitized air, cool and flowing with regularity, as he sucked in a startled breath.

Sitting up, Alexander spread his arms from his side, groping and shuffling around for answers. Was he in prison? The room was a tiny, cramped space with a low ceiling and windowless walls. A door at the other end stood closed, perhaps even sealed shut.

Had he been captured by the Republic? Thrown in the back of an Enforcer Transport and drugged until he reached the end of the line for him—a reprogramming camp at the borderlands of Solterra?

Alexander tried gathering his thoughts, but it was no use. His mouth instantly salivated for relief from the narcowafers he had run out of just before—

The end of the world as he knew it.

A collection of memories began surfacing, wicked memories of grim darkness and pregnant with despair and hopelessness.

The darkened sky and blood-red moon. The stars falling and fading, along with the fiery explosions upon the earth's quaking surface.

Father Jim and Ford and Sasha, Lucy and Rebekah and Jin—the people who had come in that yellow submarine to save him. His friends who had come for him after he had abandoned them.

Then the attack by Republic Stingrays and the deep submergence station, with that woman and those people who were part of some Ichthus Resistance carrying on the work of the Ministerium to protect the Church and prepare Christians for the apocalypse.

Which had been ratcheted up to the second circle of hell when the sky rained down an onslaught of fire and blood, torching the earth's vegetation and laying waste to presumably a third of the world's trees and grass.

Right before someone had made reference to the hidden Remnant of the Order of Thaddeus they had been hunting for over a year—of which he was their Master.

Alexander ran a shaking hand through his thick, gnarled hair, heart pounding at the possibilities and head aching with the volume on his anxiety maxing out.

Something stirred across from him, lumpy and curved.

He backed up slowly, the plasticky cushion squeaking under his movement before his back hit a wood-paneled wall. He clenched his hands into a fist and raised them toward mid-chest. No telling who could be sitting with him in that Republic hole.

But then the motion grew until a dark figure shimmering

under the dim light rose from underneath a thin blanket, hair short against the head with perfectly formed cheekbones and a scar running across the cheek that told a story he'd heard before.

"Rebekah?" he whispered.

She smiled, that perfect set of pearls set against dark Alkebulanan skin shining in the faint blue light. Infusing him with hope and settling his nerves some.

Now he regretted thinking she looked lumpy! Curved in all the right places, more like it. Which put a smile on his face knowing she was with him in whatever mess he had gotten himself into.

But wait. That meant—

"No, not you as well..." he moaned.

She sat up straighter, stretching with arms bent behind her head and closing her eyes with a casual calmness that Alexander couldn't understand. How could she act so cavalier under the circumstances! And what was she wearing? Some sort of beige burlap dress getup and a dark brown shawl wrapped over her head and thrown across her shoulders.

Then he realized he was wearing something similar, his chest itching from a shirt of the same material but with his standard white linen pants and a simple cloth hat. What manner of prison garb was this?

"Not me as well what?" she grunted as she completed her stretch.

Alexander's mind was swirling with confusion. He could hardly form the words, could hardly give voice to the wicked reality foisted upon them. He bowed his head and held it, heaving a breath of despair.

"How did it happen? My head is so foggy from it all..."

She sat up; the blanket slid off to the floor. "When did what happen? What on earth are you going on about?"

He looked up. "Th—The Republic. The reprogramming camp they stuffed us away in."

She giggled, throwing him a furrowed brow and disbelieving smile. "Are you for real? Republic reprogramming camp." She rolled her *R*s in a way that sent his heart soaring with delight, a welcomed shift.

A sudden shift in the gravitational force within their cell gave him momentary pause for his theory. As if they were slowing down from some supersonic speed, gravity working against him, tugging against his body and his bottom sliding forward on the slippery plastic seat.

Then it hit him.

Personal submergence vehicle. Zooming through the Mediterranean on their mission from Father Jim.

The door slid open, startling Alexander and sending him to his feet.

It was Jin.

"We're approaching the docking station. Get ready."

The docking station. That's right!

Alexander's head pulsed with memory now, the exhaustion from having run on a trace charge of adrenaline after forty-eight hours of non-stop mayhem catching up to him, the fraught nature of it all fraying his every nerve.

Now it was all coming back, what he had gotten himself into—as well as Ford and Father Jim.

Ford was insistent on getting back to his Noramericana homeland. He said he thought the Ministerium should get boots on the ground for themselves to see what the unsealing of the sixth seal and the launching of what was purportedly the beginning of the Great Tribulation with the first trumpet blast —what it all really meant for the world, and Ichthus. Alexander figured it was mostly an excuse to see what it all meant for his people, his family. Although he couldn't really blame him. Made perfect sense; didn't judge him for it in the slightest.

Father Jim was fine with that, so off the man went with a midsize SeaQuester and Nia, Sasha, and Lucy for backup. They were tasked with scoping out the damage up top on land and hunting down the Ryder Reeves character who seemed to have some knowledge of the Remnant they'd been trying to track down the past several months.

But that didn't end it for Padre. He had other plans for Alexander and Rebekah, who had become quite the intrepid time-travel pair through their last two missions retrieving the Church's history. Getting stuck in the past will do that! He suggested they take the Ministerium's yellow hydrocraft to the far side of the Mediterranean and jump back to AD 325—to the gathering of Ichthus's first ecumenical council. The Council of Nicaea, where Arius had been trounced and deemed a heretic. The very heretic his father seemed to want to leverage for his own designs for Panligo, and Solterra Republic.

The way Padre figured it, what would sustain the Church during Solterra's darkest hour would be the Creed that sat at the heart of their faith. Combined with the Holy Scriptures, the foundation upon which the apostles and Church fathers built and sustained the faith, with Christ at the head, retrieving the essential creedal components of their faith would anchor Ichthus in what was true, what was real about what they believed—helping Ichthus persevere through the worst of the apocalypse by holding fast to and standing firm in their trust in Jesus Christ's obedient life, redeeming work on the cross, and his victorious work through the resurrection.

Except the last time any of them had seen the former historic site, the Republic laid waste to it with a pack of Quellers that dropped an arsenal that pulverized it into dust! And what little intelligence the Ministerium was still able to gather indicated Enforcers were still stationed nearby several months later. With the Stingrays that had tracked them down and the Republic's continued Purge campaign waging away, Alexander thought it was suicide to try their hand at jumping back to the future with all that was going on.

Yet there they were, racing toward destiny once again, Ichthus and the faith on the line. And Alexander was charged with leading the effort to defend and protect all the Church held dear.

An ache began needling Alexander's temples, his mind pulsing with another memory from when he had last jumped back to the future from Smyrna after Polycarp's martyrdom. This pain wasn't quite the blooming agony that had sent him to his knees and doubled him over in that beachside shack. What he had feared was some sort of emerging bodily reaction to time travel. Jumping back hundreds of phases seemed to have triggered it, but he wasn't sure, and he hadn't mentioned anything to Father Jim or Sasha.

But now...with the ache needling him again, whether from anxious dread or the vestiges of the somatic response reactivating—now he wished he had mentioned something, the thought of that crippling pain returning sending an alarming shudder through his body.

Lord Jesus Christ, Son of God, may your hand of protection guard us this day. And keep my head from exploding!

"Looks like we're reaching our destiny," Rebekah said. She stood and offered Alexander her hand. "Shall we?"

He smiled and took it, pulling into a stand. "We shall."

Jin handed him a slate device. "Before you go, you should see this. Came in a bit ago."

Alexander took it with a frown. *What has the Republic cooked up now? What has his father?*

He expected to find Solterra's familiar logo spinning on its face, the Pangea supercontinent globe surrounded by olive branches. Instead, there was a light gray anchor set against a charcoal background, a ring of Greek characters that had become as familiar from over a year ago.

The insignia of the Order of Thaddeus, stamped on that medallion Master Theophilus had passed to him before he breathed his last.

He traced the lines cut into a V at the top (upside down) and bottom (right-side up) and the stem joining them at the center.

An anchor. A symbol of stability and hope that the earliest Christians adopted, based on a verse from Hebrews 6: *'We have this hope as an anchor for the soul, firm and secure...'* Jesus Christ, and faith in him and the Church's accompanying beliefs, were that anchor-hope.

"The Remnant..." Alexander said on a startled breath. He looked at Jin. "What is this? Where'd you get it?"

The man explained, "It was sent over from the Resistance, shot by the Order's paramilitary arm known as—"

"SEPIO..." he interrupted.

"You're familiar with them, then?" The man pushed his oversized black glasses up the bridge of his nose and gave a laugh. "I mean, I suppose you should be, given you're the Order Master and all."

Alexander frowned. "No, not familiar. I had heard something about it earlier from Nia, aside from being given the name by the former Order Master as a sort of passcode. What are they?"

He took a breath and nodded, as if stalling, searching for words. "Stands for *Sepio, Erudio, Pugno, Inviglio, Observo.* We've learned a bit more about them from the Order Remnant Kareema you met since...well, never mind. Apparently, it's Latin for—"

"Protect, instruct, fight for, watch over, heed."

The man brightened. "Hey, you're good!"

"I had training in the dead language like every other seminarian. But what does this have to do with anything?"

Alexander took a breath, chiding himself for snapping at the man. He glanced at Rebekah and saw the same look of embarrassment on her face, which reddened his with further embarrassment himself. His nerves were frayed, he was exhausted, but he didn't have to take it out on anyone else around him.

"Sorry for snapping. Just give it to me straight, will you, Jin? I'm a bit knackered at the moment."

Jin pushed his glasses up his nose again. "I understand. Well, as you also probably know, *sepio* is Latin for 'surround with a hedge.' That was the mission of a certain project launched something like 150 years ago by the Order of Thaddeus. Project SEPIO, as it was apparently named, was tasked with surrounding the memory of the faith with a hedge. To preserve and protect objects and relics of the faith, as well as the memory itself. Later, the mission got a bit creepy."

Alexander twisted up his face. "Creepy? What, like weird and scary?"

Jin laughed. "Didn't catch the double entendre...Anyway, more like mission creep, but weird fits too. They basically started going all Knights Templar, taking more militaristic, militant measures to protect Christians and churches around the world."

"What's happened?" Rebekah said, seemingly trying to move things along. "What's the slate device for then?"

Jin frowned and gave a short, quick nod. "Righto." He reached over the top and double-tapped the Order seal. It dissolved into a page with several icons. He double-tapped on a file and brought up a video.

"An operative with SEPIO sent it over," he explained, "who happened to be in the right place at the right time."

The video started playing, a shaking camera walking through a bombed-out street, hazed by billowing smoke and smoldering buildings—and no doubt smoldering remains.

Rebekah leaned over Alexander's shoulder. "What's this about? Looks like more of what we saw earlier."

Jin corrected, "It's not apocalyptic. Looks like the Republic has stepped up its game."

Looked that way. No doubt at the behest of Alexander's father, the new Sacradi of that pagan religion.

Alexander swallowed hard. "Where is this?"

"Britannia. The province of Londonista, specifically. Those ruins are the Westminster Cathedral, the great symbol of Protestant Orthodoxy built a quarter millennium ago. Leveled by a Queller attack."

Alexander didn't want to look at the images, but he did. A burned-out husk still smoldered with memory, most of the historic cathedral having collapsed in on itself. Another image panned across the rubble. Peeking through was a pale doll, head covered with bright yellow hair and a red bow and a smile to match smudged with black ash. Then an arm, blackened and bloodied.

Not the doll. Human. Small, childlike.

Images of the children from his previous parish back in Tripolitania suddenly flooded his mind. The ones that had met the same fate as the girl whose doll that belonged to those many months ago from a terrorist attack. More images came into view on the slate, some sending his bowels watery with grim disgust at the lengths the Republic would go in their Purge to either rid the world of Ichthus and its great architecture or bring it in line with their pagan agenda.

Alexander clenched his jaw with disgust, a new resolve

flooding his veins. He even made a fist, anger rising at what his father and the Patron were conspiring to bring against Ichthus, the world even. Knowing that they were also fixing to bring down the Church's central Creed concerning Jesus Christ himself—it was all too much.

And too personal, with his father at the helm of it all.

But he wouldn't let them. Wouldn't let *him*.

Time to stop letting his anxiety about the future—his future—win over the needs of others. Time to trust in the Holy Spirit to carry him through.

"Let's do this," Alexander said, handing the slate back to Jin.

CHAPTER 16

SOMEWHERE IN THE ATLANTIC.

ANOTHER SUBMARINE, another outpost. Seemed to be Ford's new lot in life.

Not that he was complaining. He'd signed up with the Legion because that's what all the kids did back home in Noramericana after the Great Reckoning, but the Republic navy was where his heart truly was. Much more of a fish than a fox, so zooming around the underwater world in hydrocrafts that would knock ol' Jules Verne's socks off was definitely childhood wish fulfilment. *Twenty Thousand Leagues Under the Sea* had nothing on the watery world!

And all of it was his oyster. At least in service of the Ministerium and Ichthus, and the whole Resistance movement against Solterra.

Ever since he was a boy, Ford had dreamed of piloting a contraption like the sleek sweet piece of Ministerium ingenuity that had been docked at Nia's outpost and was now getting refueled at the mystery station she had brought them to. Or whoever made it. Probably Asiatica, knowing their technological prowess. The undersea world had been a childhood obsession of his, reading old books and watching old shows that plumbed the depths of the ocean blue. From Jules Verne to

SeaQuest on that now-defunct peacock television network. Anything he could get his hands on to feed his curiosity and tickle his fantasies about one day driving his own sweet submergence ride.

Not that his pump had been primed to assume command of the things. He'd been as nervous as a nun in a brothel when he first grabbed hold of the reins of that yellow submarine. Or was that a saloon? Whatever it was from way back when—he was it when he first piloted the dang thing. But after navigating another hydrocraft to the seedy port of the outpost they were traipsing through at the moment, he was starting to get the hang of it—and loving every minute!

And quite the port it was, for some backwater mystery outpost at the edge of Blake Ridge sitting off the North American continental shelf. Rows of airlocks received visiting personal submergence vehicles neatly arrayed one after the other. Even had a pair of automatons that looked oddly like grizzly bears guiding the PSV hydrocrafts into port, lights blazing to lend a helping hand by cutting through the darkened void of the ocean.

Not that it was anything more special than the others littered throughout the Republic after replacing airports. But it still felt like science fiction—with that whale-like deep submergence vehicle they'd nearly crashed into pulling into the Mid-Atlantic Ridge Station hours ago to refuel, and all the other little bitty car-like submarines zooming about, going this way and that from land to deep sea submergence stations. All thanks to the Patron and his Republic cronies who'd commissioned the investment under the Solterra Earth Oceanic Organization, and before that the United Earth Oceanic Assembly.

Planes had been abandoned for a century after the world's climate broke from too much CO_2 and the oil reserves finally ran dry. That was Solterra's official story, anyway. Ford never bought any of that propaganda mumbo jumbo. Discerning minds like his thought it was more about controlling how people moved about the Republic through carefully curated transportation access points than anything to do with power or pollution. Such was life under the watchful eye of Solterra—all *'For Humanity!'* of course.

The world had planned for such a development long before it arrived, having dived headlong into the seventy-one percent of Earth's surface yet uncolonized. As a wee lad, Ford had been something of a student of the world's deep-sea colonizing efforts. While most kiddos dreamt of space after the 21st century's second decade saw humanity finally establish its first lunar colony after the former Asiatica nation-state China beat his American people to the moon, Ford's heart was under the water.

Like a kid in a candy store, he was as giddy as could be commanding his own hydrocraft. Which, truth be told, wasn't all that special considering humans had been shuttling these contraptions around for the past century anyhow, after the undersea world was colonized in the 2030s. And while China's claim to fame was the moon, the former U.S. of A's was the first Deep Sea Submergence Station. Atlantis DS3.

Of course, the Asians followed up their lunar landing with their own DS3 version. Never one to let America get a leg up on the whole global hegemony business. But then a string of undersea conflicts nearly derailed the utopian dream of owning a plot of Davy Jones's Locker. Leading to the UEOA charter in 2045, the national and transnational peace and trade accord governing stations and outposts.

It also led them to clomping through the narrow corridors of one of those said outposts to meet some mystery person Nia insisted they meet before reaching Noramericana. Something about needing to do something personal. Didn't say who or why, but Ford had learned to keep his yapper shut and choose his battles carefully with that one. Besides, they needed one more fuel up before landing in Noramericana anyway, so it worked.

Laughter echoed up ahead behind some bluesy notes that sounded like a tenor sax, followed by the *rat-a-tat-tat* of a drum set and oddly the *pitter-patter* of the vibraphone. Ford cocked his head and strained for a listen as they continued winding their way through the cramped corridors of the undersea outpost. Who were they covering?

Ford had been a jazzman back before Solterra Republic yanked the plug on such artistic pursuits. Never played an instrument himself, other than giving a half-assed attempt one summer at the trombone. Although suppose his own pipes counted, which was his forte. No one not never heard 'em either. Not in recent years. Not after that reprogramming camp, anyway...

He snapped his fingers and smiled.

Milt Jackson! That ol' vibe-master who could work the mallets on those metal bars like it was nobody's business.

There it was again, the vibes stronger now. Pretty good, too. Suppose you need something to do stuffed down inside a tin can underwater. While hot rodding through the ocean had been pretty sweet, Ford wasn't so sure about living *under* the ocean, with the cramped quarters and no sunlight and millions of pounds of water hanging over your head. Hydrocrafting felt different. Probably because you had more control, were more mobile and had more freedom to roam. Which was how Ford rolled.

They turned a corner and a hot breeze from somewhere blew past them, leaving a whiff of something strong and sour. "This place smells worse than the last joint we came from,"

Ford mumbled with complaint as he continued following Nia through a darkened corridor of gunmetal gray steel.

He scrunched up his face as they brushed past a pair of seafarers jawing it up in some tongue he couldn't make out, a whiff of an over-ripened body adding to his misery.

"A cross between boiled cabbage and a diaper pail."

"Do you always complain this much?" asked Nia, taking a sharp right and picking up her pace, clearly knowing the lay of the outpost land.

"Just when my olfactory is concerned. How you stand living down in these dumps is anyone's—"

Nia spun around, that damn Scythe of hers poking in his face. "You better be watching it, mister. I'm armed, and I am knowing how to be using it."

Ford stopped short, his nose nearly missing the end of her Scythe glowing purple. He threw his hands up and complained, "Whoa, sister, chill! Just not as accustomed to life in your neck of the Republic, that's all. More the landlubber type."

"Clearly." She frowned and spun back around and resumed the lead.

Ford turned to Sasha, who shrugged, then followed after the gal. "I am getting to like zipping around in those kick-ass hydrocrafts, though."

"Yeah, well, don't be getting too used to it. Most of them are illegal and liable to get you thrown into a reprogramming camp."

Ford didn't know that! Sent up all sorts of alarms ringing in his head. "What are you talking about? Thought the Patron blessed underwater travel, compared to the airlines that the Republic banned after the Reckoning."

Nia replied, "*Da*, the deep submergence vessels that are

being the size of whales. Personal submergence vehicles, not so much. Too much freedom."

"So we're riding around in vehicular contraband?"

"*Da*. Anyway, we're almost there."

"And *there* is where, pray tell?"

She ignored him, turning a corner that got them closer to that Milt Jackson wannabe who wasn't half bad the closer they got. Looked like some sort of clearing up ahead, with lights and voices filtering down. A club perhaps. At least the joint had that going for it. Could use a paint job though, with its sad gunmetal gray steel. He wanted to slit his wrists it was so depressing, especially with the low-key yellow lighting making the place feel like one of those carnival fun houses he'd go to as a kid.

Why deep submergence outposts were made of the iron alloy was beyond him. Seemed like something lighter would be better, like titanium. Looked better too compared to the dystopian vibe of steel, with all of its angsty gothic darkness. Although, considering Solterra life, he figured steel made sense. He also supposed the point of an underwater outpost was to sit as far under the ocean as possible, out of the prying eyes of the Republic where less-than kosher happenings went on off the Solterran radar.

Hence their little rendezvous with another abandoned station past the Mid-Atlantic Ridge Station they had left hours ago. AquaSphere 13 had been its official station signature back in the day, which didn't sit well with Ford, given his past superstitions with the number. Although the sufficiently vanilla 'AquaSphere' name made up for it, sounding more like an all-inclusive resort for Europan and Californian yuppies than some backwater outpost for hiring mercenaries and dealing in black-market thingamajigs and exchanging the latest gossip or top-secret intel among the Republic's elite.

Nia picked up her pace now as they neared what was surely some sort of club, the band switching to a Jimmy Smith tune. "Root Down," if he heard it right, the vibe-master switching it up to jivin' on the organ. Even sounded like the Hammond B-3 the jazz master was known for.

Place was packed too, men and women laughing and drinking, some dancing a boogie-woogie vibe in front of the stage with bright lights illuminating the wide dim space, wood tables and velvet-covered chairs all splayed around. A long wood bar stretched nearly the length of the joint, four or five men in smart tuxes working the line slinging bottles they pulled off glass shelves in front of mirror backs lit by blue light. The whole thing looked like something out of the mid-twentieth century. Wholly out of place in some dump on the edge of the North American continental shelf under half a klick of water.

Suddenly, Nia stopped short between two empty tables at the edge of the club. She was looking around on her tiptoes, clearly searching for someone. Then she started weaving through the crowd, bumping into a group grooving to the music. She kept at it, Ford apologizing as he and Sasha followed from behind with Lucy making up the rear.

She stopped again, scanning the room.

Ford sighed. "Who you lookin—"

Her face brightened and she ran off. Guess she found who she was looking for.

Darting for a circular booth of red velvet in a corner off stage right, a man in long dark hair stood. Broad shouldered and tall, he clearly hadn't shaved in days, a wide smile appearing behind the scruffy face. He was wearing a black fedora and a black trench coat, black turtleneck underneath.

Ford thought it all a bit too on the nose for a mystery man in some backwater outpost at the edge of the Republic. But what did he know?

"*Dzhoshie!*" Nia cried out above the din of the club.

What he did know, though, was that the fella looked a bit young for Nia, who was now fully enveloped in the man's arms. Looked to be half her age, maybe a little older, mid-twenties.

The man cried out with something in what sounded like Nia's Muscovia tongue before embracing her. Mystery Man took off his hat as Ford, Sasha, and Lucy walked up, plopping it on Nia with a laugh, the two continuing in their foreign tongue. The man nodded toward the trio who looked on, Nia seeming to introduce them and continue carrying on in a rush.

Sasha looked on, face fallen and sad. Like he'd suddenly realized any chance he had with the Ukrainski chickadee was doomed by having to compete with the man in black.

"Looks like Nia's got herself a man," Lucy said.

Ford elbowed the poor guy in the ribs. "Little young don't you think, doc?"

He heaved a breath and sighed. "*Da.*"

"But you can take him. No problem. I've got your back."

The band finished their number and got a resounding round of applause. Mystery Man slid into the booth with Nia at his side.

"Come, sit!" She gestured for the trio to take the chairs opposite the group.

Ford went to the chair nearest Nia; Sasha sat on his left with Lucy at his side. Before he sat, he stuck out his hand toward Mystery Man. "Joshie, I presume?"

The man chuckled and gave a sideways glance to Nia, who giggled as well. He took the hand, giving it a hard shake.

"Joshua is fine."

Ford nodded and sat. "Pleased to meet ya." Then he leaned toward Nia, adding: "So what's he? Boyfriend? Husband?" Thought it made sense to get it all out in the open at the start.

Nia twisted up her face, leaning back and looking at Joshua before busting out with a laugh. *"Nyet! Moy syn!"*

Ford turned to Sasha for a translation, whose face had suddenly brightened some. Must be good news.

"What's she babbling about?"

"He is being her son," Sasha said.

Ford turned back with a raised brow. "Well, there you go. Didn't take you for the motherly type, but—well, there you go."

Sasha chuckled. "Yeah, you're also looking far younger than —" He stopped, then started again: "Well, from what I would be expecting of...well, someone such as yourself."

Poor guy was blushing redder than a tomato. Ford leaned over and said, "I'll take that shovel of yours back now."

Sasha muttered something to himself, shaking his head.

Nia giggled. "It is being fine. I know what you are saying. I am being used to it when people think I am being too young to have a son who is being twenty-five."

"Twenty-five?" Ford and Sasha both exclaimed.

"Da. I had him when I was fourteen, before I committed myself to Jesus Christ and was becoming part of Ichthus." Her smile faded, and she looked up at the stage as the band readied their next song. She continued, "Nearly sent him to an exposure pile, too, had it not been for a kind couple of women who said they would help offer food and clothing for my little *malysh.*"

She paused to take a breath. Glancing to her little Joshie, her smile returned and she drew a hand to his face. "And now look at you, *Dzhoshua.* The head of the North American Resistance and chief of station for Blake Ridge Outpost."

Ford whistled. "Head of the North American Resistance *and* chief of station for Blake Ridge?"

Joshua chuckled and nodded, dipping his head before

giving his mama a look that all kids give their parents when embarrassed at the show of pride.

"Well, bravo. Nice joint you've got here, kid."

The man held his head up and puffed his chest out some. "Thanks. It was originally another research station that morphed into a mining operation," he explained, his accent far more polished than his mama's. "When the ridge gave up its last minerals, the Ministerium purchased the place for Ichthus business. Using it as a place of ministry training, a place of furlough for missionaries and whatnot. Then when the Purge started, we transformed it into a hub for Resistance activity."

"Makes sense why you'd wanted us to meet up," Ford said to Nia. "And saying hidey-ho to your boy was an added bonus, I'd wager."

She smiled and nodded. "Yes, well, we needed to be adding more fuel to our hydrocraft anyway, so it was being no trouble."

"Just hope the Republic didn't follow us here," he said with a chuckle.

Joshua's face fell, and he leaned forward with narrowed eyes. "Why would you say that? Why would the Republic be following you?"

Ford's face slid, and he glanced at Nia. "No real reason, other than they'd sicced some Stingrays on us a few days ago. But far, far from here. Back in the Mediterranean before we docked at Nia's joint."

"And then you left there to come here a day later, with no trouble?"

"Exactly! See, no biggie."

"How did you evade the Stingrays? They're the Republic's finest underwater tracking vessels. Much like the Tracker drones up top, but manned. And armed."

Ford shrugged. "We just sort of lost 'em. Out maneuvered them and outfoxed them."

Joshua leaned back and folded his arms, then scoffed and shook his head. "You don't out maneuver and outfox Stingrays, friend. I hope you did not bring them to our door."

"Do not be worrying, *Dzhoshua*," Nia said. "They didn't follow us."

"How can you be sure? Solterra has been trying to track us down for months."

"I can assure you, partner," Ford added. "The Republic ain't gonna pull one over on me. We made a clean ride."

Joshua went to keep pressing when Nia intervened, offering some more Muscovia that seemed to shut the kid up. He sighed and leaned back, taking a swig of his drink.

"Now, what news do you have from the front?" asked Nia.

The man threw back another swig and shook his head. "Not good. Everyone is pretty much on the same page that the events of recent days are connected to the Book of Revelation. They're just not sure what they mean, or what to do with them."

"What do you mean by that, partner?" Ford wondered.

"What I mean is, many believed that Christians weren't supposed to endure the apocalypse. That Jesus would rapture Ichthus away before the Great Tribulation, before God poured out his wrath."

Ford snorted a laugh. "Yeah, I was brought up on that version of the end times, as they call it. Suppose if I didn't know any better—which is really only thanks to Father Jim—well, I'd wonder if I was truly saved after the finer points of John's Apocalypse started manifesting themselves."

"Exactly. That's what's happening in many of the communities. To the point that some believers are actually ending their lives in a state of depression, their minds and souls breaking with reality at the dearth of clarity on the subject."

"Golly, that's sad," Lucy said, sitting back and shaking her head.

"*Oy...*" Nia exclaimed, shaking her head as well. "What a tragedy."

"Yes, Mama," Joshua went on. "And now with the Republic ratcheting up the Purge, dismantling less prepared Ichthus communities and dragging them off to reprogramming camps as Unfits..." He trailed off, draining his drink and adding: "I'm afraid we're coming to a precipice in short order."

"And that's why we're here, partner," Ford said. "To hopefully bring some of that clarity."

"In what way?"

"We made contact with one of the Remnants of the Order of Thaddeus."

The man seemed to perk up at the mention of that. "Really. Where?"

"Noramericana. The Georgia province. We're fixin' to get some boots on the ground to not only see for ourselves what's gone down, end times style. But also connect with an asset that had some intel to pass along to the Order Master who was with us—"

"Order Master?" Joshua exclaimed above the din of the crowd, the band striking up the next tune now. He looked past Ford into the club. "Where is he? Is he here?"

Ford shook his head. "Should be about two thousand years in the past right about now."

Joshua stared at him dumbly.

"Don't worry about it. Point being, we're hoping the Order can fill in that knowledge gap you're talking about and get some solid answers about what's been happening."

"Good. Because knowledge and understanding about the nature and extent of the apocalypse is exactly what Ichthus has been missing."

. . .

They chatted some more, mostly Nia and Joshua catching up. Soon Ford and the crew were heading back to the docking sector of the outpost. The mother-son pair embraced and said their goodbyes, then they descended back into the hydrocraft.

Ford navigated their PSV out of the docking bay, leaving behind Blake Ridge Outpost and aiming for the Hinesville Hydroport, the main port into southern Noramericana after Savannah and Brunswick were submerged beneath the flood waters of Armageddon, the catastrophic climate change event from the middle of the 21st century. Which he found a little ironic, since they were headed to the province after the place was torched during the start of the apocalypse. Go figure.

He announced, "Setting our cruising at a comfortable one fifty hundo miles per hour and at a cool depth of two hundred and fifty feet. Should get to shore in no time. An hour tops." Then he engaged the autopilot and went to fix himself a drink at the minibar in the back. They were riding in style with this hydrocraft!

"And in kilometers and meters, for us non-Noramericanan people?" asked Nia from behind in the passenger seats.

He twisted up his face. "How should I know?"

"Just over two hundred and forty kilometers per hour and just under eighty meters deep," Sasha said proudly next to her.

Ford rolled his eyes as he poured some whiskey in a tumbler. Show off. But he supposed the lad had his work cut out for him. "All that matters is we're on our way—finally. And we should reach shore in just over an hour. So settle in for the ride. But keep your seat upright and trays stowed in case we encounter some turbulence."

"I just hope your friends are being able to retrieve the sounds and images of the past with that cockamamie invention of theirs. Because if what *Dzhoshua* says is true, then we are needing the truth of the past now more than ever."

"They'll pull it off," Ford said. "No worries there."

"It is being *my* invention, by the way," Sasha said. "I can share more about the cockamamie invention, as you are putting it, if you like."

Trying a bit hard, but points for trying. Ford returned to his seat and settled in for the long haul.

Nia shrugged and yawned, stretching and settling in for the ride herself. "Sure. Why not?"

Sasha grinned and rubbed his hands together, the fella clearly relishing the opportunity to school his new chickadee in the finer art of time travel. He said, "Most people think of objects as having length, width, and height, right? Think of a book, with length and width, then the spine is being the height."

"You are speaking about an object taking up space, *da?*" she asked.

"*Da!* But what most people don't realize is that the book also occupies a place in time. Which I am calling *phasement.*"

He lifted his hand upward and traced an imaginary line downward. "Which means you can travel along this line down into time. When you are taking a book from the bookshelf, that's one phase. Then when you are placing it on the couch, that is being another phase in time. The fourth dimension is recording this placement along time in the past, just like the x, y, z dimensions record its occupancy of space in the present. We used to be thinking that solid, liquid, and gas were the only kids on the physics block. Not anymore. A new phase of matter called time crystals was discovered."

Nia scrunched up her face. "And what is being this...time crystal, as you are calling it?"

"A totally new state of matter whose atomic structure

repeats through time as regular matter repeats in space—or even changes, which is where things get remarkable."

She stared back at him blankly.

Lucy leaned over and said, "Don't worry, sister. Went right over my head the first time I'd heard it, too. And I've got advanced degrees from Stanford!"

Sasha waved his hands in the air. "Let me try this. At the normal state of water, it's a liquid. Add energy to it, and you have steam. Reduce the amount of potential energy, you are having solid ice. So three states of matter and its *placement* in space. But a professor from California theorized that if you could move the atoms from their original position in some way, then it would break time-translation symmetry and transform its *phasement* as well."

"And it wasn't until the good ol' doc here—" Ford gave Sasha's knee a good slap, "—that the technology finally got small enough to harness the time-travel capabilities of mankind into the belts Alexander and Rebekah are donning in Nicaea. He's not only a looker, the man's a *doer* to boot!"

Sasha reddened and laughed nervously. "Yes, well, it wasn't all my doing, requiring me to combine the insights of a few more theoretical physicists. But in essence, a fusion reaction inside the device unleashes enough energy to open a wormhole in the space-time continuum—warping a local region of the continuum with an electromagnetic field."

"A wormhole?" Nia asked, brow furrowed. "Is this guy being for real?"

"As real as a hamster with wings..." Ford muttered.

She leaned forward with wide eyes now. "And how does this...electromagnetic field thingy work?"

Seemed to be getting into it now—and getting into the good doc. Go Sasha!

Sasha flashed a grin and leaned forward as well. "Well, my

baryshnya, the electromagnetic field not only transforms the matter of the host into a new phase of matter that transcends the continuum, but also envelops them inside the warped region of the continuum, the wormhole—a thin tube of space-time that flattens the phases of history into a next-door region you can just zip into through to the other side."

"Iznik 2125 to Nicaea 325?" she asked on an in-awe breath.

"That is being correct! Using a highly sophisticated algorithm, the belt warps the local region of the space-time continuum by focusing the energy stored in the belt onto a single point. Like folding a piece of paper and punching a hole through the center, bringing the two dots from two locations along the plane of the paper into one single phase."

"What about the return trip home?"

Suddenly the hydrocraft trembled, cutting off his answer.

Ford swung his attention toward the instrument display, his glass rattling now and confirming what he felt wasn't an illusion.

Their hydrocraft was trembling under the ocean.

Something was making their hydrocraft tremble under the ocean.

Shucky ducky!

Now what...

CHAPTER 17

A RIGHT ANGRY rattlesnake is what it was.

There'd been plenty of those menaces around Ford's peanut farm as a youngster on the plains of Noramericana. Timbers, cottonmouths, copperheads, pygmys, corals, diamondbacks—and those were just six of the forty-one varieties making the Georgian province of Noramericana their home that were venomous! There had seemed to be an especially high explosion of them after Armageddon, the catastrophic climate change events of the 21st century that ratcheted up the temps and the sea levels. Rattlers were especially beholden to such climate variables.

And now it felt like they were riding the back of one after being scared crapless.

The tremors continued, picking up pace now with a deeper tremble than the one they had felt at the Ministerium's DSS outpost, ratcheting through the cotton-pickin' thing with such a shudder Ford thought his teeth would fall out.

"What is happening?" Sasha said with a squeak.

Ford resumed manning the PSV as it continued its antics, latching on to the control wheel in order to wrest the hydrocraft under control. It was no use. The thing kept shuddering and now it was bobbing and weaving and dipping something fierce!

Nia looked over his shoulder. "Yes, what is happening?"

"Haven't a clue! But it's like that earthquake we experienced on your submergence outpost over in the Mediterranean."

"Earthquake?" Sasha squeaked again.

"Thing's rocking this way and that, like something's got a hold of it. Can't imagine it could be anything but."

"Submarine earthquakes, they're called," Lucy said, leaning over Ford's shoulder.

Ford turned toward her and smiled. "That's right, sassafras. Sounds like you're in the know."

She shrugged. "Not all us Californian chicks are valley girls."

He laughed and returned to the controls. "Anyway, these sorts of things rumble and tumble down at the floor of a body of water and can produce powerful waves. Tsunamis even."

Another Sasha squeak: "Tsunamis?"

Nia said, "You sound like you are being an expert or something."

Ford shrugged. "I might be a Noramericana peanut farmer hick, but at least I'm a well-read one."

There went another shudder ratcheting through the fish, the bolts feeling like they would pop right out of the dang thing! He clenched his jaw and held onto the controls with tight, taut muscles as he tried to wrestle the fish from its drunken stupor.

"It's like the thing is being possessed or something," Nia muttered.

Ford shook his head. "Not what we need right now, Negative Nancy. Besides, I think I've got the hang of it now and getting it under—"

The PSV dipped at a wicked angle, nosediving toward the seafloor and sending everyone shouting with frightened protest —as if the tentacles of some sea monster had latched onto the rig and were dragging it to Davy Jones's Locker.

Maybe Davy Jones himself!

Ford's face slammed into the controller from the force of it all, blood blooming from his nose.

That'll leave a mark.

The other three tumbled into one another, falling into the display panel and knocking their heads together. That'll leave a double mark.

"Kill the engines!" he commanded.

"Are you being crazy?" Nia exclaimed from the floor.

Ford turned to her. "For your FYI, no! Because we'll get front-row tickets to Saint Pete's pearly gates with those engines blaring the way they are at the rate we're being sucked down by—"

What were they being sucked down by?

He shook his head. "Just do it, would ya?" Then he returned to the controls.

Thankfully, Nia didn't put up a fuss. Reaching up from the floor, she killed the engines down to idle speed.

Yet down the fish went, the digital depth gauge crashing into oblivion the farther they dropped.

Ford thought he was going to puke with the way his stomach was being put through the wringer. Like one of those roller coaster rides he loved as a kid. Devil's Dare, it was called, an eighty-degree plunge down thirteen stories standing up in some crazy-ass harness.

But back then he was a teenager with a death wish. Now he was more than twice as old with irritable bowel syndrome and a back that barked during summer storms from too much football. He was not up for a replay of Devil's Dare! Especially with three others on board.

The pair of Vostokana nationals were jibber-jabbering at each other in their Muscovia tongue, trying to get off the floor as the hydrocraft kept plunging farther down into the depths of Hades itself. Lucy was rubbing her head and wincing.

Thankfully, the fish had stopped shuddering. At least they had that going for them. Although Ford would have taken that over the nosedive any day of the week!

"Do something!" Nia shouted, finally managing to stand.

"I am!" Ford shouted back.

"Well, be doing something else," Sasha joined in the complaint.

"Not that I want to pile on or nothin'..." Lucy said, standing on wobbly feet, "but giving our hydrocraft a good kick in the backside would be mighty nice right about now."

Ford clenched his jaw tighter; same for his hands around the control wheel. It was nothing doing.

"Controls are totally useless!" he grumbled. "I can't make the cotton-pickin' thing climb for shucky ducky!"

Jesus, take the wheel!

But then something entirely unexpected happened.

His prayer was answered.

As quickly as the hydrocraft dipped, it started soaring toward the surface. Up, up, up it went. As if caught in the tractor beam of one of those laughably wrong futuristic DiviNet bargain-bin ebooks from last century.

The Vostokana pair tumbled backward to the floor again, cursing in their motherland tongue but managing to upright themselves while Lucy held on to Ford's seatback as the fish continued its climb.

Sasha laughed and slapped Ford on the back. "Way to be telling the PSV who's the bossman!"

"*Da*, I've got to be handing it to you," Nia said, offering her own congratulatory pat. "You certainly know how to handle a hydrocraft."

Lucy squeezed his shoulder. "Yeah, Ford, some fancy footwork you got there!"

Ford manhandled the control wheel again, straining against yet another powerful tug, a pit growing in his stomach at what was happening.

Didn't make sense in the slightest, what with the force propelling the fish forward, toward the surface, with the engines cut to idle.

Sucking it upward, toward the surface at the speed of hyperspace from one of said laughably wrong futuristic DiviNet bargain-bin ebooks from last century.

"What is it?" Nia said, nodding to Ford and making a motion with her hand at her face. Clearly she saw the confusion written all over his.

He said, "Thanks for the attaboys, but it ain't me."

"Huh?" Lucy said, staring out the front windshield.

Nia joined her. "What are you meaning that it is not being you?"

"I mean—" Ford hit the display panel with his fist, twisting up his face in anger before trying to wrestle the control wheel again. "I ain't in control!"

"Then what is it that you are doing?" she asked with confusion.

"Guys..." Sasha said, but the pair ignored him.

"Nothing! That's the point!" Ford exclaimed, motioning toward the display panel again.

"Then how is it that we are climbing so quickly after we were plummeting toward the ocean floor?" Nia asked in frustration.

"Guys..." Sasha said again, still being ignored by the pair now going at it.

Ford mumbled a curse under his breath. "I don't know! That's what I'm trying—"

"Guys!"

"*What?*" Ford and Nia both shouted at their companion.

"L–L–Look!" the man said, pointing a wavy finger toward the front window.

Ford and Nia followed his arm.

But it was too late.

Lucy sucked in a breath and muttered, "Golly..."

Ford spotted it as well—a bright blue that reminded him of Bondi Beach in the South Pacific. The most peaceful and serene picture of paradise he had ever seen in his life while hunting down a group of Unfits in the Australian outback. Stopped over at the famous beach for a little R&R, digging his toes in its powder-white sand and leaning against a palm tree with a damn-good mojito, just staring into that pool of blue, mesmerized by how rich and thick its shades were in all its reflective brilliance of the sky.

And there it was. Same blue brilliance, same bright sky filtering down into the ocean just a hundred yards away now.

Which shouldn't have been there, considering they were supposed to be shrouded by the deep, dark navy blue more typical of life beneath the ocean's surface.

That's when the show really began.

Ford stood, mouth agape. "Uh...what the hot Hades is going on?"

Nia said some Muscovia gibberish but got the point across.

She clearly didn't have an answer for him.

If Ford had to guess, they were sailing toward the surface of the ocean on the back of some wicked, unseen force.

And fast.

Only a few feet now before—

"Here we go..." he muttered.

The hydrocraft popped out to the ocean's surface like a champagne cork sailing from a bottle.

Right before crashing down and sailing forward some more in a phantasmic show of surreal maritime showmanship.

The trio lurched forward as the fish leveled out.

And that's when the mystery really began.

"What is happening?" Sasha asked on a frightened breath. Same question as before, just different equation.

"Not what," Lucy said, matching his fright. "How..."

Now *that* was indeed the question of the day. Ford didn't know the answer to the second—didn't much care. Didn't know why, either. What he figured was the *what*.

And the what wasn't anything good.

"Tsunami..." Ford said, voice dry from the chaos.

"What was that you are saying?" asked Nia.

He swallowed hard and answered, "I think it's a tsunami! A massive wave formed up when a large volume of water is displaced by a massive seismic event."

"Like an earthquake?"

"Like an earthquake."

She sucked in a frightened breath. "*Bozhe moy...tsunami.*"

"And we're riding its crest toward...who the hot Hades knows!"

"We are being like a surfboard?" asked Sasha.

Ford nodded, saying nothing, mouth open in disbelief with a strong feeling he knew exactly what was happening.

And how.

They were indeed sailing on a crested wave, engines still killed to nothing yet catapulting toward who knew where, several stories up above the ocean water below under a cloudless sky, sun high and mocking with hope.

He chanced a glance out the front at what they were dealing with as they continued riding the wave—the taste of copper instantly flooding his mouth as cold adrenaline spread through his body at the sight below.

Several stories was right!

Seven or eight, maybe even ten by his count! A gigantic ball of energy must have slammed into the earth to cause that much force. And the massive wave was gaining steam now by the second, the mound of water they were riding stacking up higher and higher as it picked up pace, rushing faster and faster in all of its powerful blue brilliance on toward—

"Shore..." Sasha muttered.

Ford turned to him. "What was that, doc?"

"Sh–Sh–Shore!"

He spun back toward the front—catching what he hadn't noticed before.

Various shades of brown, smattered with some dull shades of green were coming into view now through a haze on the horizon, compounded by the gunmetal gray of buildings from the past century.

There it was.

Shore.

And they were barreling toward it like a fox leaving a henhouse at the first shout of gunfire!

"Shore!" Ford exclaimed.

"That's what I was saying!"

Ford ushered the Ukrainski pair toward the belted seats along the walls of the hydrocraft. "We've got a hot minute to brace for impact. Strap in, compadres!"

They did. Nia and Sasha took the wall opposite of Lucy and Ford, who had a hella time getting the straps on his seat loose enough to slide into.

Still fumbling with the nylon restraints, he chanced a glance outside.

Wrong move.

They were closer now, which sent him into a panic. The Grip, as he called it that had plagued him since childhood, seized him. Jumbled his thoughts and concentration something fierce! Which gave him four left hands as he tried to get the damn restraints to cooperate—all the while a complete disconnect between mind, body, and spirit left him paralyzed, a condition that had been cured during his years with the Legion by Grandpappy's moonshine. Not a drop of that to be found as they barreled toward—

"Ford!"

He snapped his head up. It was Nia; she was smiling.

"Close your eyes and take a breath, cowboy."

His cheeks flushed hot and pink with embarrassment at being found out. But she was right. He didn't have a hot second, so he took half that. Which gave him just enough of a realignment to kick the bad habit to the curb for the time being and slide the connections in place to secure him for the tumble of his life.

"We are going to be dying. We are going to be dying. We are going to be—"

"Sasha!" Ford yelled, cutting off the doc's panic. "We're going to be fine. No one's going to die."

He chanced another glance out the front—his bowels growing weak at what he saw rushing toward them with dizzying horror.

The finer details of land were now clearly visible, palm fronds from trees waving a greeting at them while little stick figures ran for their lives at the wall of water coming in hot and heavy toward the houses and storefronts and high rises.

Ford wasn't so sure he was swallowing his own medicine.

He shook his head. Didn't matter. It was on him to bring his troops in safely.

Whether the damn ocean cooperated or not.

Lucy helped him sort his belts and get them snapped in place. He smiled and nodded in thanks.

Cinching the restraints with one final pull for good measure, Ford instructed, "Whatever you do, don't open your mouth. Keep it shut tight, or you're liable to bite your tongue or lip clear off when we land."

"O Mama..." Sasha squeaked before launching into a panicked mumble of Muscovia.

"Hold your restraints at the chest," Ford instructed, "and bring up your legs against the base of your seat."

Nia said on a nervous breath, "You sound like you have been doing this a time or two."

"Not on no hydrocraft barreling toward shore on the head of a tsunami. But twice with the Legion when riding in hot and heavy on a Queller to grab some Unfits when our airship went crashing to land."

The Ukrainski pair stared at him with open, frightened mouths.

Ford waved a dismissive hand. "Never mind. Point is, I lived to tell about it, and so will you three."

He glanced outside, widening his eyes.

Time to put that promise to the test.

Right about...

Sasha yelled out some Muscovia gibberish.

Now.

Riding high above the shore, the hydrocraft crested above the sand and trees and roads edging the ocean on toward the more worrisome land features.

Narrowly missing a twelve-story apartment complex, they

cruised farther on toward a hillside rising in the distance that Ford hadn't seen from farther out at sea.

If they were lucky, they'd make it just over the lip of the hill and slide to a stop without issue.

Except the lip started rising ever so slightly toward the heavens.

Which meant gravity and that dang wall of water were doing exactly what they didn't need!

Shucky ducky.

A loud scrape echoed from underneath the hydrocraft and sent it bolting toward the sky. Sending Sasha into another yelling fit.

They were descending more quickly now, tumbling toward the ground as the tsunami weakened.

But that dang hillside kept growing closer—brittle bushes and naked trees that hadn't seen a good bottle of water in a decade and grass that was a brush fire in the making coming too close for comfort.

Gonna be close....

Jesus, take the tsunami!

And then he did. Or so it seemed, the wall finally collapsing and the hydrocraft suddenly dropping back to Earth like that Devil's Dare roller coaster ride.

Hitting something hard, the fish rocked from side to side. Something else slammed underneath that offered a clanging jolt, then another.

Sasha yelled. Nia told him to shut it. Lucy offered a mumbling prayer with eyes closed.

Ford thought he was gonna be sick, his constitution not like it had been when he was a pimply faced adolescent.

Another thud, then a dip that sent them spinning—around and around, then around again before the PSV flipped over once, then twice, then a third time before the tumbling force of it all gave one final dose of grace to right them on their belly.

Ford thought they would go one more round when they slid sideways to a stop, the water rushing past them and churning all around them, sloshing against the hydrocraft with muddy indifference something fierce so that he thought they'd capsize again.

But they held steady, and soon the tsunamic hell retreated somewhere behind them out of view.

"We made it," Nia said with a sigh, as if disbelieving the truth of it.

Ford understood completely, sighing himself before throwing his head back with relief. He closed his eyes and took several stabilizing breaths, then lolled his head toward the front again.

The nose of the hydrocraft had dug into the hillside and a cluster of bushes bunched up in front, their pale brown leaves and spindly branches looking like a kid in a candy store with all that water. Nothing much to see out the front window coated brown, leaves and sticks and squished fish stuck and not going anywhere soon.

All that mattered was the truth of what the Ukrainski chick had said.

They'd made it. And in one piece.

He leaned forward and began fiddling with his straps. "We better get up top to check the damage."

The other three released their buckles and climbed out of their straps.

"You best grab anything you wanna take for the road," he commanded. "No telling what's up top." They did, the others scrambling for their backpacks.

Securing his own bag on his back and slinging a Neutralizer around to join it, Ford led the way to the red ladder that led to the hatch on the roof. Climbing up, he inputted the release code.

Gears ground from inside, the hatch not budging.

Shucky ducky.

There was a warning buzz before the gears stopped trying.

But he wouldn't give up. He punched in the release command again, praying to the Lord Almighty the Man Upstairs would throw 'em a bone.

Gears worked their best, seeming to give it an extra dose of college try.

Then the lock popped, and the hatch eased open on automatic hinges.

Had to put his shoulders into it to help it along, but Ford managed to push the hatch open and push through to the outside, the breeze hot and smelling of acrid smoke and fish and sulfur.

Climbing out on top of the hydrocraft, he turned around to help Nia climb through.

When he faltered from the view.

His face fell, going white while his bowels went watery, leaving Nia to her own devices.

Putting a hand to his forehead, he mumbled, "What the hot Hades?"

Bearing that wicked Scythe staff thing of hers, Nia pushed her way to the surface and helped Sasha out, then Lucy, along with a jumbled mess of backpacks, not paying attention to what Ford was mumbling about.

Until she did.

Catching sight of what he saw.

Or, in their case, what he didn't see.

"Where'd the ocean go?" he said on a breathless mutter.

Lots of questions that day. Very, very few answers.

It had completely receded after dumping them on land.

Not uncommon for tsunami waves to peel back into the ocean, their original power growing from earthquakes and oceanic volcanoes and then receding after spending itself pushing and spitting and thrusting umpteen gallons of water out on shore.

But this...

It was as if the ocean had disappeared.

Completely.

"Look!" Sasha yelled with a frantic gesture.

Ford refocused his gaze forward, squinting and following his arm.

The horizon.

Where a massive plume of smoke bloomed, and fiery light glowed hot.

"*The second angel blew his trumpet,*" Ford muttered, channeling his meemaw's end-times crazy talk that didn't sound so crazy anymore, "*and something like a great mountain, burning with fire, was thrown into the sea...*"

The worm had turned.

For a third time in as many days...

CHAPTER 18

BYZANTIUM, ARABIA-PERSIA.

HERE WE GO. Again.

Alexander said a quiet prayer still standing in the rear sleeping quarters as Jin returned to the front of the hydrocraft to retake control from the AI-assisted autopilot.

For as soon as he voiced his desire to step out in faith, stepping up to the plate to take a swing at Solterra and protect Ichthus and the faith, trusting in the Holy Spirit to carry him through, doubt was hot on his heels. Such was the pattern in his spiritual life, going back ages. Wanting to live for Christ and step out in faith, while doubt and discouragement were close at hand.

He sighed, frustrated with himself, wondering if he would ever get it right.

He guessed it had something to do with what Saint Paul himself had voiced: *'Although I want to do good, evil is right there with me...What a wretched man I am!'*

Wretched indeed!

But then he was reminded in the quietness of the moment of what Paul had also said: *'Who will rescue me from this body that is subject to death? Thanks be to God, who delivers me through Jesus Christ our Lord!'*

Praise God indeed!

Part of Psalm 46 came to Alexander's mind as well, something he had often offered as a centering prayer while pastoring his parish church. He offered it as a prayer in that moment of rising worry: *Be still and know that I am God...*

Again, but shorter: *Be still and know that I am...*

Still more: *Be still and know...*

Then again: *Be still...*

And finally: *Be...*

A hand rested on his back. "You alright?" Rebekah asked.

He took a breath and nodded. "Sure."

"Then after you, Master Zarruq," she said with a wink, motioning toward the open door.

He smiled and went to join Jin. They had been resting for the journey in a private cabin at the back of the PSV. Ahead, Jin resumed the controls and guided the hydrocraft into a private docking port at the hydroport in Byzantium, Arabia-Persia. Alexander spotted their time-travel gear, two black cases resting near the red ladder leading up top. As Jin finished the docking sequence, he unlatched one of them and double-checked the equipment.

One neural core sensory receptor, a black cap that retrieved the aural and visual brainwave information. One time travel belt, the black thing ringed by donut-like discs powered by fission material that opened up the wormhole for them to jump phases back through time.

"All look in order?" asked Rebekah, bending down next to him to check her own case. No black cap, but same black belt.

"Looks that way."

She stood. "And looks like we're ready for our return trip back to the future."

"How does that equipment work, anyhow?" Jin said from the front, the PSV slowing to a gliding stop and a loud, echoey clang from above confirming they were docked. "Never did get the word on how the whole time-travel thing happens."

Alexander stood and grabbed his case. "The way Sasha described it, imagine three people playing jump rope: you and me holding a rope while Rebekah here jumps in the middle."

"Why can't I be in the middle?" Jin complained. "Always loved jumping rope."

He chuckled. "Fine. You're in the middle, Rebekah and I are spinning the rope."

Rebekah raised a brow. "Spinning?"

"I think it's twirling," Jin said.

"Or maybe skipping—"

"Either way..." Alexander interrupted, Rebekah adding a mischievous giggle. "*Playing* jump rope—how about that—our arms make a full rotation every two seconds. As Sasha described it, that two-second motion sets the time-translation symmetry, where the period of time the rope comes around again is two seconds, like clockwork. But what would happen if our arms rotated four or five times, but the rope only made one rotation?"

"I would have to jump only once," Jin said, "and the time-translation symmetry would be broken?"

Alexander nodded. "You're a quick study. Since our motion rotating the rope would be out of sync with your motion of jumping—in essence, two separate phases of time."

"Something about breaking the time-translation symmetry, isn't that right?" Rebekah asked.

"Right, through the creation of an electromagnetic field adding laser pulses. Something about ions and matter existing in two phases of time. But it wasn't possible or practical until Sasha's invention."

Alexander held up the belt that would create the wormhole through which he and Rebekah would travel back in time to the

Council of Nicaea. Holding up the black cap device, he added: "And this retrieves the sound and sight data from our brain waves to record the information. An AI algorithm translates that neural data into images and sound, allowing us to retrieve the actual events of Ichthus's memory before jumping back to the future."

"Easy as that, huh?" asked Jin.

All of a sudden, the pain returned with a throbbing ping, offering up a timely reminder. He scoffed. "Easy nothing. You try zooming through time at faster than light and see how you turn out."

"Don't forget the awful smell!" Rebekah said. "Oo-wee does time stink."

He laughed. "And that!"

"Sounds like a blast. But alas," Jin sighed, "I'm stuck guarding our hydrocraft while you two get all the glory."

Alexander put a hand on his shoulder. "For which we are eternally grateful."

"Speaking of which," Rebekah said, "we should probably get going. No time like the present to—"

"Jump to the past?"

She smiled. "Exactly."

The trio embraced and said their goodbyes. Soon, Alexander and Rebekah were surfacing onto a grated deck bathed in white light, a door standing shut at the end of the narrow private corridor.

Alexander opened it and popped his head out. The hallway leading out was empty. Relieved, he motioned for Rebekah to follow, and off they went. He recalled the first time he ventured this way with his original handler, Tara Rodriguez. He got into a scuffle with a very large man, with the epithets *mystik* and *sanguinazi* slung his way. He hoped this trip would prove far less threatening.

The pair followed the flow of humans and humanoids out from the cool, sanitized hydroport of clean lines and pallet of ocean colors, Rebekah slipping her arm inside Alexander's arm.

He startled and turned to her. "For our act, of course," she said with a smile. "A couple traveling from Alkebulana to Arabia-Persia on holiday."

One end of his mouth curled upward. "Our act. Of course." He wondered if there was hope it would move beyond that.

Soon they emerged into stifling, sweaty Byzantium, the regional capital of Arabia-Persia at the center of the reconstituted ancient empires under the terms of the Reckoning. Temperatures had to be in the low hundreds, compounded by the suffocating humidity made that much more unbearable by the stench of rotting fish and seaweed and garbage wafting in from the sea and some ungodly part of the city.

He breathed through his mouth, shielding his nose with his arm, but it was no use. The present stunk just as bad as the past! Solterra liked to style itself as a utopian paradise, where everything was in unified order and done *'For Humanity!'* as its citizens were programmed to intone. But most people knew better. Pax Solterra of the singular, united Earth may well indeed reign from sea to shining sea; that he'd give the Republic credit for. But much of the world seemed no better off than the days of the Roman Empire from two millennia ago.

Exhibit A: the stench.

A mishmash of soaring ultramodern buildings of gleaming glass and titanium towered above them. Ancient few-story ones of stone and steel still standing from the previous centuries were sandwiched in between, creating a claustrophobic feeling Alexander could definitely do without. The sight made him long for Tripolitania, where two, maybe three stories were the norm, with wide open spaces and views for miles. Most would call it quaint, destitute even. He called it home, and it was where his heart still was.

Alexander took Rebekah's hand and made for the terminal pickup zone of queued magnacar cabs, a vacant cab hovering at the front. It had seen better days, the body dirty and pockmarked and vehicle leaning to one side, but it would do.

The up-door unfolded as they approached, like one of those ancient DeLoreans he had obsessed over as a boy. So he slid into the backseat that didn't fare much better than the outside, the scuffed blue upholstery and a strong whiff of something sour making him think twice about his choice. Rebekah was close at his side, then the doors closed. There was something familiar about it, something he couldn't quite put his finger—

"Where to?" a rather large humanoid grunted, a plebe as they were affectionately known among the human types for being of the lower-class AIs in the Republic.

That voice...Something about it also rang familiar.

"Iznik," Alexander said, the ultramodern town of the ancient one known by the Church as Nicaea.

The rotund AI humanoid twisted to face him in a herky-jerky movement. "You. Again!" he grunted with derision.

Alexander furrowed his brow as he stuffed his long, lanky legs in place, staring at the mechanical human that creepily seemed to recall who he was.

Then it hit him.

The gruff, grande plebe from his mission with Tara racing to the conclave that started it all, and again when he returned after his first mission.

His face fell. He closed his eyes and sighed. *Of course...*

Both times the AI put up a major fuss for the long drive to Iznik. And both times the plebe had extorted from him digital *merca* credits. A thousand quids the last time.

Now a third time around this block? This was not going to go well.

And definitely did not bode well.

"Where's your master, little doggie?" it said with a creepy grin, a plasticky mouth widening to show a full set of pearly white teeth and a thick, gray tongue.

Little doggie. The insult the AI had lobbed at him the last two times around.

Great.

"Again, you pay in full at start!" the plebe yelled.

Yep. Not good at all.

The humanoid brought a stiff arm to its chin. "Although, you gave me good tip last time." It tilted its head awkwardly, then shrugged. "So ten percent discount."

That was unexpected. Goes to show what a little kindness can do in the long run. Especially when you're dealing with humanoids programed with perfect memories. Although he would never get used to the cheap imitation of humanity. Nothing came close to the Imago Dei; the image of God in humanity was far better than anything we could come up with shoved inside silicon and silicone.

"Deal," Alexander said. He whipped out his mobile, the face of the thin sapphire device asking for the nine hundred Republic credits. He jammed *Accept* then stuffed it back in his pocket, cursing under his breath as his hard-earned digital money from that wharf zipped across DiviNet from his account into the humanoid plebe's bank.

Gruff Grande Humanoid offered a growly chuckle before turning around and throwing the vehicle into gear. It lurched forward on a bed of air before drifting into the traffic exiting the hydroport.

"What was that about?" Rebekah whispered. "The humanoid seemed to take a fancy to you."

He chuckled. "You have no idea."

The driver lumbered through the city before making his way on the O-4, the local nickname for the main Anatolia Motorway stretching through industrial parks and barren wastelands. The pair said little on their journey, partly because of the interest in discretion, partly because Alexander was nauseous from the deep-sea journey combined with the cabbie's high speeds and hairpin twists and turns. He fell asleep, and soon the magnacraft was jerking to a sudden stop.

Alexander snorted awake. "Are we there already?"

"Not exactly, little doggie..." the humanoid grunted.

A hand dug their nails into his leg, jolting him awake now. He turned to Rebekah, who was pointing out the windshield. "Looks like trouble."

He followed her gesture. Looked like she was right.

Large, boxy charcoal magnacrafts were anchored at the end, angled in a V and letting traffic through one vehicle at a time.

Destroyers.

A checkpoint, set up by Enforcers.

Which meant several months after destroying the Ministerium the Republic was still keeping the area under lockdown.

The magnacraft lurched forward, three figures coming into view wearing similarly colored charcoal garb, thick helmets of angled, reflective visors hiding ill intent. It wasn't until another pair clad in crimson joined the trio that Alexander's heart began matching the cab's lurch.

"Enforcers and Purifiers?" Rebekah said. "Dear Yahweh from on high..."

Alexander agreed. Which meant nothing good.

They were still a ways behind, nine or ten magnacars. But the sands of time were running down to nothing. Soon they'd be next.

Then all bets were off.

He turned to her. "But why the show of force? This doesn't make sense in the slightest. Didn't the Ministerium abandon the blasted site months ago?"

"Certainly, and no one has returned since. From what Father Jim had described, the self-destruct mechanisms the Ministerium put into place should have decimated the former HQ. There was no reason to return."

"Then why are they here?"

The pair went quiet, their quickening breaths and the plebe's grunting mumbles the only soundtrack for their contemplation.

A muffled cry broke the silence, followed by a shout and shrilly shriek. Outside, up ahead.

Alexander looked up in time to find a tall man with bronze skin putting up his hands just as the familiar blast of a Neutralizer sent the man sprawling backward. Saw it before he heard it, three electrical charges spitting bluish-white balls at the man before the dreaded *chew-chew-chew* sound echoed toward their magnacar.

Rebekah gave a shrieking gasp of her own as he leaned forward for a better viewing, glimpsing the man writhing on the ground as blueish-white tentacles flickered across his body.

Not good.

His tongue tingled for a narcowafer, but he was fresh out. He settled for a panicked prayer for the Holy Spirit to calm his nerves and pave the way for their safety.

"We need to get out of here..." Alexander mumbled.

The magnacraft lurched forward again, the offending polis's own craft having been hauled off the road and another interrogated by another set of Enforcers.

He turned to Rebekah, grabbing his black case with a nervous rattle and hoisting her own case upon her lap.

"Now! Get ready to slide out."

"What, here?" Rebekah exclaimed, face falling and eyes widening.

"What about the ride?" Gruff Grande Humanoid complained, gesturing with a bloated hand out his rolled-down window.

Alexander said, "I've already paid you the *merca* credits up front. Remember?" He pointed against the glass window outside, adding: "We can use that clump of cypress trees over there as cover. Hopefully, anyway..."

Rebekah looked past him out his window. "You're bloomin' mad if you think we can just waltz out of here under the nose of a platoon of Enforcers."

"The little missy's got a point," the plebe said.

Another lurch of the car; another several meters closer to a date with an Enforcer.

Running a frustrated hand through his unkempt hair, Alexander sighed. "What choice do we have? What do you think those Purifiers are going to do when they go rummaging through our cases?" He held up his case and rattled it for emphasis. "We've got five, maybe ten minutes until we find out, and I'd rather not press the Holy Spirit's powers of intervention. So unless you've got any better ideas, we need to get to it."

The pair jerked again as the magnacraft lumbered to their next place in the queue of magnacars. Not long now, and their getaway clump of trees was closer now.

Alexander offered Rebekah his hand. "Now or never. Will you trust me?"

She looked at his hand and sucked in a breath. For a second, he worried she was planning on riding it out, rolling the dice to see what came up at the checkpoint.

But then she slapped her hand on his and clenched it tight. "Let's do this."

He grinned, then said to the plebe cabbie, "Another four hundred and fifty quid are in store for you if you keep your mouth shut. That's a fifty percent tip for never mentioning a word of our existence. We were never here, understood?"

The humanoid heaved his form around for a look, staring a beat before saying, "Six hundred."

Alexander frowned. "Four fifty."

"Five."

Rebekah rested a gentle hand on the plebe's doughy arm. "Four hundred and fifty is a good tip." She smiled, adding: "Please, help us..."

Gruff Grande Humanoid licked his lips, as if some pre-programmed impulse raced through the humanoid on par with human lust. He nodded, then turned around, agreeing with a grunt as he drove to his next spot.

Six from the checkpoint.

Now it was definitely time to get to it!

Alexander gathered his case and prepared to jump. "Deal. I'll add the tip once we're cleared of the checkpoint and it's clear you kept your word. Look for the extra funds in an hour."

And with that, he threw open the door without another word, the plebe cabbie offering a grunting protest about the terms of their agreement, but it was no use.

Alexander was gone, with Rebekah close behind.

Praying to the good Lord above he'd made the right call.

CHAPTER 19

ALEXANDER DARTED out onto the hard, packed brown earth dried in the kiln-fires of the cataclysmic climate changes Solterra had suffered under the past few decades, the dry heat slapping him in the face like the mawing mouth of an open oven. Hunched over and hugging the black case to his chest, he stumbled up a berm he hadn't noticed from the car before beelining it for the cypress cluster.

He drove for the grouping of trees that were farther away than he had anticipated. The heat was doing a number on him as he sprinted toward the target, shirt soaking with sweat and the stifling, staid air refusing his lungs purchase.

Panting, he dove inside the cypress cluster, praying he hadn't been seen.

Had he just made the biggest mistake of his life? Running away from a Legion roadblock filled with Enforcers and Purifiers who would love nothing more than to add his scalp to their belts had to rank right up there with stupid. What the Republic wouldn't give than to not only round up a pair of Christian Unfits, but a pair of Ministerium members at that. And the Master of the organization tasked with defending and protecting Ichthus's faith.

Master of the Order of Thaddeus.

But he made it, hunching over and hustling into the clump of trees that was mercilessly fewer and farther between than he had originally thought. He crouched in the poor excuse for a thicket and set his case down at his feet, Rebekah coming up fast and doing the same.

"We made it," Alexander said out of breath.

"Don't count your chickens before they've hatched," Rebekah warned on the same shaky breath.

The pair crouched still—waiting, intuiting, discerning their next moves as they gulped down the hot air.

The line of cars moved again, then brake lights screamed suddenly as another couple were dragged from their magnacar. This time a taxicab like their own, their suitcases torn open as the man and woman were shoved into the back of a Transport that had lumbered into view.

Oddly, the couple looked like it could have been him and Rebekah. Both young and two differing shades of Alkebulanan skin, their opened black suitcases cast aside.

Was the Republic searching for them?

As if his heart rate wasn't already ratcheted up from the run and their mission, his ears started humming with cardio overdrive, and chest started constricting with lack of oxygen.

"We need to go..." he said lowly.

"But where?"

"Anywhere."

Two Purifiers appeared again, then another as the queue of cars moved forward, Gruff Grande Humanoid's magnacraft next in line now.

And all the reason to grab Rebekah by the arm and shuffle out from the cluster of cypresses, their fanning branches kicking up a fresh, clean aroma as they pushed through and out into the open, the herbaceous, spicy, and woody evergreen scent carrying with them on a hot breath of desert breeze.

The land sloped down into a rocky basin of hardened earth that stretched for several kilometers, parched and void of any life. They would be sitting ducks out there, easy to be seen and picked off if anyone cared to look. But Alexander figured the Republic's finest were more than preoccupied with their searches.

At least he hoped that was the case.

Because if not, if they were spotted fleeing from a line of magnacars waiting to be interrogated by the Enforcers and Purifiers stationed now a klick or two behind the running pair— then the suffocating heat and their sweat-drenched clothes and the unwieldy black cases that seemed to grow heavier by the step would be the least of their worries.

Alexander and Rebekah went about their escape in silence, scrambling down the rocky, sandy embankment before dashing south. Partly because it was tough enough work lugging their black cases across the wilderness in the blistering heat without adding talking into the mix. Mostly because they thought any sound they made would surely somehow find its way back to the Republic's version of the Nazi's SS.

Spent a good hour making their way south, using the embankment as a buttress, hoping the scraggly bushes and boulders up above would enhance their covering. Soon the hill curved left, and the basin opened up to the city farther ahead that had been roadblocked by the Republic Legion.

A ridgeline of businesses and shops butting up against the dried-out basin was across the way now, coming into view. Much of this edge of the city looked last century, made of brick and rotting wood and corrugated metal. Facing away from the rest of the city of gleaming glass and polished titanium high-rises, their back ends butted up against the vacant land, as if their faces were looking on mournfully at the rest of the world that had left them behind.

The sun was dipping behind them now, offering a modicum of relief from the unrelenting sun still high in the cloudless sky. Alexander pointed ahead and picked up the pace. "We should get a move on. No telling what happens at nightfall, and we need to get the lay of the land anyhow."

Promising something more than the wide openness they were trapped in, he led the charge toward the shelter, drenched and sweltering and aching from the mad dash. Hated how exposed they were, and he prayed to the good Lord that they hadn't made a very bad decision.

Looking toward the city's edge where they had come, very few magnacraft were moving. Mostly going, but very few coming. It was probably a good sign that no Destroyers were meeting them at the edge of the embankment and the sky was free of Tracker drones—that he could see, anyway. Gruff Grande Humanoid must have done his job. If not, they surely would have been neutralized and on their way to a reprogramming camp now, cancelled even. Guess that meant he was going to be out another four-fifty *mercas*.

Almost there now...

They came up fast to the embankment edge, slamming into it and scrambling up its face. A foot slipped under Rebekah, her chin catching on a large rock and cutting a line of blood. She gave a cry but recovered. Alexander grabbed underneath her arm and pulled her back to her feet.

The pair continued up the embankment, far steeper here than the one they slid down, rocks and dirt and the detritus of the city falling with every foothold and push toward the surface.

Until finally the ridge appeared.

Alexander shoved his black case over the edge, then pushed

himself over. He took Rebekah's case from her and helped her over as well.

"We made it," she said with a shaky breath, a hand wiping her sweat-drenched forehead.

He smiled and gave a thumbs up.

Heaving desperate breaths after the sprint of their life, they embraced and laughed, celebrating their success at evading the Republic.

Then he heard it.

The faint whirling buzz he had caught back at his parish in Tripolitania when all of this blasted business with the Ministerium began over a year ago.

"Tracker..." he said on his own shaky breath.

They were large enough to see, filled with all kinds of gadgets for listening to and scoping out the polis at the whims of the Republic. But he couldn't see it in the blinding sun. Could be coming toward them from the basin; could be coming in from the city.

Wherever it was, the Lord's good graces were about to run dry if they didn't get to it.

A dock with a rusting garage door anchored the center building, a freshly paved magnaroad winding between another trio of shops and into the city. Looked as good as any place to escape, its door raised enough to fit underneath. Maybe...

Alexander ran toward it. "Come on!"

Rebekah followed without hesitation, the whirl growing, the buzz sending fear worming into them with dreadful possibility.

Hopping up to the dock, he grabbed Rebekah's outstretched arm and pulled her up. They scrambled underneath the mawing door, squeezing along the concrete floor and barely sliding through.

Just as the whirl grew and a shadow passed at the embankment's edge.

The space was clear, a garage of some sort with a high ceiling. The smell of mildew and chemicals mixing with the hot, humid air threatened to undo them both. It sent Alexander's head into a dizzying spell, bile rising and filling the back of his mouth with the taste of sour copper at the combination.

Rebekah ran toward the back, to a door. Alexander followed.

She tugged at its knob, then again, but it was no use. Locked solid, a dirty glass window with a wire mesh mocking them, staring out into a long sunlit hallway leading to another door with a window that peered out into the world.

Another door offering possible escape.

Alexander turned back toward the mawing gap lighted by the sun, the whirling muffled now by the garage door.

They were trapped.

With the Republic just outside.

Like caged animals.

No, worse.

Like one of those Jews Alexander had read about during primary school from two centuries ago. Those deemed the detritus of Europa who were hunted down like dogs, rounded up, humiliated and dehumanized in worker camps, before being tortured and gassed and incinerated.

Yes, like that.

Except in their case, Christians who were being Purged from Solterra by ultramodern means and dragged away to reprogramming camps before they themselves were either purged of their beliefs or cancelled for them.

No one really knew what that was like, either the camps or the cancelling, since no one had lived to tell about it or escaped.

Except for Ford...something he would have to circle back to later given the stakes Ichthus was now facing.

That he and Rebekah were facing. Then and there!

But how did the Republic know to look for them? That was the question...

The humanoid cabbie? Didn't seem the type that was all that beholden to the regime. Although you could never trust a noid. Always looking out for themselves with no thought of anything else or any*one*. That was the design defect in those imitations of humanity: You can't program empathy.

Perhaps someone else had spotted them dashing across the dried-out lake basin and called the Patron himself. Probably a big, fat reward for ratting out *sangunazis*, the epithet used to label those who claimed allegiance to the faith of Ichthus. Stretching back before even the Reckoning, the term of derision began popping up on the pre-DiviNet internet before making its way into the mainstream. It was a way to mock those who claimed the name of Christ as 'blood-eaters' who practiced superstitious ways and bigots who believed regressive ideologies harmful to the Republic.

Or maybe worse: There was probably an even larger reward for *mystiks*, those known within Solterra as the clericati class of Ichthus who led church services and conducted Church business and guarded the Christian faith.

Or maybe still they weren't looking for them at all. Just a routine patrol given how buttoned down the city seemed to be with the interrogative roadblock and all.

Regardless, they were screwed if they didn't think of something. And fast.

A *whap-whap-whap* right before the sound of shattering glass broke Alexander's concentration.

He startled, covering his head thinking it was weapon fire before whipping it toward the mawing garage door even as his heart bolted toward the concrete floor, the light slicing into the darkened garage but offering nothing more.

"Give me a hand, would you?"

Alexander whipped his head back toward the smaller exit door.

It was Rebekah. She had managed to shatter a hole through the glass with a pipe, and now it was stuck in the rigid wire mesh.

Alexander grabbed hold of it and clenched his jaw, giving it a good yank, then another before it popped loose. He used the end to bend the wires and enlarge the opening. Enough for a small arm to fit through and unlock the other side.

"Looks about your size," he said, tossing the pipe to the ground with a *clangity-clang*.

She gave it a wincing glance. "Might not want to do that, mate, with Solterra scrounging around outside."

"Yeah, bad form." He gestured toward the opening. "Care to do the honors?"

She made a motion at her temple toward her ear, as if following through an unconscious tick that used to put a stray lock of hair back into place. Which meant she'd had a full head of hair before she shorn it down close.

As Rebekah gently reached inside the hole, being careful not to get caught on the stray, jagged wire edges, Alexander wondered who she had been before she signed up with the Ministerium. Wondered who she had been before she cut her hair short. He knew from some of the story she shared that she was the daughter of the Minister of Peace, Mbuto Kony, the former warlord who had been conscripted after the Reckoning to manage the defensive—or rather, the peaceful efforts of the Republic. She had also been sold into slavery by her father, though why wasn't clear. Perhaps it was then that she let her locks go, literally cutting off her former life. Or maybe while she was enslaved or afterwards after what she had done as a child soldier when Mama Mara found her.

Regardless, he wanted to know her more, wanted to *understand* her more. He was grateful for another chance to work closely together to make both happen.

There was a *click*, and the door popped open.

"Success," Rebekah exhaled before turning the knob.

The infamous whirling returned behind them, pausing her advance.

Both turned back toward the propped open garage door. This time joined by a new sound.

Grunting and growly.

Then the opening of doors, and the thudding of boots on the ground, and the slamming of doors before voices were heard giving out commands.

Enforcers!

"Now or never, Alex," Rebekah said.

He turned to her and smiled. "Hey, that's my line."

She returned the smile. "Where do you think I got it?"

No more talk. Time to act.

Grabbing their black cases, they shoved through the door and ran down the corridor toward the front entrance lit with their way to freedom.

Until a shadow passed across the open window up top, a helmet blocking the sun from shining through.

Stopping them dead in their tracks.

Blocked. Again.

Alexander grabbed Rebekah's arm and dragged her down a hallway as voices carried through the entrance door before a *jingle-jangle* of the handle.

Now they were officially screwed!

A set of stairs took them to another floor.

"Where are we going?" Rebekah said.

"Haven't a clue!" Alexander answered as he paced the darkened space, air hanging heavy with heat and dust and even thicker with the tension of the moment that had gone from bad to crazy in no time flat.

Windows lined the back with a view of the bone-dry basin, along with a massive charcoal magnavan resting on the ground and an Enforcer milling about. Boxes were stacked and strewn about, clearly a storage room with titanium and chrome parts for magnacars glinting in the sunlight.

"Check it out," Rebekah said at the bottom of a ladder. She was pointing toward a door in the ceiling.

Alexander joined her. "Where do you suppose it leads?"

She laughed. "Uh, how about the roof?"

He frowned. "Funny. But let's get out of this mess before we go back to busting my—"

A thud echoed from behind at the room's entrance, down the stairs.

The pair looked at each other with wide eyes.

Enforcers had entered the premises.

Looked like the only way out was up.

Without thinking or waiting for more, Alexander grabbed his case, grabbed hold of the ladder, and started climbing. A square door was latched at the top.

But not locked.

Thank you, Jesus...

He pushed through with his black case, the door giving a creaking protest on stiff hinges, praying there wasn't a Tracker waiting for them on the other side.

Sun blinded him, and a gust of heavy heat slapped him in the face. But he climbed onto the roof, helping Rebekah and gently shutting the door behind.

"Now what?" he asked, assessing their options that had pretty well dwindled to nothing. The roof was what he expected: flat and black and dotted by a few vents and an HVAC unit that rattled and coughed and sounded like it was on its last leg. Not that he minded, as it would hide the sound of their movements.

Rebekah edged to the end of the roof near the building's rear before skipping back. "Another Destroyer looks like it just rolled up. Another handful of Enforcers spreading out."

"Which means they are having it in their heads that something worth a platoon of Enforcers is worth their time."

She nodded, saying nothing.

"But how do you figure it?"

She shrugged, edging to one of the sides butting up against another building. "Maybe our cabbie talked."

Alexander smirked. "See if I give him any of that tip we negotiated."

"Or maybe the Tracker caught enough of a look at us before we were able to get inside. Our pictures are surely in the Republic's database of Unfits." She glanced at him, adding: "Yours especially."

He leaned toward her, mouth running dry at the possibility. "Why, because I'm the Master of the Order of Thaddeus? You really think the Republic knows?"

She peered over the edge into an alleyway that ran between the two buildings. "Not sure, but it's the only explanation."

Alexander ran a frustrated hand through his hair. Not only were they trapped, there was a good chance they were being hunted. He looked in the sky, shielding his eyes from the blinding sun, searching for the Tracker that had sent them scurrying into the building to begin with.

Nothing.

Either it had moved on or was too high to see or hear. Either way, they were screwed if they didn't figure something out.

And fast.

"I think we can make it," she said, putting one foot behind the other and rubbing her hands together, facing the gulf between them and the other building.

Alexander furrowed his brow. "What, you mean jump?"

"No other choice, especially—"

There was a bang against the door leading back down inside.

They looked at each other and nodded.

Now or never.

Then ran.

CHAPTER 20

R EBEKAH CLEARED the lip of the building first, tossing her black case to the other side before sailing across and landing hard on the adjacent roof, but on both feet. She recovered as Alexander made his jump, tossing his black case to her and making a running start before leaping.

Landing off balance closer to the edge.

He leaned forward to compensate when a foot slipped overboard, sending his knee crashing into the edge. Pain lanced up his thigh and snatched any balance he had left.

Then he slid down over the edge and started tumbling.

When a hand grabbed him and held him firm.

Allowing him to grasp the edge and pull himself up with Rebekah's help.

Just as the door on the other side creaked open.

Now or never!

Alexander pushed himself up with all his might as Rebekah tugged, the rattly HVAC offering enough cover for them to complete the scramble before diving for a larger ventilation unit that sat near them.

They dove behind it as a pair of Enforcers in charcoal

armor climbed out of the hole and began scoping the roof on the other building.

Alexander held his breath, fearful merely breathing would alert them of their presence on the other side. Rebekah looked like she was doing the same, her hand digging into his knee as they sat bunched up behind the HVAC unit and wedged against a wall to a covered entrance that led down below.

Felt like an hour, but within a few minutes, the Legion soldiers seemed satisfied and went back down below, the door crashing closed with another protesting creak.

Alexander exhaled a heavy breath and heaved another one, closing his eyes and running an anxious hand through his hair as he sat recovering.

"That was a close one," Rebekah said, searching for her own breaths.

He chuckled. "You think?"

They stood, squeezing out from their hiding place and making for the door.

Alexander took a breath and tried it. The knob turned without issue and the door opened. He gave Rebekah a relieved smile, thanking the Lord above for his providential protection. They slipped inside and descended a musty stairwell that led into a utility room. Mops and buckets were thrown in a corner and the smell of cleaning chemicals hung in the air.

Exiting, it looked like some small-part machine shop, an open floor plan with a low ceiling. They ran to a door at the far end, the opposite side of the garage they had just come from. An office sat empty, and a dirty window with a mesh wire similar to the one they broke through earlier looked out onto the street from the door.

They came up to it fast, leaning out of its viewing on either side but able to see the street.

Completely clear.

No cars, no people. Which made sense, given the city seemed to be locked down tight. Not even the platoon of Enforcers were out in front, which seemed too good to be true.

Rebekah had the best angle of view toward the garage. "Anything?" Alexander asked her.

"Nothing. Must be milling about inside or gave up."

They waited some more, but Alexander wondered if they were pressing their luck. Best to get out while they could before the Republic sought answers from adjoining buildings.

He took a breath and nodded to Rebekah. "Shall we?"

She moved to the other side of the door behind him. "After you."

He flipped a deadbolt to unlock the door and grasped the handle. Turning it slowly, he eased the door open. Popping his head outside for a look.

No Enforcers yet, but a few people were walking briskly across the street. One solitary elder, a couple huddled together, and a trio of women with heads bowed and mouths moving in hushed tones. A group of children scampered from the other way with a ball, nearing the garage and heading their way. What you'd typically expect in a city, but the adults seemed to be on edge.

As the children neared, Alexander saw his window. Without consulting with his partner, he stepped out onto the street and motioned for Rebekah to follow.

The kids rushed toward them with laughter and taunts, the ball being passed from front to back in some sort of game.

Alexander closed the door. The pair rushed out ahead of them, hugging their cases tight against their chests and hoping the kids would offer some protection from behind as they made their way down the street, holding their breaths and praying for safe passage.

They made it two blocks before the kids hung a right

toward the basin, taking their ball with them and their protection from Enforcer eyes.

The pair quickly crossed the street toward a bakery that looked already closed for the day and slid inside a covered doorway, looking back and assessing their options.

"Looks like the Republic gave up then," Alexander said, thankful they escaped with their lives.

Rebekah replied, "Think we fooled them enough to think they had nothing in the first place, or do you think they know we were there and they missed out?"

"Either is possible. With the door window busted, they have to know people were inside at some point."

She looked at him and nodded. "We better get going then."

He nodded and led the way, darting around the corner and down a road that led back toward the Ministerium HQ ruins.

The plan was to get close to the former headquarters to a park that sat a kilometer away. They figured it would serve the best staging ground for their journey knowing they were near enough to the original site of the Church's ecumenical meeting while being far enough away from watching eyes. Then again, they could end up in the middle of some home like last time—or worse: end up in the trunk of a tree or said home's wall! Sasha didn't think it worked that way, that phase jumping would sort of course correct itself, but it was all speculation.

Either way, Alexander felt conspicuous in their back-to-the-past getup weaving toward the jump site, Rebekah's burlap dress with matching headscarf and his simple burlap shirt and linen pants with that cap seeming like red beacons now blaring their subterfuge intent and drawing everyone's attention to them. Not that there were many people out and about to notice them, given the city was still locked down and Enforcers were roaming for whatever reason.

They cut across several blocks using alleyways between a

smattering of last-century buildings of stone and wood and ultramodern ones of gleaming glass and titanium, making their way toward the park and nearing the direction of the Ministerium's ruins.

So far, so good.

The sounds of activity were floating toward them through the streets up several blocks, more of the same grunting and rumbling, but it was hard to tell what direction. At least they hadn't seen any sign of the Republic.

Alexander remembered the first time he had been dropped off with that gruff, grande taxicab humanoid over a year ago now, with that Tara Rodriguez character who would later betray the Ministerium to the very forces now fighting against them. Could hardly believe his eyes when Father Jim brought him down below the Church of the Dormition and then on to the conclave that met in a reconstructed Sistine Chapel several stories beneath the city. It was magical, if not a bit surreal taking part in yet another historic meeting of Ichthus's minds to help right the Christian ship after a rise in apostasy threatened to undo the Church.

And there he was, heading back to the area to continue that work, ready to jump headlong back in time to—

Rebekah yanked his arm, pulling him backward with a jerk as they rounded a block.

"What the—"

She wrapped a hand around his mouth to quiet him. Then she pulled it away and put a finger up to her lips and pointed around the corner.

Alexander leaned around and spotted it.

Roadblock. Totally missed it in his daydreaming and focus on getting to the park.

Just one Destroyer with two Enforcers milling outside, then another up top manning one of their powerful Raycannons.

Lots of firepower for a simple roadblock. Why, was the question. Seemed more like they were cordoning it off. Again, for what reason was the question.

Then he realized where they were.

It was only a few blocks beyond that the Ministerium's HQ used to sit. He stole another glance and saw the devastation now, which was a blank slate of dirt and some trees. All the rubble from the Ministerium's security measures that detonated the building had been cleared away, the crater filled in. It was as if it had never sat there to begin with for all those centuries. The Republic made sure Solterra was wiped clean of its memory.

And Panligo, no doubt—even his father.

Now some makeshift structures stood behind the Republic's roadblock, several Legion officials and other unmarked personnel going about their business.

Rebekah poked her head over Alexander's shoulder. "Why the firepower for an empty lot with a handful of tents?"

He went to answer when a magnacar, sleek and silver, rushed past them from behind toward the roadblock.

They startled and stumbled back, their heads and chest filling with alarm at being spotted. They stood clear of the entrance to the street, recovering their breath and waiting for a response, some sound of rushing boots or shouts of intercepting command that would alert them they'd been seen.

Nothing came.

"Let's get out of here," Alexander said.

Rebekah nodded. "Agree."

She edged to the building corner, then waited for an all-clear visual, making sure the Enforcers were busy with something other than looking their way. Getting it, she darted across, clearing the threshold into the next alleyway.

She put up a hand for Alexander to wait while she ensured

the coast was clear. Took a minute, but she finally motioned for him to come.

He did, darting across the street but not before taking one parting glance toward the cleared ruins of the Ministerium HQ.

And spotting someone he absolutely did not expect to see in those parts.

He almost faltered his steps at the sight, disbelieving his eyes, but he made it across, heaving a breath and sighing before reaching around the corner for another look.

"What is—"

This time Alexander put up a finger to quiet Rebekah. He glanced back and put two fingers toward his eyes, then motioned around the corner. He stepped back for her to confirm what he had seen.

The startled breath confirmed it.

"Is that who I think it is?" she asked lowly.

A cold dread spread down Alexander's body at the sight of exactly who she thought it was, her wide eyes telling it all.

Apollos Nicolai.

They stole another confirming glance. It was him, tall with wide shoulders and that mane of blond hair, with high cheekbones and the equine nose.

Coming up behind him was Dominic Weiss, the former Ministerium cardinal who had architected the schism in Ichthus and helped birth Panligo. Or so they had thought before they learned Alexander's father, Martin Zarruq, was the true brains behind the religion's hostile takeover of all others, including the Church. Weiss rested a hand on Apollos's shoulder and whispered something in his ear.

With wide eyes, he and Rebekah looked at each other, communicating the exact same pressing question.

What were they doing here?

Apollos and Dominic. Riding together into an area secured by Enforcers. Into the former Ministerium HQ!

Alexander and Rebekah simply watched them for a while from the edge of some convenience store—waiting, discerning, intuiting what it was the former members of the Ministerium were playing at. For a while they simply convened with some of the personnel milling about the site. The pair couldn't make sense of it, given how far away they were.

Alexander ran a frustrated hand through his hair. "What the heck is going on? I can't make anything of their conversation."

Rebekah turned to him with a raised brow. "What, you're not a mind reader, Master Zarruq?"

He smiled at her. "Very funny. What, pray tell then, do you suppose they're going on about? Why are they here, at the grave of our former HQ?"

She shrugged. "Beats me. Perhaps there is some excavation work going on? Trying to sift through the rubble of our ruined headquarters for intel on the goings on of the Ministerium? Knowledge is power, as they say, and what better way to run the Republic's Purge than to leverage what we left behind to wage their war?"

Alexander considered this, eyeing the men engrossed in some conversation with a tall, broad-shouldered Legion with combed silver hair in a cream-colored suit, patches on his chest showing him to be of some rank.

Perhaps...

He said, "But weren't Father Jim's countermeasures supposed to eliminate such a problem, incinerating and destroying the evidence?"

Rebekah nodded. "That's what I had understood. But supposed to eliminate and actually eliminate are two different scenarios. Obviously, something's brought them back to the site of Ministerium operations. For what...that's the question, isn't it."

Yes. It was.

Couldn't make sense why Apollos and Dominic would be back at the leveled Ministerium HQ. Now he didn't care. Only thing that mattered was stealing into some hidden place that would let them jump to the past and retrieve the memory to the central element of Ichthus's faith: the Nicene Creed, defending the deity of Jesus Christ. That's what mattered, so they couldn't take their eye off that ball.

But where? And how would they avoid the Enforcers roaming around, much less make the jump back to the past?

Rebekah grabbed Alexander's arm. "Look..."

He peered around the corner again to see Apollos and Dominic back at their magnacar. Some sort of case had been hoisted up on its hood. Silver and not much bigger than their own cases they had been lugging around all day.

"What the bloody hell is that?" Alexander muttered, squinting for a better view but not finding any.

"Whatever it is," Rebekah said, "maybe it's the reason they returned to the Ministerium's HQ."

Perhaps...

He glanced behind toward the west, the sun beginning to edge toward the horizon now and cast long shadows across the city with a deep orange glow.

"Regardless, our time is running out."

Rebekah smacked her case. "Pretty sure we've got all the time in the world with these things."

He laughed. "Good point. But the longer we stand around, the greater chance we have to being picked up by those roaming Enforcers."

The grunting rumble of a Destroyer echoed from up the

block, the darkened nose of the menacing beast poking out and bending toward them down the magnaroad.

Alexander pulled Rebekah back inside the block in time, but it also sent him jumping into action.

"Come on!" he said, snatching his black case from the ground and motioning farther inside the alleyway. She did the same, the pair running until they slipped inside a narrower corridor slicing between a high-end clothier and a wine bar.

The rumble echoed back toward them through the corridor of buildings, but then it passed, the beast moving on.

He sighed and leaned against the wine bar wall. "That was close."

"I'm not so sure the park is a good idea anymore," Rebekah said, taking a breath herself. "With these Destroyers and the Enforcers roaming about, I doubt we'd even make it there, let alone make the jump to the past."

"Agree. But now that our jump point is pretty well cut off, now what?"

Rebekah turned back toward where they had come. "How about the basin we traveled across to make it into the city?"

He turned to follow her gaze. "What do you mean?"

"If I remember it right, it used to be a massive lake. Lake Ascania. Seems like it has served us well in past missions making the jump through time along waterfronts."

Alexander snorted a laugh. "I seem to recall how well that served us on our jump back a mission or two ago, me nearly drowning at the bottom of the Mediterranean!"

Rebekah shrugged. "Good thing I was there to save you."

He smiled, the memory of her giving him mouth-to-mouth surfacing. "Yes, good thing. But the Enforcers, what about them?"

"I'd imagine they've moved on. Besides, we've gone fifteen, sixteen blocks over by now. I'd say we head straight back that way—" She gestured down the street toward an open front that edged the basin. "Then go from there."

Alexander considered this, frowning at the thought of returning anywhere near the swarm of Legion knuckleheads, but it was clear it wasn't much better where they were at.

Another rumble grunted toward them from behind, much closer now—sending them scrambling farther into the shadows.

It roared past but wasn't a Destroyer. Just an aging, sagging magnacar model from last century. But all the reminder that they needed to move out.

So they did, hustling down a magnaroad that led toward the basin, weaving inside covered doorways and alleys if they suspected danger, darting across blocks to other streets. Running toward the basin now, it appeared to be a park the closer they got, which meant there would be a bathroom or maybe a maintenance building they could use for cover from unsuspecting eyes.

The trees were tall and full of leaves, the grass long and soft and green, smelling of lilacs and honeysuckle coming off a warm breeze gusting through the paradise. An unexpected find but not entirely, given that parks were a major feature of the Five-Year Plan Solterra offered pretty much every five years since the Reckoning a few decades ago.

Blessedly, the park was empty. Not a soul to be found. Again, made sense given the roadblocks and checks, even the Legion seemed absent. Probably too preoccupied with the pair of preening knuckleheads back at the former Ministerium HQ. Regardless, Alexander was just grateful for the providential light shining down on them now, considering what they had endured earlier.

And there was what looked like a bathroom! A small structure painted brown down at the far end of a path along the edge of the basin nestled inside a grouping of three rather large oaks, boughs thick and bending, offering a canopy that would shroud the facility from view.

He followed Rebekah toward the building. She came up to it fast and went to open the door, glancing around first for signs of prying eyes. Alexander joined her, holding his breath as they waited.

Finding none, she tugged at the handle.

Moment of truth.

It swung open.

They let out a collective sigh and rushed inside. There wasn't any lock they could find, but a large single handicap stall offered enough privacy. It stank from lack of ventilation and air conditioning. Gaseous refuse clawed at Alexander's nostrils, feeling like defecation was clinging to his lungs. He was just thankful for the open door, and ready to get to it.

Latching the stall door that mercifully fell with a privacy wall to the floor, they quickly opened their cases and assessed their equipment. All seemed in order. Was a cramped space, with their gear and the toilet, but it would do.

Rebekah helped Alexander with the black cap, the familiar tentacles attaching to his head and world going dim before returning to normal—the transmitter attaching the signal to his neural core momentarily affecting his eyes and ears. Then he helped her with her belt, securing it around her waist and turning it on.

It hummed to life, the screen showing the familiar green Cyrillic characters.

Alexander smiled, giving Rebekah a thumbs up. She returned the glance, taking a breath and smiling herself. "Show-time, I suppose."

"I suppose so."

He went to ready his device when the sound of a *purr-purr-pring* from a mobile device sliced through the silence of the restroom—the echoey shrill sending his pulse lurching forward at the sudden turn, his worry ratcheting up to match.

He caught his breath and huffed a frustrated sigh, then dove for the black case that had stowed his time travel belt—and his mobile. Mumbling a curse, he snatched the device as another round of *purr-purr-prings* started up.

Silencing it, he glanced at Rebekah and held his breath—waiting for a platoon of Enforcers and Purifiers to come busting into the restroom to haul their butts to a reprogramming camp.

The seconds ticked by as the mobile device continued dancing for attention in Alexander's clenched fist.

Rebekah nodded toward it, saying lowly, "Perhaps you should answer it. It might be serious."

He nodded and glanced at the device's face, a furrowed-brow Father Jim greeting him.

Looked serious enough.

Alexander knelt to the floor and answered the call, putting it on speaker between him and Rebekah who joined him on a knee and turning the volume down low.

"Hey, Padre. We were just about to make the jump back in time. Is everything all—"

"It's happened. Again!" Father Jim said in a worried rush, voice strained and faltering, face white and crestfallen.

Alexander glanced at Rebekah, who seemed to match the cardinal's own fright.

"What's happened again?" he asked, though he pretty well knew it could be one of two answers.

Either the Republic was on the move again against Ichthus.

Or the Lord Almighty himself was moving against Solterra —again.

Either answer didn't bode well.

"The second angel has blown his bloody, bloomin' trumpet," Father Jim exclaimed. "That's what's happened!"

Again, the strained, faltering voice, and the whitening, falling face.

Alexander's breath caught in his chest, his stomach sinking and veins freezing with icy flight-or-fight adrenaline, sending his pulse galloping forward again.

"The second angel, Cardinal?" Rebekah said, shaking her head. "What are you going on about?"

"*'The second angel sounded his trumpet,'*" Alexander intoned, knowing exactly what Padre was playing at, "*'and something like a huge mountain, all ablaze, was thrown into the sea. A third of the sea turned into blood.'*"

She looked up at him from the mobile device. "You're quoting Scripture."

He nodded, saying nothing.

"The Book of Revelation."

Another nod. "Chapter 8, verse 8. About the unfolding of the next phase of the apocalypse."

Father Jim nodded from the device. "That's right. We are firmly inside the Great Tribulation now."

"How? What happened?" asked Rebekah.

The cardinal told them, relaying all that had happened in the last few hours according to the eyewitness accounts of Ford, Nia, Sasha, and Lucy that the Ministerium agents had relayed through a panicked call into the deep submergence station back in the Mediterranean.

"Dark times ahead, I'm afraid," Father Jim went on. "Not only for the Republic, but for Ichthus as well. Though not directly, the unfolding of these judgments will affect many of our brothers and sisters, with family and friends and colleagues experiencing the wrath themselves—dying even."

Alexander ran a worried hand through his thickened hair. No escaping it now. Solterra Republic was coming under the full weight of God's judgment.

Padre continued, "Which makes the urgency of your travel back through time to the Council of Nicaea that the more urgent! The Church will need the retrieved memory of one of the most consequential of gatherings of Christian leaders in history to stay the course, to run with perseverance the race marked out for us, fixing our eyes on Jesus, the pioneer and perfecter of faith."

Rebekah grabbed his hand, tears brimming her eyes and mouth curling into a trembling grin, clearly trying to keep it together while bearing the weight of their mission.

Alexander smiled back, squeezing her hand with a grin of his own and trying to hold steady, to hold it together—for both their sakes.

"This memory will also serve as the torch we bear as witnesses to this faith, casting the light of Christ in the fast-darkening corners of the Republic. After all, the purpose of these wrathful trumpets is to bring the world to repentance—to embrace the gospel by believing in Jesus Christ for the forgiveness of sins and salvation of the soul. I pray you are successful in your journey, you two."

Alexander took a breath and nodded. "You and us both."

The cardinal said a quick prayer of safety for their journey, then signed off.

Stowing the device back in the black case and closing the lid, Alexander stood, offering a hand to Rebekah and bringing her back to her feet.

"You ready for this?" he asked.

Rebekah wiped her eyes and swallowed hard, then nodded. "Ready as I'll ever be."

"For Ichthus," he nodded back.

"And the Republic."

Indeed...

Time to make the jump back to the past.

It was the fifth time now, and he had to admit: As much as he had pitched a fit to Father Jim for his return jump, especially after their run in with the drunkard from the past over a year ago, and coming up against the limits of future technology, and nearly being marooned in the past—in spite of the memory of that fraught experience and all the inconveniences and smells of the past and frightening things-get-worse present, he was beginning to sort of love the adventure of it all.

Loved the full-on sensory experience, loved the high he got from jumping across phases. A far greater high than his narcowafers ever gave him—from the humming vibrations along every fiber of his being in the familiar long, undulating waves to the thunderstorm static-charge smell; from the blinding luminescence to the soundless void.

He just hoped his head didn't explode, or implode, or sizzle from the frequency of visits. Because the way it felt after the last jump, with the instant pain lancing back and forth between his temples—he prayed to the good Lord to shield him from any deleterious effects of the time travel.

Alexander fastened the time transport belt around his waist, then engaged the screen situated on the front while Rebekah did the same. A little screen on each of their devices displayed a Cyrillic word in green for 'GO,' indicating all was ready to jump phases.

His heart leaped, a shot of adrenaline shooting through his veins at the memory of what he had experienced the last time he'd jumped phases to the past—and what they would experience again. He started breathing heavier as his pulse started picking up pace, realizing this was it.

The moment of truth. Again.

Alexander grabbed Rebekah's hand, nodding at her with a reassuring smile before the two punched their blinking green buttons.

Jumping them hundreds of phases back to Nicaea, circa AD 325.

Arguably the birthplace of Ichthus's faith.

For the sake of the Church's faith—and his own.

During the rising apocalypse, no less.

CONTINUE READING SEASON 2

You've just finished episode 1 in the religious sci-fi apocalyptic thriller *End Times Chronicles Season 2*, the first book in the four-episode series, *Apocalypse Rising*.

Think of it like your favorite Netflix, HBO, or Hulu show, where the story unfolds in installments. Each book can be read as a complete story with a beginning, middle, and end—but it ends on a cliffhanger that naturally flows into the next episode, fitting within a larger four-part tale.

Continue binge-reading the adventure by diving into the next episode now!

APOCALYPSE RISING • *Season 2*

Episode 1
Episode 2
Episode 3
Episode 4

Building a relationship with my readers is one of my all-time favorite joys of writing! Once in a while I like to send out a newsletter with giveaways, free stories, pre-release content, updates on new books, and other bits on my stories.

Join my insider's group for updates, giveaways, and your free novel—a full-length action-adventure story in my *Order of Thaddeus* thriller series. Just tell me where to send it.

Follow this link to subscribe:
www.jabouma.com/free

A big thanks for joining the Ichthus Remnant on their adventure saving the Church—and the world!

Enjoy the story? Here's what you can do next:

If you loved the book and have a moment to spare, **a short review is much appreciated.** Nothing fancy, just your honest take. Spreading the word is probably the #1 way you can help independent authors like me and others enjoy the story.

Continue binge-reading the adventure by diving into episode 2 in the epic saga of *Apocalypse Rising*, season 2 of *End Times Chronicles*.

If you're ready for another adventure, you can get a full-length novel in my thriller series for free! All you have to do is join the insider's group to be notified of specials and new releases by going to this link: www.jabouma.com/free

Group X Cases Supernatural Suspense Series

Not of This World • Book 1

The Darkest Valley • Book 2

Against These Powers • Book 3

Luck Be the Ladies • Novelette

End Times Chronicles Sci-Fi Apocalyptic Series

Apostasy Rising / Season 1, Episode 1

Apostasy Rising / Season 1, Episode 2

Apostasy Rising / Season 1, Episode 3

Apostasy Rising / Season 1, Episode 4

Apocalypse Rising / Season 2, Episode 1

Apocalypse Rising / Season 2, Episode 2

Apocalypse Rising / Season 2, Episode 3

Apocalypse Rising / Season 2, Episode 4

Antichrist Rising / Season 3, Episode 1

Antichrist Rising / Season 3, Episode 2

Antichrist Rising / Season 3, Episode 3

Antichrist Rising / Season 3, Episode 4

Faith Reimagined Spiritual Coming-of-Age Series

A Reimagined Faith • Book 1

A Rediscovered Faith • Book 2

Mill Creek Junction Short Story Series

The New Normal • Collection 1

My Name's Johnny Pope • Collection 2

Joy to the Junction! • Collection 3

The Ties that Bind Us • Collection 4

A Matter of Justice • Collection 5

He Will Direct Your Paths • Collection 6

Find all of my latest book releases at: www.jabouma.com

J. A. Bouma believes nobody should have to read bad religious fiction—whether it's cheesy plots with pat answers or misrepresentations of the Christian faith and the Bible. So he tells compelling, propulsive stories that thrill as much as inspire, while offering a dose of insight along the way.

As a former congressional staffer and pastor, and award-nominated bestselling author of over forty religious fiction and nonfiction books, he blends a love for ideas and adventure, exploration and discovery, thrill and thought. With graduate degrees in Christian thought and the Bible, and armed with a voracious appetite for most mainstream genres, he tells stories you'll read with abandon and recommend with pride—exploring the tension of faith and doubt, spirituality and culture, belief and practice, and the gritty drama that is our collective pilgrim story.

When not putting fingers to keyboard, he loves vintage jazz vinyl, a glass of Malbec, and an epic read—preferably together. He lives in Grand Rapids with his wife, two kiddos, and rambunctious boxer-pug-terrier.

Connect at: www.jabouma.com • jeremy@jabouma.com

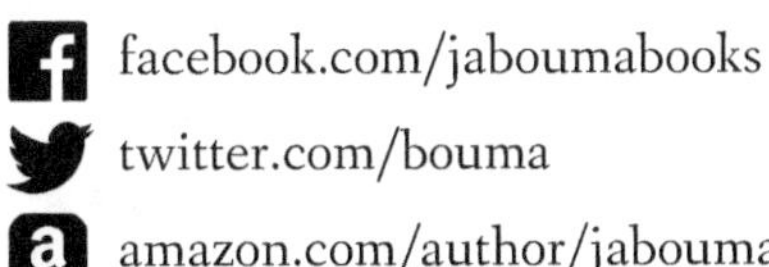

facebook.com/jaboumabooks

twitter.com/bouma

amazon.com/author/jabouma